Gone With the Wine

POUR DECISIONS

Book 2

Kelly Jamieson

Ebook ISBN 978-1-998717-11-8

Print book ISBN 978-1-998717-10-1

Editing by Kristi Yanta

Cover design and formatting by P.G. Forte

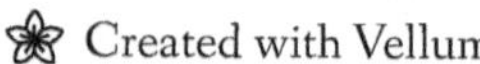 Created with Vellum

About this title...

Where there's a wine, there's a way.

Jansen

I'm trying to start over after a soul-crushing end to my hockey career and my marriage—so I buy a winery. I have no idea what I'm doing, but at least I have a reason to get out of bed in the morning. I hate asking for help, but when I meet the wine-maker next door, I'm jacked to have an excuse to see her again. She's gorgeous and full of life, with grape juice-stained hands, a sunburnt nose, and long legs in cut-off shorts. But Bianca's not so eager to help a grumpy rich celebrity who thinks he can just buy a winery and become a winemaker.

Bianca

Holy crap, I've inherited part of the family winery. That should be a dream come true, but I left Napa to get away from my family baggage. I have no choice but to go home and help my sisters get through harvest season, but I'll be making a quick exit back to my rising star wine career in Argentina. Meanwhile, our new neighbor is a tall, dark, and ripped temptation. He needs a winemaker, and I need a laboratory—so we make a business deal. But while we work together picking, crushing, and fermenting, the attraction between us is causing another chemical reaction. And with wine and with life, it's not healthy to keep things bottled up...

Prologue

Bianca

I pick up my phone and check the time. Still too early.

I press a hand to my quaking stomach. My arms and legs are tingling as if I'm cold, but out here on the terrace at Castillo Lorenzo Winery it's a comfortable late summer temperature with afternoon sun warming the stone and scenting the air with bougainvillaea. I don't know why I'm nervous about this video call with my family.

Oh wait. It's my family. *That's* why I'm nervous.

I gaze out at the rows and rows of malbec grapes stretching into the distance where the snow-capped Andes Mountains rise against the clear blue sky. Absolutely breathtaking.

It's harvest time here in Argentina, and I've taken a break from the frenetic pace for this call. Obviously, I couldn't go home for this right now.

I've been living and working here just outside Mendoza, Argentina, for years now but the beauty never fails to affect me. The elegant wine-tasting terrace is shaded with vines, shrubs, and Jacarandas that bloom velvety lilac in November, and brightly colored flowers spill out of big pots. Guests are enjoying their samples of malbec, syrah, and cabernet franc.

My phone buzzes with the notification. I start and drop my gaze to the screen, tapping it and moving to the far side of the patio away from guests. The face of my older sister Rosa appears. She's sitting in the Napa, California office of James Davenport, the Lamberti family lawyer. Also in the room, although I can't see them, is our Uncle Geno, Aunt Janet, and our cousins Gianni, Vittorio, and Leo, Jr. Leo's the son of our Uncle Leo, Geno's brother, but he passed years ago.

"Hi!"

"Hi, Bee!"

We make stilted small talk, acutely aware of the other people in the room with Rosa. Still no Allegra, our younger sister.

"Are you sure you sent Legs the link?" I ask.

"Yes, of course I did. I just have no idea what time it is over there. Could be middle of the night."

"Nah, closer to eight or nine pm. Barely dinner time."

At that moment the screen splits in two, Allegra joining our three-way call.

God, I miss them.

"Hey, Bee!" my younger sister says. "And Rosey Posey. Sorry I couldn't make it back. How are you holding up, Rosey?"

"I'm fine," Rosa says. "I'm sorry you couldn't be here, too."

Allegra shrugs a shoulder. "You know how it is. I'll try to be there for the memorial."

She'd better do more than try. I catch Rosa's exasperated eye roll. We both love Allegra, but she's never been what you'd call dependable.

"You've got time," Rosa says. "We won't hold the memorial until after harvest season at least. But you really should be here for it, Allegra. After everything Grandma did for us. Pay our respects."

Allegra nods, her face shadowed by the late afternoon sun behind her head. "I'll see what I can do."

Nonna raised us herself, after Daddy died and Mama ran off to Italy with Sergio. We owe her so much. My heart squeezes with grief.

"Where are you this week, Legs?" I peer at my phone, taking in the gorgeous old buildings behind Allegra. "Greece?"

Allegra shakes her head, curls dancing. "Gibraltar." She waves a hand behind her. "I might actually get some time to look around before I move on."

"That's so cool." Rosa smiles.

Allegra couldn't be much farther away from me.

When I left Oak Creek Canyon in California eight years ago for college, I was happy to escape. I wanted to be on my own in the world, not part of the Martinelli-Lamberti family, not the girl whose mom ran away to Italy with a man, not the invisible middle sister. I was eager to make my own mark in the world, and I've been working hard ever since to achieve that.

My full scholarship to Cornell University was a dream come true and my ticket out of Napa. Waaaaay out of Napa. Then I decided to do my internship in Argentina—even farther from Napa. When I was offered a job at the winery where I interned, I took it. I've been the assistant winemaker here ever since, working with Milenko Torres, an elite winemaker who's been producing internationally awarded wines including his amazing malbec.

And I'm starting to be known, too, as Milenko gives me the freedom to develop wines of my own. It's what I've always wanted—to be known for something I've accomplished myself, something that's not just brushed aside or ignored, not something that belongs to the "family." That's what they did to

Nonna. She never got credit for her creations; they were always "Belmonte" wines. I want to create elegant, complex, delicious wines and I'm on my way to doing that.

Rosa holds up a finger to her lips, indicating we should be quiet. She turns her iPad and I see Mr. Davenport walking into the room.

He takes a seat behind the wide, official-looking desk at the front of the room, then looks directly at Rosa's iPad. And frowns.

"Hi, Mr. Davenport," Rosa says. "I know this is a little unorthodox..."

"But so are we," Allegra adds with a laugh.

I hear Rosa's sigh. She's never had much patience for Allegra's antics.

"Sorry, sir," she says to Mr. Davenport. "You know my sisters, Bianca and Allegra."

"Quite well," he answers.

Allegra waves. "Hi, Jimmy!"

I hear someone snort, then cough in a feeble attempt to cover laughter. I, too, have to bite my lip on a smile.

"As I was saying, Mr. Davenport," Rosa continues seriously. "My sisters Allegra and Bianca are both out of the country but want to participate in the reading as well."

"That's fine."

Rosa turns her tablet around again. Mr. Davenport takes his glasses out of their case and slides them on. "As long as you don't disrupt the proceedings." He directs his attention to the phone with a raised eyebrow.

We've known James Davenport almost our entire lives—he's been the family lawyer for as long as anyone can remember. And he knows us. Sometimes to our embarrassment.

"Yes, sir," I reply.

"It'll be just like I'm there in the room," Allegra adds.

"That's what I'm afraid of," he says drolly. "Just—be appropriate, please."

"Yes, sir," Rosa says.

"Thank you. Is anyone else joining us virtually? Your mother, perhaps?"

I wince.

Rosa says, "No, sir."

One corner of my mouth kicks up. Yeah, Mama wants nothing to do with this family anymore.

It's not our fault Mama decided to run away to Italy with a man soon after her husband died. But we've always suffered the consequences of that. I swallow a sigh.

"Thank you all for being here," Mr. Davenport lays a hand on the stack of papers on the desk in front of him. "I know this is a sad and difficult time for the whole family."

He takes off his glasses and rubs his eyes briefly.

Damn. He was Nonna's friend as well as her lawyer. Of course he's sad, too.

Clearing his throat, he taps the papers again. "Your mother" – he nods at Uncle Geno – "and grandmother" – he glances around the rest of the room, his gaze encompassing Rosa, Allegra and me via the smartphone, and our three cousins – "was a remarkable woman. She will be greatly missed. She also lived a full life, loved her family, and had very specific thoughts about her will and what would happen after she passed. Her greatest desire was that you remain a family, supporting each other, regardless of what's in these papers."

Nonna used to say family is the core of everything. I miss her so much already. My eyes sting and I bow my head as I blink back tears.

Mr. Davenport starts reading the documents in front of him, details about safe deposit boxes, life insurance, bank accounts. I don't know why everyone has to be present for this.

Uncle Geno has been running the family business since Papa passed away. Mama wasn't interested in sticking around, so she gave up any connection to the business once she left the country (and her daughters) behind. Our generation? Well, except for Allegra and me, they're all working for Uncle Geno in some capacity, or will eventually, but it's going to be decades before they actually take the reins. To clarify—Uncle Geno's sons will take the reins. Rosa already works for Uncle Geno, but I don't see him giving her any control. I'm loving my life here in Argentina, working with a talented, knowledgeable mentor, making amazing wines. And Allegra? She's busy traveling the world and when she's done, who knows where she's going to land.

"In regard to Belmonte Winery."

Yeah, yeah, get on with it.

Mr. Davenport reads Nonna's words from papers he holds. "'Geno, you have been a faithful steward of the family winery, and I trust you to keep that tradition strong for future generations. All holdings from your father, and his father before him, are passed down to you.'" He pauses and flicks his gaze up, presumably toward Uncle Geno. "'I have every hope that your sons, my beloved grandsons, will carry on that tradition on the land bequeathed to your lineage. I love you all.'"

Just what I expected. I've been overlooked my whole life, as the middle child, but being overlooked by Nonna in this way stings. Ah well. I've followed a different path, and it's fine.

I hear Uncle Geno speak. "Thank you, James. I know how hard—"

"We're not finished," Mr. Davenport interjects.

"Excuse me? You've gone over everything—the accounts, the financials, the properties..."

"One property." Mr. Davenport sets that paper aside and

glances down at the one remaining in his hand. "Belmonte Winery."

I frown, my fingers tightening on my phone.

"These are the final wishes of Maria Carmela Bianchi Lamberti, in her own words. 'My dearest children and grandchildren. I love you all and wish I could have remained with you forever, in our little patch of heaven on earth. I have loved every moment together, and wish you all nothing but peace, prosperity, and happiness.

"'As you know, when I married my sainted Leo, I brought my family birthright, Caparelli Vineyards, with me. It had been passed down to me by my mother, God rest her soul. And though I allowed my sainted Lorenzo to run both wineries as one, it has remained my birthright throughout our marriage and beyond. Geno, when you took over for your father, you continued to treat them as one entity, as agreed upon previously. But now, in my twilight years, I wish to rebuild the tradition started by my mother, and pass Caparelli Vineyards on to the next generation of wine-making women in our family. My dear daughter, Caprice, has chosen to live and work overseas with her second husband, and has shown no interest in Caparelli for many years. Therefore, I leave my vines, my property, and my birthright to my three granddaughters, Rosa, Bianca, and Allegra, to carry on the proud matriarchal tradition of Caparelli.'"

I smack my hand over my mouth as I gasp.

"'I also leave a modest bank account –" Mr. Davenport holds up a folder "– to provide some cushion should they choose to bring Caparelli back from disuse. I hope with all my heart that they do. My darlings, my tre sorelle, I wish you all well in your new adventure."

Holy shit. What? I press a hand to my forehead, suddenly hot and dizzy.

Mr. Davenport folds his hands on the desk and looks at each of us in turn. "Any questions?"

"What the hell is that?" Geno's voice is loud enough to be clearly heard on my phone.

I'm wondering the same, Uncle Geno.

"Your mother's last will and testament. It is quite legal, and she was of sound mind and body when she wrote it. There will be no point in challenging it."

"But it makes no sense. Caparelli and Belmonte have been combined for decades! Caparelli can't exist on its own. You agree with me, right?" Rosa turns her phone and he's looking directly at her—and us—hands planted on his hips. "You've been working for the family for years. You see how the two are intertwined."

Rosa doesn't answer and there's a long silence.

Yes, they've operated as one organization for as long as I can remember. But I also remember the stories Nonna used to tell us, of growing up on Caparelli's grounds, how proud she was when it became hers, how she chose to share it with her husband while still retaining that birthright for her own. And she's entrusted it to us? I can't...I...

"Besides, there's no way you'll be able to get it up and running on your own in time to save the grapes," Uncle Geno says.

"She's not on her own," I snap.

"Excuse me?" Uncle Geno frowns.

"She's right," Allegra says. "There are three of us. She's not on her own."

I shift my focus to the tiny image of Allegra on my phone as she weighs in from across the globe.

Uncle Geno waves a hand dismissively. "Whatever. Not like you'll be doing much from your little European vacation. Just like your mother."

I hear Rosa suck in a breath as I wince. Uncle Geno's always been a little crotchety, but why is he being such a jackass?

"Belmonte needs the grapes. We have plans for them. And if you don't allow us to harvest and use them, they'll rot on the vine."

What? He really thinks we can't do it! He thinks we can't harvest the grapes ourselves.

"Then we'll just turn them into raisins and make a profit that way," Allegra says.

"Allegra!" Rosa's mouth falls open.

I grin. Oh my God. Allegra is known for saying what's on her mind. Sometimes second by second.

Uncle Geno's smile is fake. "Our arrangement has worked just fine for decades. We've even honored the history of Caparelli vineyards through our Carleo Cabernet."

The Carleo. The "tribute" wine Uncle Geno has been selling for years. The one where Nonna's contribution has been reduced to a side note. She was a gifted winemaker, but never got the credit she should have. These days, lots of women are working in the wine business.

I think I get my love of winemaking from her. I think I have talent, too. But I've always been disregarded by Uncle Geno. His son is Belmonte's winemaker and Uncle Geno won't have it any other way. And honestly? My sisters never really paid much attention to my wine creations, either.

"There's no reason to fix what isn't broken," he says.

Rosa finally speaks up. "I think...I'll have to talk to my sisters about it."

"But—"

The image on screen jiggles and shift as Rosa stands.

I speak up, too. "Yes, we have to discuss our options. All of them."

"Girls!" Uncle Geno booms. "I must insist—"

"Nope." Allegra laughs through the phone. "Pretty sure you don't get to insist anything. Andiamo, sorelle mie, let's discuss our options."

"We'll be in touch about the financials," Rosa says to Mr. Davenport.

She sounds like a winery owner already. I smile.

Winery owner. Whoa.

I own a winery.

The image shifts again as Rosa walks out of the room. Once outside the building, she holds up the iPad so we can see her face, blinking a little in the bright California sunlight.

"I have just one thing to say," Allegra pipes up, her eyes wide on my smartphone screen.

"What's that?" Rosa asks.

"Holy shit."

Chapter 1

Bianca

4 months later

I'm so gross I can't stand myself.

I feel like I've been traveling for a week, and I probably look and smell like it, too. Ugh.

I'm dying for a shower and a nice bed and I'm almost there, but as I get closer to Oak Creek Canyon, the knots in my stomach tighten and my hands stick to the steering wheel of the car I rented in San Francisco.

I'm almost home.

All my life as the middle kid I felt, well, unnoticed. My older sister Rosa was perfect—well-behaved, top marks in school, just *good*. Then there was Allegra, the youngest, the baby, fun-loving, energetic, impulsive. I loved wine and wine-making and I had ideas but was brushed off as just a kid. Just a girl. I had a period of rebellion, much to my eternal chagrin. But I also loved my chemistry and biology classes and quietly made small batches of wine that I sometimes snuck into tastings when I was working at Belmonte. People liked them. They were good.

The wines I've been making in Argentina are good, too.

Then Nonna died.

Something pinches in my chest. Yes, I left Oak Creek Canyon, but I always knew Nonna was here. Wherever my sisters ended up, wherever I ended up, Nonna was here. She was regular emails and FaceTime and even hand-written birthday cards. She was there for all three of us when both our parents were gone, and I loved her.

I slow the car to drive through the town of Oak Creek Canyon. I may have abandoned my hometown, but I have to admit it is pretty—tidy tree-lined streets, masses of rose bushes, pots of flowers overflowing with colorful blooms. I drive past the marketplace with its red awnings and charming stone walls draped with ivy, a spa with silvery olive trees shading its entrance, the three Michelin Starred restaurant, Old Dove House.

Then outside the town I prepare for the turnoff that will take me to Caparelli.

My winery.

A laugh escapes me. That's so just so incredible, and yes, my laughter may have a touch of hysteria.

It's not just my winery—my two sisters and I now own it. I'm not the only one freaking out about this.

I pull in a deep breath and make the turn.

This should be another dream come true—owning my own winery. But it's more like a nightmare, because Nonna is gone. And also because I'm building a successful career in Argentina that's important to me and I had to leave it.

Memories of growing up in Oak Creek Canyon flood back, always feeling overshadowed by my sister and cousins, ignored (other than that incident involving beer, weed, and peer pressure when I was a teenager) and less-than. And now—we apparently have a fight on our hands, because Uncle Geno is pissed that he didn't inherit Caparelli. Since he learned that at the reading of Nonna's will, he's been actively trying to sabotage my sister Rosa's efforts to clean things up. And Nonna is no longer here to act as a steadying influence on our sometimes-hotheaded family.

No Nonna.

My throat aches.

But I'm here. And I'm pissed. Since discovering Nonna left Caparelli to us, Uncle Geno has been playing shitty games with us. He overlooked me one too many times. I'm back and I'm going to make myself noticed whether he likes it or not. I owe it to my sisters.

I spare a glance down the road toward Belmonte before turning into the driveway of Nonna's old home, a big old Victorian structure. I remember running around inside it and playing outside among the vines. But now...well, it's seen better days. I slow to a stop and gaze at the house.

The bones are good, but my God, the old girl needs some work. Peeling paint and curling shingles give the house a rundown look, but man, I love that porch, wrapping around two sides of the house. The paint on the columns may be flaking, but their shape is charming, and they look solid. I can picture it with wicker furniture, comfortable cushions, and hanging pots of flowers. And a glass of wine. Of course.

So many memories. After my father died and Mama ran away in a scandalous move people still talk about, Nonna took in my sisters and me and raised us here. But once we grew up and left, she ended up moving in with her son, my Uncle Geno, so the house hasn't been looked after for years.

The grounds are overgrown, although I can see some efforts have been made to tame things. I let my gaze roam around, taking in tangled vines, thick shrubs, and sparse flowers. There's still a magic about the place—a feeling of bygone times, family legacy, and heritage. The entire region has a rustic ambience that blends with the history and refined charm of wine.

Another deep breath. But I'm also excited to see my sister, in the flesh instead of on a screen. She doesn't know I'm coming today. I'm not exactly trying to surprise her, but I didn't want a big deal made of it.

I slide out of the car, leaving my belongings, and the distinctive clap of the car door closing reverberates around the yard. As I stroll toward the house, a head pops up in the front window—what used to be the parlor. I grin and wave.

I watch Rosa's face transform, her mouth dropping open, eyes flying wide open. She freezes for a moment, then disappears, reappearing as she throws open the front door, a heavily carved oak door. "Bee!"

She's so pretty, with her dark hair pulled back into a ponytail that accentuates her perfect bone structure and shows off big brown eyes.

I quicken my step and we run to each other, wrapping each other up in the tightest hug. The scent of her hair, the berry scent of the shampoo she's always used, is so familiar.

"You're here!" Rosa squeals. "Why didn't you tell me you were coming?"

"I don't know. I didn't know how all the travel would go and I didn't want it to be a big thing."

"It *is* a big thing! You're here!"

"I promised I'd be here for harvest."

She squeezes me again. "I've missed you so much."

"I missed you, too, Rosy Posey."

"Ugh. Do you have to call me that?"

I grin. "Sorry, it slipped out. How are things here?" I fling out a hand toward the vineyards.

"Uh...well, you've been talking to Jake, so I know you're up to speed on what he's been doing with the vines. Come on, let's go inside."

Ah yes, Jake. Her ex-boyfriend who has suddenly reappeared in her life again. I have so many questions.

We walk into the foyer. With the oak floor, original oak doors and trim, the big oak staircase with the carved newel post, and flowered wallpaper in dark shades of burgundy and navy, it feels gloomy in here. "This place needs some work."

"I know." Rosa sighs. "I've done a little. Come into the parlor. I managed to clean up in here."

I follow her into the room. Rosa *has* fixed up this room, and it's bright and inviting with late summer sunshine pouring through the window. I plop myself onto the couch. "I'm so tired. If I'm not making any sense, that's why."

"That's why you should have told me you were coming! I could have had a room ready for you. Are you hungry? Thirsty?"

"Maybe? I don't even know what day it is."

She laughs. "It's Wednesday and it's nearly noon. I'll make us a salad in a few minutes. Where's all your stuff?"

"I left it in the car. I'll get it in a bit." I adjust a cushion behind my head and stretch out lengthwise on the couch. "Aaaaaah. It feels so good to lay down."

"Do you want a nap? I can make up the bed right now."

"I probably will need a nap, but not now. Let's catch up. So yeah, Jake's filled me in on some things. What I want to know is...what is happening between you two?"

"Well, uh." She runs a hand over her dark hair and looks away, her cheeks getting pink. "We've, uh, kind of discovered that the, ah, chemistry between us never really went away."

I eye Rosa curiously. She's usually so composed, it's funny

to see her all flustered and stammering. This tells me a lot about what's happening with her and Jake.

She and Jake were high school sweethearts, but he left abruptly after high school and that was the end of that. Dealing with Rosa's broken heart back then left me a little pissed at him, to be honest. When I heard from Allegra that Jake is working here and not only that, living here in the house, I was startled. He broke Rosa's heart years ago and my first worry was that he'll do it again. I told Rosa that on the phone, but she quickly changed the subject.

"That was a long time ago," I say slowly. "And there's still chemistry?"

She nods. "Yes. And—"

"You graduated high school and he fucked off to parts unknown almost immediately," I remind her. "I'm surprised you're even talking to him, to be honest."

"It's complicated."

"No shit."

She lifts her chin and straightens her shoulders. "There's another thing. The reason it's complicated is that...we're married."

My jaw drops and I sit bolt upright. "What?"

Rosa licks her lips as her eyes flicker. "It's a long story."

I swing my legs over the side of the couch and lean forward. "You can't be serious. When did you get married?" I nearly shout.

She sucks in a breath. "Ten years ago."

I fall back into the couch cushions, gaping at her. I literally have no words. I am dumbstruck. Speechless. After a moment of thick silence, I frown and shake my head. "How can that be?"

"I was supposed to be on that high school graduation trip.

Jake and I detoured to Vegas, and, well, it was impulsive, but we were in love."

"Sweet buttery Jesus on a breadstick. A Vegas wedding. I cannot believe this." I lean forward again. "Why did none of us know about this?"

Her lips thin and she drops her gaze. "Uncle Geno got involved. He convinced me that it was a mistake and I owed it to the family to have the marriage annulled. Then he told Jake that I didn't want to be married anymore."

My eyes snap wide open.

"We both signed annulment papers and Jake left."

"Ohhhh." Relief sweeps over me. "So you're not really married?"

"But..."

I tense up again.

"Jake never filed the papers."

"Oh my God. I can't believe this." I swipe a hand across my forehead. "This is a soap opera."

Rosa flashes a tight smile. "I know, believe me. I thought the marriage had been annulled. I didn't believe Jake when he said we were still married, but he kept insisting so I went to the Court House, to Public Records, and it's true...there was no annulment ever filed."

"Holy shit." My heart is racing unevenly. "I think I'm having some kind of cardiac event."

She eyes me with concern.

I suck air into my lungs. "So Jake shows up here and tells you you're still married, and there's still 'chemistry...'" I make air quotes with my fingers. "So you move into together and... what? Doesn't this seem like another impulsive move?"

"I know it might seem like that. But we love each other." She drops her gaze to her twisted fingers. "I tried to forget him, but I didn't. I never got over him. And he never met anyone else he was serious about either."

I blink at her. I remember how heartbroken she was when he left. I had no idea that they'd actually gotten married. But I did know she really loved him. And honestly...I kind of loved Jake, too. He was a great guy. He was good to Rosa. And then I was pissed at him for how he treated her. "I'm having a hard time absorbing all this."

"I know." She swallows but meets my gaze steadily. "All that time apart because of Uncle Geno. He convinced me I'd failed the family by impetuously getting married. I felt like I had no choice but to do what he said. My foolish, impulsive actions had harmed my sisters, my grandmother, my family. I had to make it right. So I spent ten years trying to make it up to him. And by doing that, I hurt Jake."

I see the anguish in her eyes, along with a pleading look for understanding

She still loves him.

Now I'm even more pissed at Uncle Geno. "Does Uncle Geno know Jake's back? Of course he does."

"Yeah. And he knows we're still married. And he's furious."

My eyebrows tug down. "Why? What does it matter to him?"

"Why do you think?" She rolls her eyes. "He thinks Jake could take Caparelli from us."

"Ohhhh. Of course." I exhale a long breath.

"I set him straight." She lifts her chin again.

"Good for you," I murmur. Uncle Geno isn't the easiest person to deal with, especially when he's angry. "Why didn't Jake file the annulment papers?"

"He says..." Her face softens. "He didn't want an annulment. He says since he went to all that trouble to marry me, it seemed like a stupid idea to give up that quickly."

My heart turns to custard. I may be a little cynical when it comes to our family, and when it comes to love I know I keep walls up, but seeing Rosa so in love and clearly happy melts those icy barriers. "I still have questions," I croak. "But come here and give me a hug."

I stand and she rushes over and we squeeze each other tightly for a long moment.

"I'm sorry," I say eventually. "I'm sorry Uncle Geno did that to you. Made you stay here and give up your life for the family. And I'm sorry I didn't know."

Rosa's an adult and the big sister who looked after Allegra and me. We were never "best friends," but we're sisters and I love her.

"It's okay, Bee." Rosa's face lights up and her smile is soft. "We're okay. Really."

She looks...happy. Really happy. Glowing happy. "Sure. All right. Well. Wow." I shake my head. "Where *is* Jake?"

Rosa waves a hand. "Out in the vineyard. They're checking for downy mildew."

Since he left Napa ten years ago, Jake's apparently been traveling all over, working at different wineries. He's now an experienced viticulturalist, and we needed someone to look after the vines if we want to be able to harvest grapes this year. His family used to own the winery next door to Caparelli and he always thought he'd work there, but they just recently had to sell the place, sadly.

"These two kids he hired are working out okay?"

"Yes! I'm so grateful to them, too. I've been working on things here at the house and also business stuff."

"Which isn't good."

She grimaces. "Not great, no. But now you're here, we can really make some plans. We can make wine!"

"Well, not really. Uncle Geno has the wine. What the fuck

is that all about, anyway? Nonna left us this winery. That wine is ours."

Rosa frowns. "Well, he's been running both vineyards as one for years."

I shake my head. "Without the wine from last year's harvest, all we have are grapes, and it'll be a long time before we're ready to bottle the juice from them."

We need that wine. I push back my shoulders, my muscles tightening with readiness for battle.

"I know." Her lips droop. "And winemaking is what you do."

"True. But there's lots to do after the crush. Lots of testing to make sure fermentation is happening properly, too fast or too slowly. Checking sugar and alcohol levels. You know." I wave a hand. We both grew up in a winery. We knew this stuff by the time we were twelve.

"Yes."

"And of course I can help with the harvest."

"So much work." Rosa sighs.

"There's something so special about the harvest, though." I love it when the leaves turn gold and the days grow shorter and cooler. I love finally seeing the results of the growing season, seeing the fruit ripe and heavy with the sweet juice that will become wine, thinking about the possibilities of the wine...it excites me and inspires me.

The decision of when to pick the grapes is so important— they have to be the perfect ripeness to make clean, balanced wines. Leaving the grapes too long ends up with flabby wines that lack structure. Nobody wants a sugary, unctuous Zinfandel.

I didn't want to come home. But family is important, and the lure of being handed a winery and being able to call all the shots is too good a chance to pass up. I have to admit I'm excited to be part of the decisions this year.

I don't plan to stay long. I promised Rosa I'd come back for harvest, despite being busy at Castillo Lorenzo. But being here, seeing the vines and the house and the outbuildings with potential for creating a beautiful wine tasting experience, with all its memories and history, gives me this weird urge to make something of this place. To make something *special*. For Nonna's sake.

We've hauled my suitcases up to my room and I've unpacked, had a short nap, and I'm in the kitchen hoping for food when Jake walks in. He's tanned from the sun, and a little sweaty and dusty. We both go still and look at each other across the room. He's older—a little heavier, with an attractive beard and eyes that hint at suffering and regret. But when he smiles, crinkling up those eyes, it's genuine and warm. "Hi, Bee."

I huff out a breath and move toward him for a hug. "Hey. Good to see you."

After we separate, he says, "Where's Rosa?"

"I don't know. I just woke up. I'm a little jet lagged."

"No doubt. That's a long trip."

"Yeah." I eye him. "Rosa told me about you two."

He keeps his expression neutral and holds my gaze steadily. "Yeah? That's good."

"I was worried about you being back in her life after you ditched her without a word all those years ago."

"I understand."

"I don't want her to be hurt again."

He dips his chin in a brief nod. "Neither do I. I promise...I love her."

"I believe you," I murmur. "But ten years...you were *married* and you left for ten years."

"Yeah. I thought she didn't want me."

"Uncle Geno."

"Yeah."

"I am so pissed at him."

"You and me both. I hated him for making decisions for Rosa. For forcing her to sign the annulment papers, for making her feel guilty and telling her what to do."

My heart squeezes. "Yeah."

"I still get pissed thinking of her here in Oak Creek Canyon all that time, feeling guilty and like she had to make up for something that wasn't hurting anyone else." His voice deepens with emotion. "But I also realized that I was just as bad as Geno."

I frown.

"I kept her tied to me," he says quietly. "All that time. I would have known if she was involved with someone else," he adds quickly. "I would have done something then." In answer to my unspoken questions he says, "My mom kept me up to date."

I nod.

"Geno took Rosa's choice away from her by making her sign the annulment. And I took her choice away when I didn't file the papers." His voice deepens with emotion.

I blink. That's true.

"So I gave her the annulment papers. So *she* could make the choice."

"Oh." My heart climbs into my throat.

"And she ripped them up."

My eyes sting. I swallow. "Thank you."

He nods, a half-smile on his face.

Rosa comes in the back door then and halts, looking between us. "Oh."

I smile at her. "Hi. We're just catching up."

"Are you threatening him again?" she demands, going to him and sliding her arm through his.

I laugh. "No. Hey, could we eat? I'm starving."

"Me too," Jake says.

Rosa's on top of that, with food in the fridge—marinated chicken breasts that Jake puts on the grill along with some potatoes and other veggies. She and I assemble a salad and soon we're sitting at the big kitchen table eating.

"What happened with Take Flight?" I ask Jake.

He tells me about how his mother got sick, how the medical bills piled up, and how his parents decided to retire and sell the winery. I can see it's painful for him. He loved that winery. It was always assumed he would take over, but...he wasn't here.

Because of Uncle Geno.

More anger flares inside me. I have many things to talk to Uncle Geno about.

"You want to see the grosso grapes?" Jake asks.

"Ohhh yes. I didn't realize we had those growing here."

He mentioned them to me on the phone a while back. A lot of the vines here were originally planted by Italian immigrants in the late 19th Century, which is why there are merlot and zinfandel and sangiovese grapes growing here. Grosso grapes are not well known. They're high in acidity and tannins and are only blended with other red varieties that produce fuller, fruitier wines. I'm super curious about them and what we can do with them.

God, I love wine.

Chapter 2

Bianca

It's my second day in Oak Creek Canyon and it's girl's night at the Golden Cougar Bar and Grill. The name is unfortunate, but it's been around for generations and is named after the actual cougars that inhabit the valley. I'm meeting my two besties from high school, Millie and Ana.

I walk into the bar. "This place hasn't changed," I murmur, looking around the rustic room with wood posts and beams and faded signs. It's packed with people at the long bar and tables. I spot Millie and Ana and head toward them across the scuffed concrete floor, smiling.

"Hiiiii!" They stand up and we exchange a round of hugs and greetings.

"It's been so long!"

"You look amazing!"

"I can't believe you're back!"

Finally, we all take seats on dinged-up metal stools at the high-top table. I settle myself into place, emotion pushing at my ribs from inside, my eyes stinging a bit. "It's so good to see you."

They beam back at me. "You, too," Millie says.

I've told myself I didn't miss anything from home, but the truth is—I did. I've missed my friends, these two women I share so much history with. There's nobody else in the world I have the same relationship with as them. Even my sisters; with Rosa being older, the perfect big sister, and Allegra the baby everyone doted on, as a kid I gravitated to connections outside the family.

"I'm so happy to see you," I admit honestly, reaching out to squeeze a hand of each of them.

A young guy approaches to take our order.

"Oh, I don't know what I want," I say. In the heart of wine country, this place always focused more on beer selections. But I enjoy a beer sometimes and it's been a while, so.... "I'll have a Hoppy Ending."

He nods and Millie and Ana order Baby Got Bocks.

I see the looks I'm getting from people in the bar. I doubt anyone recognizes me; I've changed since I lived here. No doubt they're wondering who the stranger in town is. One of the downsides of small town living that I remember so well.

"I'm sorry about your grandma," Millie says. "She was so special."

"Yeah." I drop my gaze briefly. "It still seems weird that she's not here." The vibe has taken a downturn, so I square my shoulders, lift my chin, and smile. "How are wedding plans coming?" I ask Millie.

Which of course reminds me of the astonishing news about Rosa and Jake.

I hear all about Millie's upcoming wedding and Ana's job at the local veterinary clinic. I fill them in on my time in Argentina and Tomás, the hot cowboy I was with for a few months while living there.

"Speaking of boyfriends," Ana says, leaning closer. "Mark Watson is over there."

I blink. "Oh." Mark was my high school boyfriend. "I'm not looking."

Ana laughs. "Okay. But he's single again! He and Marnie were together for...how long?" She looks at Millie.

"Over a year."

"Right. They just broke up," Ana says.

"I'm not here for romance." I make a face, lifting my beer. "I'm here to help Rosa and figure out what the hell we're going to do with Caparelli." And to turn the tables on Uncle Geno, but I don't mention that.

To be honest, I'm not looking for romance anywhere. After being abandoned by my father (well, he died, but still, I felt abandoned) *and* my mother, then passed over by my family, I'm the poster child for abandonment issues and avoidant attachment style. Yes, I've been to therapy.

"That doesn't mean you can't have a little romance." Millie lifts her glass.

"Or a little bit of bam bam in the ham," Ana adds.

Millie and I stare at her then crack up laughing. I almost fall off my stool. "I'm probably only going to be here for a couple of months."

"Oh." Their faces fall.

"I thought for sure you're back to stay," Millie says slowly.

Ana pouts. "Me, too."

I shrug and smile. "Well, who knows. We have a ton of work to do and Uncle Geno isn't making it easy for us."

"I've heard the rumors." Millie wrinkles her freckled nose. "I don't get it. Family is family, right?"

"Right." I press my lips together. "We're going to make this work. We're determined. It's what Nonna wanted."

"I agree," Ana says with a firm nod. "I loved your Nonna."

"Thanks." I smile.

We order snacks and more drinks and get caught up on life in Napa and Oak Creek Canyon. They tell me about friends from high school who are married and having babies. "Brittany Fox married Josh Hunter and now her name is Brittany Fox-Hunter."

I let out a little cackle. "No!"

"And..." Ana leans in. "They just had a baby and named her Ima."

I gasp. "You are kidding me."

"True story."

"Ima's an unusual name to start with, but with that surname...that poor child." Millie shakes her head.

"Do you think if you were born with a different name, would you have a different personality?" I tap my chin.

"Hmmm. I don't know. I never really liked Millie. Maybe if my parents had named me something cute like Ashley or Ella I would have been super popular, with boys after me all the time."

I make a face. "But would your personality be different?"

She tilts her head. "Maybe I would have been more confident? That would make a difference."

"What if I were named Olga?" Ana muses. "Maybe I'd be tougher."

"When I was a kid, I hated all the Italian names in our family," I share. "I wanted to be Siobhan."

Millie giggles. "Irish?"

"Yes. It means 'full of charm' so I thought I would be Irish and charming." I shrug.

Ana tips her head. "I thought your Italian family was so glamorous and so big and boisterous."

"Big and boisterous is correct." I make a face.

After we pay our bill and head outside, we wander down Laurel Street past cute little shops that are now closed. We pause to admire a display in the window of Poppy's Vintage Collectibles.

"I want that chair," Ana says, staring. "It would be perfect in my bedroom."

"It would," Millie agrees.

We move on and stop at The Dancing Grape, a gift shop with all kinds of wine-related stuff.

"Look at those wine aroma kits!" I point. "That's amazing."

"Not like you need it," Millie says.

"You should try those wine lovers' chocolates," Ana says. "They are delicious."

"Sounds yummy."

I walk a little farther and now it's my turn to drool in front of Lavender Lingerie. This is a new store in Oak Creek Canyon, and wow, it's hitting my weakness for anything purple. "Oh my God, look at that slip dress!" I gaze at the pansy purple silk garment with embroidered bra cups. It's my favorite color and so luxe looking. "Wouldn't I look sexy in that?"

A noise beside me has my head turning. I'm face to face with a man I do not know.

Almost face to face—he's tall. And he's eyeing me with a startled expression.

Heat rushes up into my face. Where are Ana and Millie? "Uh. Sorry. I thought you were my friends. I mean, I thought I was talking to them."

Deep-set hazel eyes stare at me, his thick eyebrows drawn together above them.

Whoa. This is one attractive man.

I blink, in a flash taking in his firm jaw, carved cheekbones, and strong nose that's just a bit uneven. Also wide, wide shoulders and lots of hard-packed muscle. "Uh..." I say again. "Sorry."

This would be a good time for a big sinkhole to open up in the ground beneath me and swallow me up.

Millie and Ana appear next to me. "Oh hey, Jansen," Millie says. "How are you?"

Wait. They know him?

His closed expression relaxes when he looks at them. "Hi. I'm good, thanks."

Millie looks back and forth between us. "You've met Bianca?"

Now his lips twitch. "Sort of."

"Oh my God, I thought it was you two beside me and I started talking to him," I babble with a nervous laugh. "Oops!"

"Bee, this is Jansen Beck. He bought Take Flight."

"Oh." My scrutiny of him turns chilly, despite the pleasing width of his shoulders, the drape of his T-shirt over flat abs, the veins running down strong forearms to the backs of his hands.

"Bianca is an amazing winemaker," Ana tells Jansen. "You two should talk! Jansen's going to need help. He's never owned a winery before."

I blink at that. "Wow. That's...amazing. What happened to Randall?" He was the winemaker at Take Flight for decades.

"Retired," Jansen says.

"Ah."

"Bianca Martinelli," Millie finishes the introduction. "She owns Caparelli Vineyard."

"Part of it," I mumble.

"The competition, then," Jansen says.

I lift my eyebrows. "You must be new here."

He frowns. "Well, yeah. Why?"

"We're not all competitors. In Napa, we all help each other." I ignore the resentment that pushed to the surface when I learned who he is. He's an outsider. The one who took over Jake's heritage.

"Ah."

"I mean, we all help each other and learn from each other. A rising tide floats all boats. That kind of thing." More blabbing.

"*Lifts* all boats," he says.

"Right. Right."

"We?" Millie says, arching a brow.

I go still. "Did I say that?"

She grins. "You did."

"Well, I just meant—"

"Never mind." She bumps her shoulder into mine. "We know. Anyway, like you said, Jansen needs winemaking help, and here you are!"

Like I want to help him! But I kind of dug my own hole here with my talk of neighborly teamwork. I grit my teeth on a smile. "Of course! Happy to help!"

He doesn't smile back. "That's nice of you, but not necessary."

Fine. He can figure out how to make wine on his own. Good luck with that.

"Okay! Nice to meet you! We should go." I grab Millie's arm.

Jansen nods, looks at the shop window again, then back at me. "Nice to meet you, too. And the answer to your question is —yes. Yes, you would."

He smiles briefly at my friends, turns, and walks away from us down the sidewalk.

Heat rushes to my face. Oh. My. God.

"What does that mean?" Ana whispers.

I start speed walking, tugging Millie with me. "Nothing."

Chapter 3

Jansen

What in the French-fried fuck am I doing here?

Carrying a thermal mug of coffee, I stroll from the house toward the vineyard, with my dog guest running around wildly sniffing everything he can. Somehow I ended up with this mutt last week when I found him on the property, matted and dirty, thin, with sad eyes. And only one ear. When I tried to coax him nearer to me, he didn't even stand on his scrawny legs, just crawled, inching closer on his belly. And when I picked him up, he was shaking. I hated that.

I took him to the vet where Ana works. I expected to leave him there, but they couldn't find his owners. I should have taken him to a shelter. But I couldn't do it. So after paying the outrageous vet bill (I should have bought a veterinary clinic, not a winery), I brought him home. Just until someone claims him. He's a scruffy mutt, some kind of Jack Russell terrier mix, so I've been calling him Jack.

I've never had a dog. I don't know much about dogs, how to train them, what to feed them. We're in the middle of harvest, a crazy time of year. This is *not* the time to be getting a dog. People already think I'm unhinged for buying this winery.

Early morning fog shrouds the hills with a pale glow as the sun rises behind them. From here I can see the neat rows of vines climbing the hill in shades of green and gold, their curves mirroring the undulations of the land. It's pretty goddamn amazing.

This place is mine and I have no clue what I'm doing.

After I retired from the league, I bummed around for months trying to figure out what I wanted to do with the rest of my life. I was a pro hockey player, but I'm not cut out for jobs in broadcasting. I'm not a coach. I have a bunch of college courses in business, but I took those years ago and I couldn't figure out what I could do with them.

Adjusting to retirement is hard for a lot of people, but for me it was excruciating. Giving up a career you still love isn't easy. At first, I thought I'd have a whole new life of freedom and fun, but instead I was lonely, lost, and surly.

Then my wife cheated on me.

That fucked with my head and for a long time I didn't care about doing anything. Even getting out of bed.

Luckily I have a couple of good buddies who knocked some sense into me, got me to a doctor, got me back working out, and eventually sat me down to talk about my future. I wanted to stay in California after playing for years with the Long Beach Golden Eagles. Although maybe as a city guy, I should have stayed in L.A. This rural setting is alien to me.

And I got this crazy idea to make wine.

"Jack! Hey buddy! Get back here!"

He's getting a little too adventurous, which is probably what got him lost. I give a shrill whistle, and he comes trotting back on his short legs, tongue hanging out of his mouth.

"Good boy." I bend and rub his head.

I got interested in wine a few years ago when a bunch of friends and I went to a wine festival in Long Beach. I thought it was pretentious and snobby and I rolled my eyes at how they described the wines when they poured them. But then I tasted a couple that were pretty amazing. I found myself seeking out the different tasting notes, curious about the differences between wines. I wanted to learn more. I took courses. I started making wine at home.

I lean on the fence, one foot on the lower railing, and sip my coffee as I gaze out at the landscape, at the layer of fog hanging in the air. I fill my lungs with the cool, damp air.

This was kind of a wild impulse. When I said I wanted to own a winery, my sensible friends thought I'd lost my mind. My family thought I was bonkers, too, but I'm used to them being critical of what I do. When I played hockey as a kid, they were on me all the time, pushing me to practice harder, putting me into hockey camps, pointing out how good other players were. So I didn't expect them to think this is a genius idea.

Yeah, it was insane. Take Flight wasn't the first winery for sale that I looked at, but to be honest, I only looked at a couple others. This one felt right. It's small but with a quality reputation. It has amazing views and a nice tasting room, also a house on the property where I now live, which is way too big for a single guy, and needs updating, but for now it's fine. I quickly learned about yield per acre and price per ton. I bought the winery without telling anyone. Like I said, they think I've lost my mind.

Finally I have something I'm excited to get out of bed in the morning for. Something that's mine. A purpose in life. Something I can accomplish without skates and a stick.

I hope.

I take another mouthful of coffee, dark and rich, still surveying my estate. Hell yeah. I have an estate.

I'd laugh at my cockiness, but I don't laugh much anymore.

That reminds me of last night.

I was walking down the sidewalk, slowing as I approached the Golden Cougar, and out of nowhere that woman asked me if she'd look sexy in that slip thing in the window.

At first I was taken aback, but she'd been so embarrassed that I'd been amused.

Not to mention a little intrigued as I pictured her in skimpy purple silk.

Oh hell yeah. Sexy as fuck.

She was hot even dressed in jeans and a T-shirt, her dark hair cut in shaggy layers, bangs hanging over rich brown eyes with glints of copper, her mouth a little wide and tilted up at the corners.

She's friends with Ana and Millie, who I first met at a Cuban music event at El Castillo, a winery not far from here set in a stone castle. I barely know anyone in town other than the people who work for me, but I went with my buddies who came to visit and we got talking to Ana and Millie's partners, and they introduced us to a few other people. They were all friendly enough, but clearly think a hockey player buying a winery is nuts. That's okay. My family and friends think so, too.

Yeah, she was sexy.

Stop thinking about Bianca. You have wine to make.

I really don't have a clue what I'm doing here.

"Come on, Jack. We have work to do." I head past the bocce court, across the patio, and inside. The tasting room is deserted at this early hour. I walk through it and downstairs to the cellar. This is where the wine is, the reds now almost two years since harvest. We're getting close to harvest this year and the chardonnay grapes are doing well. So I'm told. I don't really know. They look like good grapes to me.

Some of the staff at Take Flight chose to stay on and some

left. I hired Diego as vineyard manager, and Antonio stayed on as cellar manager, who then hired a few more people to help them keep things going until I sold my place in Long Beach and moved here.

What I don't have is a winemaker. Much as I love the idea of making wine, I know I need someone skilled to do that.

It's cool. Soon we'll be bottling the stuff that's in these barrels. Then drinking it. And selling it, of course. Hopefully. My investments have done well enough to allow me to buy this place, but I'm going to need to make money at some point. And I need to show all the doubters that I can actually do this.

With no job, no marriage, and no future, I've been feeling like a huge has-been.

I need to accomplish something.

Somehow, I've been convinced to go to the Napa Fair.

This sounds like a lot of people having fun, and that's definitely not my scene these days. But if I'm going to live here and run a business here, I need to interact with people in the community.

I don't want to go back to that black hole of loneliness that dragged me down.

One of my biggest problems when I retired was missing my teammates and buddies. After the years playing together, traveling together, all the pranks and chirps and inside jokes, I was lost without that kind of camaraderie. But the guy my wife cheated on me with was a former teammate. That made things kind of awkward with my old buddies. And that's putting it mildly. I wanted to take him apart with my bare hands. And my teammates were the only friends I had, so I was pretty isolated, other than a couple of my closest friends, Frenchy and Copper.

This morning I ran into Miles at Café Royale when we were both getting coffee and he invited me to the fair. He and Nolan, who I met at the Cuban music event, are going, along with Millie and Ana. A county fair is a long way from the exclusive clubs and flashy night life in Los Angeles, but what the hell. It's something.

I wait for them at the entrance to the park. It's a nice warm evening and people are streaming into the venue—groups of teenagers, parents with kids, older couples. Music from the bandstand and the smell of hot dogs drift on the air.

"Hey," Nolan greets me when he and Ana arrive. "Good to see you, man."

We exchange hellos and some small talk for a little while. Then Miles and Millie show up and we do it again.

When I first met them, they acted like I was Tom Cruise or some mega-famous celebrity, all polite and careful and formal. Which was laughable because I felt like a huge nobody here in Napa, knowing nothing and no one. Now they're more at ease.

Finally, when no one makes a move to go in, I gesture at the entrance and say, "Should we get tickets and go in?"

"Just waiting for Bianca," Nolan says.

Bianca. Oh.

"Okay," I answer without batting an eye.

Suddenly this outing is much more interesting.

"Oh, there she is!" Millie waves.

Bianca sees Millie waving and strides toward us on long legs. Jesus, she's pretty. There's a tinge of gold beneath her smooth, tawny skin, her dark hair gleams in the evening sun, and her smile for her friends is warm and full of affection.

"Hiiii!"

She hugs her girlfriends, then Miles and Nolan, who I gather she hasn't seen for quite some time. It sounds like she's been away. Where has she been? My curiosity is aroused.

"Sorry I'm late," she says. "There was a dog."

A dog. There was a dog. What?

Then she looks at me. All that warm affection disappears. "Hi again." I'm certain she had no idea I was coming. I flick a glance toward Millie and Ana, hoping there's no matchmaking happening here. I mean, Bianca is attractive, but the last thing I need is another woman to screw me over.

"Hi, Bianca."

"You saw a dog?" Millie says with a laugh.

"He was so cute! You should have seen him—he had these floppy ears and big brown eyes, and he was so soft. A golden retriever puppy. And he was wearing a bow tie! I love dogs," she finishes with a sigh.

"Okay, let's go in!" Millie says.

We line up at the ticket booth and once inside with bands on our wrists, we start wandering down the main drag. The girls quickly detour into a big tent that's selling various crafts, exclaiming over jewelry and coasters and goat's milk soap or some shit. Miles, Nolan, and I meander a bit, too. Neither of these guys is part of the wine industry—Miles is a deputy in the Napa Valley sheriff's office and Nolan's a marijuana grower. They're both eager to hear about my hockey career, and I don't mind talking about that. I had a great run; it was only after I left hockey that things all went to shit.

After that, we continue our stroll past the kids' zone. Nolan spots the beer tent and makes a beeline toward it. I'm not going to object to a cold one, so we all get beers.

"Look at the rides!" Bianca says. "Wow! They never used to have this many."

"We have to go on the Ferris wheel," Millie says to Miles.

He slings an arm around her shoulders. "Sure."

"I want to go on the Shock Wave!" Ana points at a dangerous looking structure.

Bianca bites her lip. "I could do the Ferris wheel. I think I'm too old for the Shock Wave."

"You used to love it!" Ana says.

"I know." She scrunches up her face. "I was crazy, apparently."

"You sound like an old lady," Millie teases. "You're only twenty-six."

I'm thirty-six. That's a fuck of a lot older than her. What the hell was I doing, fantasizing about her in skimpy purple silk? Jesus.

She rolls her eyes. "The last time I came to the fair I was eighteen."

So she *has* been away for a while.

"Let's all go on the Ferris wheel," Millie says. "We can discuss the Shock Wave after."

"Uh, no thanks." I wave a hand. "You all go on, though. Rides aren't my thing."

Disappointment shows on their faces.

"You're going to make me go on the ride alone?" Bianca says.

Well, shit. The seats only hold two people, so of course she'll be alone.

"Are you afraid?" she asks, lifting a perfect eyebrow.

"I'm not afraid of it," I say patiently. "It's just not my idea of fun."

"Maybe the Teacups are more your speed? We can probably find a toddler to go on with you."

"Ha ha. I'm good, thanks."

"Standing on the ground watching everyone else is your idea of fun, then?"

I stare at her. "Basically, yeah. I'm the one who's old."

"Phhhht. Fine. I'll go alone." She turns her back on me and starts toward it. Ana and Millie give me a brief look of sadness, but follow Bianca.

Before I can even think about it, I start after the group. "Fine, I'll go on with you," I say as I join them in line. "So you won't be alone."

"Don't feel obligated on my behalf." Bianca waves a hand.

I cock my head, studying her face. She's all cool and condescending but a faint tightness at the corners of those pretty lips hints at nerves.

"Of course not." I shrug.

She sucks on her bottom lip, then shrugs, too. "Whatever."

She's nervous about the Ferris wheel. But she was going to ride alone.

The sounds of the carnival surround us—music and chatter and screams from folks on the Shockwave and the Zipper. When it's our turn to get on the big wheel, I let her go first and then the attendant closes the bar in front of us, locking it into place. Bianca curls her fingers over it but tosses her hair back and smiles as we glide away and up.

The sun is low in the sky now, the neon lights on all the rides coming on. We stop a few times as more people get off and on the ride, and end up stopped at the very top. We have a view of the entire fair and the town of Napa around us and I survey my new home. "This is cool."

"Yeah." She, too, looks around but her knuckles are white on the bar in front of us.

"Tell me some of the things you see," I say. "I'm new here."

"Right. Um, well, that's the river over there. The Napa River."

"Uh huh."

"That's a cemetery."

I nod.

The wheel starts up with a small jerk and Bianca jumps.

"This is so fun!" she says with a nervous laugh.

"Yeah, it's okay."

We're all loaded up and making smooth revolutions now.

"Have you been away from here for a while?" I ask. "I got that impression from things you've said."

"Yes. I went away to college in New York, and then I moved to Argentina."

"Whoa. That's quite a move."

"I did my degree in Viticulture & Enology, and then an internship at a winery in Argentina. When I finished, they offered me a job and I decided to stay."

"Wow." I'm impressed. "Why are you back?"

Her eyes shadow. "My grandmother died and left my sisters and me her winery. I took a leave to come home and help my sisters figure out what we're going to do with it."

"Are you thinking of selling it?"

She's quiet, gazing out at the view below us. "We can't sell it. Nonna loved Caparelli. She and my grandfather made some amazing wines there, years ago. It's been in the family for a long time." Then she visibly straightens and says crisply, "What about you? You just bought Take Flight. What made you decide to come here and buy a winery?"

"I needed something to do."

It's sort of a joke, if you know me, but she doesn't know me, and also I'm not good at making jokes. She gives me another chilly look. "That doesn't sound like a very good reason to buy a winery. Running a vineyard and making wine are a complicated business."

"I'm learning that."

"You've never made wine before?"

"Yeah, I made wine. At home. Also I've drank a lot."

Another joke that lands like a bowling ball.

"Sure," she says, more scorn in her voice. "That'll help a lot."

"I'm not making a good impression on you, am I."

She blinks. Then her lips twist briefly. "I'm sorry. The Wright family owned Take Flight for generations. It's hard seeing someone else take over it."

"I know. I've talked to Jake."

She starts. "You have? Oh. Of course you have."

"Just to be clear, I didn't buy it out from under them. They put it up for sale for their own reasons. I just happened to be the lucky buyer."

She levels a long, lukewarm look on me. "You're right. That's not a reason to resent you. I'm sorry again." She sighs. "I'm...well, I'm not entirely happy to be back here. My grandma died. My family is pissed at us because she left the winery to us. My uncle is apparently trying to sabotage us."

"Jesus."

"Yeah. My little sister can't be bothered to come and help deal with this. And, truthfully...I was a bit nervous about this Ferris wheel."

"No? Really?"

She shoots me a slitty-eyed look.

I shrug. I admire her honesty. "I'm kinda surprised you're nervous." She doesn't seem like the fearful type. She seems confident. Self-assured. Blowing off to Argentina must have taken guts.

"Maybe I am getting old." She wrinkles her nose.

I snort.

"I don't usually take things like that out on other people, so I'm sorry. Everything will work out."

"I'm sorry about your grandmother."

Her face softens. "Thank you. I miss her. Even though I lived far away, she was always here."

Bianca has an air of reserve about her, other than when she's interacting with her friends. You can practically see the guard she lets down with them. Not that she's cold. Nobody with a mouth like that and eyes so sensual could be cold. Now seeing a bit of softness beneath the reserve makes me even more curious about her.

As we slow to a stop at the bottom to get off the ride, she says quietly, "Thanks for coming on here with me."

Chapter 4

The others are waiting for us but instead of more rides, Ana and Millie decide they're hungry, so we head to some of the food booths. I'm starving, too. There's a lot to choose from—corn dogs, barbecue, funnel cakes. We study options, standing beneath white lights strung among the tall cypress trees around us. We all make our selections and then take them to the wine garden, where one of the local wineries is selling their products.

"I'm super curious about their wine," I say quietly as we approach the bar.

"Why?" Millie asks.

"All they make is blends."

"Ah."

Although not part of the wine business, she's lived in the valley her whole life, so she understands.

"What does that mean?" Jansen asks.

"Hang on, I'll tell you more." I smile at the girl behind the bar. "I'll try the Blackbird, please."

"Of course." She pours me a glass.

"What is the blend?" I ask.

"It's sixty-seven percent zinfandel, thirty-three percent cabernet sauvignon. Blackbird combines the robust flavors of zinfandel and the grandeur of cabernet sauvignon, resulting in a rich wine with full fruit flavors and soft, elegant tannins."

"Do you know how it's aged?"

She smiles. "Eighteen months in one hundred percent French oak, sixty percent new, forty percent neutral."

"Thank you."

We find a table and sit. I hold up my glass, swirl it, sniff it, then sip.

Jansen's watching me. I try not to be distracted from the wine. His brown hair is brushed back off his face, neat sideburns meeting dark jaw stubble, his mouth seductive, his eyes attentive.

Ahem.

I let the flavors of the wine play over my tongue. I nod.

"How is it?" Jansen asks. "Good?'

I smile. I don't describe wines as "good." "Luxurious," I say. "Flowing red and blue fruit flavors—blackberry, blueberry, cranberry. The zinfandel gives a layer of cracked black pepper and red licorice. Then there are hints of caramelized brown sugar and vanilla from aging in the French oak."

He nods slowly.

I smile brightly. "How's yours?" He chose a different one.

He takes a sip. "I'd say...dark."

I nod. "Fair."

"Blackberry. Cherry." His forehead wrinkles. "Mocha?"

Interesting.

"Want to try it?"

"I do." I reach eagerly for his glass. I'd taste everyone's if I could.

"Mmm. This one's different. I think it's a blend of several varietals. I'd say cab sauv plus syrah and malbec, for sure. And yes, dark. Deep. Voluptuous."

Jansen does a slow blink.

Heat slides over my skin at the way he's looking at me. I kind of sounded like I was talking about sex. Ha.

I hand back his wine and he takes it, eyes fastened on my face.

Damn, he's attractive.

Yes, I resented him. Not only for being the new owner of Take Flight, which I know logically isn't his fault, but for being another rich celebrity who thinks he can just buy a winery and become a winemaker. I was kind of a bitch to him even though he was nice enough to come on the Ferris wheel with me.

But even though I had a grudge against him, I felt a tug of attraction.

He has a strong presence, making me feel like the world has shrunk to this tent, this table. His gaze on me is weighty, substantial. Intense. This is not a man who goes through the motions; he's focused, purposeful, engaged.

Up there on the Ferris wheel, his strength reassured me, though. He knew I was nervous and tried to distract me from it and I felt safer because of it and maybe a teensy bit grateful.

My gaze wanders from his intent eyes down to his right shoulder, which he's rolling apparently subconsciously. His left hand holds the plastic cup of wine. No ring. His fingers are long and lean, dusted with dark hair. His hands are attractive. His thick eyebrows are attractive. Even his voice—gah. It's rich and smooth, like red wine. Like expensive sheets. Like slow sex.

I've been reliving the embarrassment of that night when I accidentally asked him if I'd look sexy in that slip, but I couldn't figure out why. Sure, it was a little embarrassing, but I've done that in the grocery store and didn't brood about it for days. It wasn't the embarrassment, though. It was him.

With his towering height and unmistakeable strength, he has a very physical presence. He's not a lean man, but he's not fat, with broad shoulders, a muscle-packed chest, and thick thighs. He's solid. And tall. He's hot.

I suck air into my lungs and gulp down wine. And choke.

Oh God.

I cough into my hand, heat enveloping me, my chest burning.

"Are you okay?" Ana asks, seated next to me.

I nod. "Fine. I was trying to breathe and drink at the same time." I was abusing that poor glass of red. Serves me right. "Spoiler alert: it doesn't work."

I cough a few more times, dab at my mouth with a paper napkin, then pick up my corn dog, all the while trying to ignore Jansen watching me from across the table.

"Tell me about the blends," Jansen says.

"Right." I focus on wine. "Well, cabernet sauvignon is king in Napa Valley. That's what most of the grapes grown here are. It used to be that everyone wanted single-vineyard wines. Wines made just from the grapes grown in one vineyard. Or even one block." Like the Carleo Belmonte still produces. From Caparelli grapes. Ugh. I wave a hand. "I can explain that some other time. Or maybe you already know. Anyway. People used to turn their noses up at blends, but I'm intrigued by them. I think bringing different varietals together can be like creating an orchestra."

"Okay, yeah." He nods.

"Are you getting winemaking lessons?" Ana asks Jansen with a smile. "I told you Bianca could help you."

I give her a look. "This isn't exactly lessons."

"I know. He could probably use your help at the winery, though."

"I've got things covered," Jansen says with a polite smile. "We're good. But thanks."

He just took over a winery and he doesn't need help? I call bullshit. But I set that aside. "Here in Napa we make reds in a Bordeaux style. And I think we can make excellent *blends* in a Bordeaux style." I lift my glass. "I'm impressed with this one. The winemaker is doing a good job." A little envy warms my stomach. God, I want to make wine.

"What were you making in Argentina?" he asks.

I sigh inwardly, remembering my work there. "In Argentina, it's all about the malbec. They make the best malbec in the world. I was also playing around with syrah, cabernet franc, cabernet sauvignon, and bonarda. Full-bodied, layered, very intense wines."

"Interesting."

I smile. "I could talk for hours about it. Don't encourage me."

"It's interesting."

"The goal in blending is to respect the character of each varietal while crafting the best possible wine." I wave my hands again, almost knocking my glass over. I grab it to steady it. "Oops. So like when one musician plays the...the flute, it can be pretty. But when you layer in more instruments and musicians who play well together, you create a beautiful, harmonious symphony."

"Right. Like a hockey team."

"A...what?"

"A hockey team. You have a bunch of guys who are good players on their own position, good at scoring goals or taking faceoffs, or defending or stopping goals, and you put them all together to make a team that works as one."

A slow smile plucks at my lips. "Yes. That's it exactly. In music you have to understand all the different highs and lows and rhythms. The different instruments. And with sports, I guess. With wine, you have to know the flavors and what individual wines contribute to the overall character. And like music, it should evoke emotion. Memories. A shared experience. A good wine is best shared."

"Also like a hockey game."

I grin. "Sure. Okay, I'll shut up now."

He almost smiles. "Thanks for explaining that."

"No problem." I bite into my corn dog. "God, this is good! I haven't had a corn dog in years."

After we eat, we go back outside.

"Come on over, folks! Win the ladies a prize!" A man at one of the games gestures at us, pointing to giant stuffed animals.

"What if we can win our own prizes?" I call back to him.

The others all chuckle and I catch Jansen's smile of appreciation.

"Skee ball," Nolan says, rubbing his hands. "Let's do it."

"Don't waste your money," Ana begs him. "You'll never win anything."

He frowns. "You just challenged my masculinity. Now I have to win something for you."

She covers her eyes with one hand. "Oh, here we go."

The three guys pay and line up.

Why is Jansen doing this? He doesn't have to win a prize for anyone. Maybe it's just fun for him.

He's tossing the ball in quick, efficient motions, his hand and eye coordination commendable, racking up points. He punches his hands in the air when he wins, then looks almost embarrassed, dropping his arms. The game operator hands him a plush panda bear.

Jansen looks down at it. He shakes his head, then looks at me. "Here you go," he says dryly.

"Oh, keep it! You won it!"

"I don't need a stuffed bear."

I reach out for the bear. I have a weakness for pandas. I stroke my fingers over the soft fur and admire the black rings around his eyes.

"Why did you play?"

"To win."

Our eyes meet.

Okay. I understand that.

He has a competitive streak. He wants to be the best. So do I.

Huh.

"I used to have a panda almost like this when I was a little girl. I named him Dumpling." I make a face. "Did you know that pandas spend twelve hours a day eating?"

"No. I did not know that."

"Twelve hours of eating. What a great life that would be."

His lips twitch.

"Is that you, Bianca Martinelli?"

I turn and see my eleventh-grade teacher, Mrs. Gerstenmayer. Oh my God. I can't find words for a few seconds as I stare at her. "Um, yes!" I plaster on a big smile. "Hi, Mrs. Gerstenmayer."

"You're back! I'm so sorry about your grandmother."

"Oh, thank you. We all miss her."

"The entire county misses her. When will her memorial be held?"

"We're planning it for after harvest."

"Ah." She nods. "Argentina! Is that where you still are?"

"Yep." I smile again. "I'm here to help Rosa and Allegra.

You probably heard that Nonna left her winery to us." Except Allegra's not even bothering to show up.

"Rumor is that you're going to sell it to Geno."

My eyes pop open wide. "What!"

She nods, lips pursed. "That's what I heard. Oh hello, Ana. Millie. How are you?"

We make some small talk that thankfully doesn't involve me, and then Mrs. Gerstenmayer moves on.

I slump against Ana. "Why did we have to run into her?" I mumble.

Ana chuckles. "It had to happen sooner or later."

"Who is that?" Jansen asks.

"Eleventh grade English teacher." I avoid his eyes. "There was this one night I was hanging out with a bunch of seniors and we maybe drank some beer and smoked a little weed and decided to steal some golf carts from the high school football team and I may have lost control of mine and drove it into her storage shed."

His eyes widen. He rolls his lips inward. "I see."

"I had to spend the first part of my summer vacation rebuilding it." I wince. "Nonna was not happy about that." It did get me some attention, but I discovered that I didn't like being in trouble and went back to my nerdy, invisible ways after that.

"Did you pass English?" he asks.

That makes me smile. And his lips are curved in what almost appears to be amusement, too. "Barely. I was more of a science girl."

"Ah."

As we meander the fair and end up sitting near the bandstand to listen to the group doing Fleetwood Mac covers, I think about Mrs. Gerstenmayer's comment about selling the winery to Uncle Geno.

I know we were adamant when we found out that Nonna had left us the winery that we would run it ourselves. But realistically, both Allegra and I have lives far away from here. We were all emotional at the reading of the will but now that some time has passed, and not hearing anything from Allegra, maybe we really aren't being practical about this.

Selling to Uncle Geno would definitely be an option.

I nibble my bottom lip as I turn that idea around in my mind. I could go back to Argentina. Allegra could stay wherever the hell she is right now. Rosa could—I don't know, I'm sure she could get a job as an office manager at another winery near here, or go back to working at Belmonte. The family would all be happy.

Why didn't we even consider that?

I need to talk to my sisters about it.

The musicians take a break.

"Should we go to the petting zoo?" Ana asks. "They have baby goats."

"Oh my God, I love baby goats!" I jump to my feet. Then I see the expression on Jansen's face. "What? What's wrong with baby goats?"

"Nothing."

"Don't tell me—petting animals isn't your thing."

"I feel like goats smell bad."

A laugh shoots out of me. "Well, maybe."

"Also goats are jerks."

My mouth drops open and I gape at him. "Take that back!"

He blinks. "What? They are?"

"They're adorable!"

"A goat headbutted me once," Miles says.

"See?" Jansen lifts his eyebrows.

"I...I...can't." I stare at him. Someone who doesn't like baby goats?

He shrugs. "I've never had much to do with farm animals."

"City boy, huh?"

"Basically, yeah. Also too busy playing hockey."

I frown.

"Didn't you know Jansen used to play hockey?" Ana says.

I give her a perplexed look. "No. How would I know that? Also, what does that mean?"

"Hockey's a sport played on ice where skaters try to score a goal with a stick and a puck." Jansen's face is deadpan.

"I know what hockey is!" I laugh and give him a little push. Oh. He's solid. Definitely.

"He was a professional hockey player," Ana says. "With the Long Beach Golden Eagles. He was kind of famous."

I blink. "Oh." I look back at him. "I'm sorry, I don't follow hockey. I didn't recognize your name."

"I wouldn't expect you to."

"So that's what the hockey team analogy was about." I tap my temple. "I like it. Different wines bring different attributes to a blend, like individual players on a team. And bringing them together elevates the game."

"Yeah. Exactly."

"Well, that's cool. Okay, let's go look at the animals."

As we stroll, my head is now full of the surprising information that Jansen is a hockey player. Or used to be. That he's famous. With hockey fans, I guess. I don't know anything about hockey. Now I want to. Which is crazy.

"Definitely smells like a barn in here." Jansen scrunches up his slightly-crooked nose.

"Don't worry, the scent won't stick to you after we leave." On the Ferris wheel I noticed the seductive scent of his cologne, something that smells like walking into the perfume department at Saks.

He rolls his eyes.

We spend time admiring and petting bunnies, goats, sheep, and the cutest little pigs! Well, Jansen keeps his distance while the rest of us pet them and feed them the food they give us. Then we all make a quick stop in the bathrooms before returning to the wine lounge for another drink.

As we take our seats, a man stops in front of me. "Bianca?"

I meet his eyes. It's Mark Watson, my high school boyfriend. "Mark! Hi!"

"I heard you're back." He smiles. "It's good to see you."

"You, too!" He was—is?—a nice guy. He still wears his light brown hair in a neatly cut style and his eyes crinkle at the corners with his easy smile. If I'd stayed in Oak Creek Canyon, who knows what would have happened with us.

We do a little catch-up chit chat, then when I mention Caparelli, he says, "I heard that Geno's contesting the will."

Once again, I'm thrown. My mouth falls open. I shake my head. "I haven't heard anything about that. I think the lawyers would let us know if he was."

"Maybe he just plans to." Mark shrugs. "That's kind of awkward, huh?"

"Oh yeah." Jeez. What the hell? I keep hearing all these things that are supposedly happening but aren't. This is one reason I was happy to escape small town life. Everybody's all up in everyone else's business. Apparently that hasn't changed here. "I'll be having a talk with Geno soon." I smile as if everything's fine. "We'll figure it all out."

Why hasn't Rosa told me about all these crazy rumors?

"How long are you here for?" he asks. "We should go out for a drink sometime."

"Oh sure. That would be great. I'm not sure how long I'm here, but at least a couple of months. I said I'd help with harvest."

"Okay. Give me your number, and I'll text you."

We exchange phone numbers.

When I turn around and sit down, I immediately feel Jansen's eyes on me. He's watching with a steady gaze and thin lips.

I smile. "Old boyfriend." I wave a hand. "Years ago."

"I should be going," Jansen says. "I've got an early morning with my vineyard manager to check the grapes."

Everyone agrees it's time to call it a night and we all walk to the exit. Now it's totally dark and all the lights in the trees and on the rides are so pretty. The faint screams of excited riders float on the breeze along with the music of the band that's playing again.

"Where'd you park?" Ana asks me.

I point down the street. "In the lot that way."

"Oh, we're this way. Okay, goodnight, I'll text you about yoga classes."

"Okay! Night, everyone."

I start walking and Jansen joins me. "I'm parked this way, too."

"Oh. Okay." After a pause, I say, "Did you enjoy the fair?"

"Actually, I did."

"You sound surprised."

"Well, to be honest, I wasn't sure about coming tonight. I've never been to a county fair."

"Ah. Right. City boy."

His lips kick up. "Right. Also, I'm pretty busy these days, trying to figure out what's going on, and do some renos on my house."

"You do have a lot on your plate. Well, this is my car." I point at my rental. I meet his eyes even though my belly flutters as I do so. "I'm glad you joined us and had a good time. Good night, Jansen."

"Goodnight."

I get into my car, reverse out of the spot, and exit the parking lot. I glance in my rear-view mirror and see a shadowy shape of a man leaving the parking lot and going back the way we came from. That's Jansen. He said he was parked this way, too. Where is he going? Weird.

Chapter 5

Bianca

"We need to have a team meeting," I announce the next morning in the kitchen.

Rosa gives me a sour look. "What does that mean?"

"You, me, and Allegra. We have to talk."

"About what?"

"About why a pizza box is square when a pizza is round." I exhale with exasperation.

"Bee!" She scowls. "Okay, I presume we need to talk about Caparelli."

"Yes. There are all kinds of rumors going around and honestly, I don't know if we've evaluated all our options."

"Like what?" Her forehead pleats.

"Let's talk to Allegra. What is the time difference? And where is she right now anyway?" I pull out my phone. "I'll message her."

To my surprise, she responds right away and says she can video chat with us. I call her, and Rosa and I sit at the kitchen table with my phone propped up in front of us.

"What's happening with you?" I ask Allegra. "Where are you now?"

"Romania!"

"Oh wow. Okay."

"What's the hockey player like?" Allegra asks. "Does he have teeth?"

I blink. "Uh. Yes, he has teeth. I think." I squint. "He doesn't smile much, so it's hard to know. But he ate a corn dog the other night with no problems."

"You had dinner with him?" Allegra gapes at me.

I wave a hand. "No. I was at the fair with Millie and Ana and they invited him, too. He's kind of a grumpy bear." A very attractive grumpy bear. But I'm not admitting that out loud.

"Ah." Allegra smirks. "Nothing wrong with a bear."

"I have no constructive response to that."

She grins. "Why did you call this meeting?"

I take a breath. "There are rumors going around town about us."

"What else is new." Allegra rolls her eyes.

"Apparently Geno is thinking of contesting the will."

Allegra snorts.

Rosa shakes her head. "James said the will was airtight."

"Did you know about this?" I ask her.

She bites her lip. "Yes."

"Why didn't you tell us?"

She averts her gaze. "I didn't want to bother you. It's just a rumor."

I throw my hands up. "Rosa! We're a team! Don't hide things from us."

She rubs her forehead. "I'm sorry. You're right."

"You have to tell us what's going on," Allegra says, thankfully backing me up.

"I know. I will."

"Has Uncle Geno said anything to you about that?"

"No."

"Do we trust him, though? After all his efforts to undermine us here?"

Rosa nibbles on her bottom lip. "No. I don't trust him."

"So he could very well be planning to contest the will."

"I guess so," she concedes. "He could tie things up for a long time."

"Let him try." Allegra waves a hand. "This is clearly what Nonna wanted."

"Well, we can't do anything about it until we're notified legally, so..." I pause, not sure where to go next. "I'm going to talk to Uncle Geno. There's another rumor."

"What?" Allegra asks.

"That we're going to sell Caparelli to him."

"What!" Allegra gasps. "No!"

I huff out a laugh. "Have you thought about it, though?" I glance sideways at Rosa.

She frowns. "No. Of course not. We've talked about that. Nonna wanted *us* to have this winery."

"Maybe we were all caught up in the emotion of it," I say slowly. "I know that's what she wanted, but I have my job in Argentina, and Allegra is in Romania. Maybe selling is a reasonable option."

Her brows twitch toward each other, but she says nothing.

"Is this what you want to do?" I continue. "Because we don't have to do this. It's going to be a lot of work, and a lot of money, and...well, obviously it would make Uncle Geno happy if we sold to him."

"Would it, though?" Rosa asks. "I think he wants us to just give it to him."

I purse my lips. "You could be right."

"No," Allegra says, unequivocally. "We are not selling."

"But you're not even here, Legs," I say gently. "Are you going to come home and help with this?"

"I just have a little issue I'm dealing with here." Her gaze slides off camera. "I'll be home. I'm just not sure when."

I swallow my sigh. Sure. Great.

"I'll admit I had the same thoughts," Rosa says.

My head snaps around to stare at her.

"Handing the reins back to Uncle Geno and the cousins would be so much easier, so much less stress." She lifts her hands. "But I don't want to see Nonna's legacy swallowed whole by the rest of the family business."

"Same," Allegra says.

"I'm prepared to work at this," Rosa adds. "Jake's here to help. You're here now."

"Not for that long, though," I remind her. "This is a lot for you to handle if I go back to Argentina."

She bites her lip. "Is that what *you* want, Bee? Do you want us to sell?"

I pause. Since I've been back, I've thought a lot about it. It would be easier. I could go back to Argentina and not worry about my sisters and this beautiful place. But... "No." I just can't do it. "But I want to make sure you two are all in with this crazy plan."

"It's what Nonna wanted, and I think we should at least try."

I meet Rosa's eyes, then turn back to my phone and stare at Allegra in the camera.

"I agree," she says.

"Okay." I nod and lift my chin. "Then that is what we'll do."

I'm not only relieved, I'm happy. I don't want to sell to Geno. But I felt we should talk about it again.

"I have another suggestion." Rosa bites her lip and her eyes meet mine then skitter away.

"What?" I ask slowly.

"We could sell the grapes."

I blink. And blink again. "Sell the grapes? Seriously?"

"Yes, seriously. It would be one way we could make money."

It's not a crazy idea. There are lots of wineries that don't grow their own grapes, or all of their own grapes. They buy grapes from vineyards and make their wines from them.

"Then we'd *really* have no wine," I say. "How would that help us bring Caparelli back to life?"

Her lips tighten. "It would just be a slower path. We could use the money to do other things this year. And then next year we could start making wine."

"I don't want to wait that long." I look at the phone and see Allegra's conflicted expression. "What do you think, Legs?"

"I don't know." She makes a face. "Okay, I do know. I'm coming home. Soon. And maybe I don't make the wine, but I want to help sell the wine. I have so many ideas! And I want to contribute. So I don't want to sell the grapes and wait until next year."

Relief slides warmly through my veins. I smile at Allegra then look at Rosa.

"Okay," she says with a hitch of one shoulder.

"Okay, the other thing." I glance between my sisters. "I met Jansen Beck, who bought Take Flight. He might need some help."

"That's not our problem," Rosa says, evidently still a little bitter on behalf of the Wright family for having to sell.

"Not, of course not. But good neighbors help each other. Although we do have a lot of work to do here."

"This is enough work," Rosa agrees.

"Well, there's another angle I thought of yesterday. Jake said Jansen has a beautiful modern lab over there. We don't have a lab at all. I mean, we have space for one, but all the equipment is either gone to Belmonte, or it's out of date. We need to test the grapes, test the juice once we've harvested. I could make a deal with Jansen that we get to use his lab in exchange for me helping him."

"Huh." Rosa tilts her head and looks at Allegra.

She wrinkles her nose. "You do what you think is right, Bee."

Yikes. I look back at Rosa.

"Well, that's a good point about the testing," she says slowly. "But we do have some money we could use."

"We're going to need funds for harvest. And barrels. And a million other things."

"The tasting room!" Allegra pipes up.

Oh boy. There was a tasting room here many years ago. "We have no wine to taste, Legs," I remind her.

"We will!"

I smile. "Yeah. We will. And that raises another question. But first—if I make that deal with Jansen, you're both okay with it?"

"Sure," Rosa says slowly.

"Of course," Allegra replies.

"Do you think I'm letting down Nonna by helping another winery and not focusing on Caparelli?" I bite my lip.

"Nonna would have wanted to support a neighbor," Rosa says firmly.

"I agree," Allegra says. "Remember the time the Crowleys had their baby way too early, right in the middle of harvest, and

Nonna went over there and helped keep things going while the Crowleys were at the hospital with the baby?"

Nonna did always do stuff like that. I smile. "Okay. I wish Uncle Geno felt the same." My lips push downward. "It's ridiculous that he doesn't want us to run Caparelli. Neighbors help neighbors. Family helps family. Right?"

"Right." They both appear dubious.

"Okay. We need to have a clear plan. Not just financial, but also branding, marketing, production."

"I have a lot of that figured out," Rosa says. "But we do have decisions to make."

"Let's do it."

We spend time going over Rosa's plans and analysis and estimates, talking about expenses, barrel needs, bottling costs, and capital expenditures. Then we move on to salaries, benefits, supplies, repairs/maintenance, utilities, packaging, bottling, and warehousing costs.

We argue about a few things; we all have different priorities when it comes to the winery. For me it's all about the wine, of course. But we manage to come to consensus on the decisions we need to make now.

"Okay, I think that's good for today," Rosa eventually says. "Next we need to work on our sales and marketing plan. We really need to nail down our branding."

"I can help with that!" Allegra says.

"Okay." I sit back in my chair. "Anything else you want to tell us before we end the call?" I ask Allegra.

She frowns. "What? What do you mean? What would I have to tell you?"

I pop up one eyebrow. "I don't know...maybe what you've been doing, who you're with, what the weather there is like?"

"Ahahaha. Funny. Okay. Gotta go. Bye!"

Rosa and I exchange glances as I tap the screen on my phone to end the call.

"She's acting weird," Rosa says.

"She always acts weird."

She snorts. "True."

Okay, that's settled. Why am I so invested in this? I don't even plan to stay long enough to see how the wine turns out.

But I care.

Chapter 6

Jansen

"How was the fair?"

Diego, Antonio, and I are walking in the vineyard. I glance at Diego. "It was okay. Kind of fun. I learned some stuff about wine blends."

"Huh. That's good."

Diego pauses and plucks a grape from the vine. He pops it in his mouth.

We're looking at the grapes to see if we're ready to start harvesting.

Diego makes a face. "I wish I had more experience with this."

Antonio tries one, too.

The grapes look good to me—fat and purple. I might as well try one, but I have no idea what I'm looking for. Yep. Tastes like a grape. "This tastes pretty good to me."

"It can taste good a while before they're ready to pick," Antonio says. "I think they need longer." He makes a face. "I'm used to working with the winemaker to decide."

Both these guys know what they're doing in their own

jobs. Antonio is my cellar manager. He was working as the cellar assistant until I bought the place, which involves a lot of stuff—moving wine, topping, filtration, cleaning and sanitizing the equipment, helping with bottling, and, like pretty much everyone here, helping with the harvest. He just doesn't have a lot of experience with actual winemaking. Diego looks after the vines—pruning them and trellising them, monitoring soil moisture, monitoring pests and diseases, and overseeing the harvest. And yeah, he knows how to assess the grapes for ripeness, but the winemaker needs to be involved, too.

Except I don't have a winemaker.

"Let's check the Brix." Diego holds up some kind of tool, then plucks a bunch of grapes and squeezes them over it. The juice drips into a well. "The sugar in the grapes is measured in degrees Brix," he explains to me. "It should be between nineteen and twenty-five degrees. We can also check the pH and TA levels."

I know most of that. "TA?"

"Titratable levels. A good target for red wine is generally six point five to seven point five grams per litre."

"This feels like chemistry class."

"Yeah, there is a lot of chemistry. But you know, there's no substitute for experience. Most winemakers I've worked with use the science but also the taste and feel of the grapes."

I was more of a science girl.

Last night I learned so much about Bianca Martinelli. I thought she was a smoke show that night I met her, but after listening to her rattle on so passionately about wine, about a dog wearing a bow tie, even about destroying her teacher's shed, I'm even more attracted. She's fun. Interesting. Seriously bangable. Also, young. Too young for me.

She's not immature, though.

"I don't have that kind of experience," Diego says regretfully. "Are you hiring a winemaker?"

I shake my head to refocus. "Yeah. Working on it. How close do you think we are to harvest?"

"The forecast is for warm weather. So it could be a matter of days."

"Shit. I won't find someone that quickly."

"Probably not. This isn't the best time of year to be hiring someone. And after we harvest, there's a lot of work to do. Testing, checking sugar and alcohol levels, making adjustments. I can do that, but it's a lot for one person."

"Okay." I rub my forehead. I have to quit fantasizing about a winemaker and actually run my goddamn winery.

"We also need to get the reds bottled," Antonio says. "Unless you want to let them age even more."

Hell if I know. "How do we know when they're ready?"

"They're ready when the cork goes in the bottle," he says.

Diego laughs.

Ah. That was a joke.

"Seriously, it's the same thing—experience. Tasting the wine. Deciding if we want to blend any of it, or bottle them as single varietals."

This I understand now, thanks to Bianca.

"Okay. Leave it with me for a bit."

They both nod.

I make my way back inside. The person who really runs the business is Carol. She's the accountant for Take Flight and luckily stayed on. She does a million other things, too, though. I stop in the door to her office. "Hey, Carol. How are you?"

She smiles. I think she's about sixty, but her deep ochre brown skin is unwrinkled and her smile is youthful. Curly hair bounces around her face when she talks and moves. "I'm good, thanks, boss."

I smile at being called boss. "How was your dinner last night?" She told me yesterday that her son and new daughter-in-law were having her and her husband over for the first time in their new home.

"It was really nice! Isabella cooked us a lovely dinner. The chicken was a little dry." She makes a face. "But I didn't tell her that. And they're settling into the house."

We chat a bit more and then I go into my own office and sit at the desk.

Bianca gave that dipstick her number last night. Lucky for me, I have a good memory when it comes to numbers. I pull out my cell phone and look at it for a few minutes.

Am I really calling her for business reasons?

Or am I calling her because I want to give her the business? Heh.

Might as well be honest. It can be both.

No. This has to be strictly business.

I hate having to admit I need help. Needing help makes you weak. So my dad always told me.

Finally I tap in the digits.

It rings a couple of times, then she answers. "Hello?"

"Hi. Bianca?"

"Yes..."

"It's Jansen Beck."

After a beat of silence, she says, "Hi, Jansen."

"I hope you don't think this is stalkerish, but I heard you give that guy your number last night. It, uh, stuck in my mind. And this morning I was talking to my guys here and we have some problems." I pause and grit my teeth. "I'm hoping you might be able to give me advice."

"Mmm." I can almost hear her thinking. "What kind of advice?"

"We aren't sure when to pick the grapes."

Another short pause. "Oh."

"Also, we have wines that need to be bottled. Antonio says we might want to blend some of them. And we were talking about that last night, and you sound like you know what you're talking about."

"I do know a little about it." I hear the smile in her voice. "We're going through the same things here. Except we don't have any wine to bottle." She blows out a sharp breath. "But never mind that. We're getting close to harvest, yes. I'm going to be helping Jake today, but I could come over there later, if that works."

Better than I'd hoped. "Sure. That's fine."

"Three-ish?"

"Sounds good. You know where I am?"

"I live next door."

"Right. Okay. Great. See you then."

I end the call. Okay. It didn't sound like she's going to call the cops on me. Although I do have a contact in the sheriff's office. Ha.

I lost some sleep last night, thinking about her. That never happens to me. Since my divorce, I've gone out with a few women, but I haven't been so caught up in someone that I keep thinking about her. Dreaming about her. Fantasizing about her.

Get it together, man.

Carol and I go over some business things and I give her approval to order supplies, stuff I don't understand, which frustrates me, but I'm learning. I spend the afternoon with Diego in the vineyard being taught more about caring for the vines.

"I want to get some owls," he says.

I frown. "How do you get owls?"

"There's a group in Napa that build owl boxes so that barn owls will nest in them. Owls eat rodents, so it helps us with rodent control."

My chin jerks down. "We have a rodent problem?"

"Not a problem, but there are always mice and rats." He shrugs.

"So much for the romantic beauty of winemaking."

He grins. "Using rodenticides is harmful to the environment, and possibly to the grapes, so this is better."

"Eco-friendly," I murmur. "Okay, let's do it."

I'm checking the time until it's nearly three, then I go to the house to wash up. My face in the mirror is already tanned from being outside in the sun. I rub my stubbled jaw. Should I shave? Change my shirt? I'm kind of sweaty. Nah. What am I thinking?

I step back outside and see Bianca walking across the yard from the line of trees that separate our properties.

Once again, I feel like I just took a poke check to the gut.

Her smile as she turns her face to the late afternoon sun. Her glowing skin. Her sparkling eyes. I feel like I'm a hundred years old, tired, dirty, sweaty, and she's striding across my yard with a spring in her step like one of those baby goats she gushed over last night.

Maybe I should get some goats.

Jesus. No.

I jog down the front steps to meet her.

"Hi." Her smile is polite. She's dressed in cut off shorts and a striped tank top that hugs her generous tits, with work boots and socks on her feet. A hot pink bra strap slides down one shoulder and straggly threads hang over smooth thighs, drawing my attention there.

My body is responding, and this is not good. I clear my throat and try to keep my expression neutral. "Hi."

She arches an eyebrow. "Are you always grumpy?"

I narrow my eyes. "I'm not grumpy."

"You sound grumpy." She shrugs. "And you're scowling at me."

"No, I'm not."

She levels me with an incisive look. "Okay." She slides her gaze up and down over me. "Um. This is how you dress to work in the vineyard?"

I look down at my striped dress shirt, dark jeans, and brown leather shoes. "What's wrong with this?"

She grins. "You look like you're ready to go to a fancy club."

I roll my eyes. "Guess I should cut off my jeans, eh." I rake a glance back over her thighs.

She laughs. "Jorts is not a good look on guys. Maybe just get some boots. So. Should we have a look at your grapes?"

"Yeah. I see you brought help." I gesture at the refractometer she's carrying. "We checked some grapes earlier."

"What was the Brix?"

I fill her in as we walk toward the vines. "And Antonio said some other testing could be done."

"Yes. I'll do that, too. We need to look at a few different areas, though. Just because grapes aren't ready in one part doesn't mean the whole vineyard isn't ready. Some rows ripen more quickly if they have more sun exposure, or less if they're exposed to a lot of wind."

"That makes sense."

We walk down a path between vines. It's quiet here, peaceful and almost spiritual. The air is soft and fragrant with the scent of grapes and sun-warmed earth.

"Also some varieties take longer to get to optimal ripeness. Chardonnay and pinot noir are early ripeners. Cabernet sauvignon and syrah come later." She leans in to inspect some of the plump, golden chardonnay grapes hanging on the vine. As she reaches out a hand, I notice dirt under her short fingernails. Is that a turnoff? Hell, no.

I think of all the manicures my ex-wife got, and her perfect white-tipped nails. I thought they looked nice. Classy. But this girl's dirty nails are weirdly adorable.

"These are beautiful." The reverence in her voice matches the hushed atmosphere. "I'm looking for any shriveling or desiccation." She gently moves bunches of grapes and proceeds down the aisle, studying them. "Now we'll taste." She pops one in her mouth in a sensuous gesture that makes my groin tighten. She bites down, chews, and swallow. "I'm checking the way the skin pops when I bite into it, then tasting. It should be more... tropical than green. Green definitely has a taste. These are still green."

"Okay."

"But very close."

I follow her as we move along and she scrutinizes grapes. Every movement of slender arms and graceful hands draws me in. When she cups clusters of heavy grapes, my balls tighten. I can't look away.

We eventually come to the cabernet grapes. She does the same there, with the same worshipful admiration of the grapes. Something stirs in my midsection at her devotion and enjoyment. "I taste cherry," she says. "But not black cherry yet."

She takes another grape, bites it open, then studies it. "I'm looking at how brown the seeds are." Then she eats the seeds, chewing them. "We check the color of the grapes, the color of the stems and the seeds. The plumper and easier they pull off the vine, the riper they are. And chewing the seeds is another clue—they're softer and chewier when ripe. And of course the taste. No bitterness. The characteristics of the varietal should shine through."

"I would never know that."

She gives me an amused look. "No."

"You think I'm an idiot for doing this, don't you." I feel like I'm failing a test. I don't like it.

She hums. "No. It's bold, I'll give you that. But you seem like someone who's determined to succeed."

I nod. "Yeah. I didn't make it to the NHL without determination."

"Exactly." Our eyes meet.

I shouldn't have asked her to come here. Did I think I could be with her and keep things strictly grape business? Ha. I'm an idiot. My hands are sweaty and my cock is taking notice of how short those cut-offs are and also my chest keeps pinging.

The moment stretches out, heat building around us. Then she blinks rapidly a few times and looks away. She swallows. "If you pick the grapes at the right time, everything else falls into place. You know when you have a perfectly ripe piece of fruit and it's so delicious, but then one day later it's overripe and mushy?"

I nod.

"You want to get the grapes at that moment—when they're super delicious and the fruit has everything it needs."

"But how do you know? That's my problem."

"Truthfully? It's a bit of magic. You can measure sugar content and pH but it really comes down to taste. The relationship between acid and sugars and tannins. When the grapes are perfectly delicious. But not necessarily sweet. And no machine can tell us that. You have to trust your palate. Intuition."

I cough. "I suspect you can't teach intuition. Or magic."

The corners of her mouth, perpetually smiling, lift higher. "No."

We check more grapes, walking the paths in the quiet sunshine, probably for a couple of hours. Then Bianca says, "Okay, take me to your lab."

I feel proud that I know I have a lab and where it is. We hike back to the building, and I lead the way to the back.

"This is nice," she says, looking around the lab. "It looks like it was recently updated."

"Yes, they told me they'd updated the lab about two years ago."

She sets about testing grape juice, making notes on her iPad, mumbling to herself and explaining things to me.

"You'll need to keep a close eye on the chardonnay," she finally says. "And the pinot noir is close, too."

Sure. I'll keep an eye on them. Despite watching her closely (very closely) today, I don't really know what I'm looking for.

"Are you ready for harvest?" she asks, looking up at me. "You have workers lined up? It's an intense time."

"Diego tells me we are. He has workers ready to come when they get the word."

"Okay, good." She sighs. "We've been having some trouble finding help. Apparently, a lot of places are facing labor shortages now, and most workers have already been hired. Or they've gone into hiding because of that ICE raid at Garrafeira last week."

I frown. I recognize the name of the winery. "ICE raid?"

She makes a glum face. "Yep. We rely a lot on immigrant labor. Anyway, I'm glad you're ready."

"Should I apologize for that?"

One corner of her mouth kicks into a wry smile.

I can't look at her without noticing her mouth. Does she kiss with as much energy and passion as she shows about wine?

"Of course not," she says. "You're running a business."

"Trying."

"Aren't we all." She pauses. "What about the reds you want to bottle?"

"Right." I slide off my stool. "Do you have time to check them?"

"Sure."

I lead the way from the lab down to the cellar with its many barrels of wine. I love this place. The vineyards have a special atmosphere, but this place is unique—dark, quiet, mysterious.

Bianca makes a soft sound of pleasure as she looks around. She likes this, too.

"Do you have a wine thief?"

"Of course." I know a few basic things. I fetch the long glass tube as well as a couple of glasses, and hand it to her.

She inserts the tube into a barrel through the bunghole, holds her thumb over the top, and pulls it out containing beautiful cabernet sauvignon. I hold out two glasses and she releases wine into each. "You're tasting, too?"

"You bet. I'm learning."

She nods, smiling, returning the rest of the wine to the barrel.

We both sip. I'm getting used to watching her search out various nuances. It's sensuous. And sexy. Once again I can't take my eyes off her.

We taste various barrels, and she offers up opinions and is firm that the wines are ready to be bottled.

"What about blending some of them?" I ask.

She pauses and tilts her head. "I have ideas."

"Of course you do."

She arches an eyebrow.

"I'll pay you," I say, desperation husking my voice. "I want to make good wines."

She gazes at me for a long moment. "I have a job already. Not to mention, my own winery."

"I know." I scrub a hand over my mouth, my gut bunched in a knot. If she says no, I'll be mortified. This is why I hate asking for help. *Keep it casual.* "I just need temporary help. I'm going to hire a winemaker, but we need to bottle right now."

"Yes," she says slowly. "You do."

"You have your own winery to worry about, I know."

"True. But we don't have any wine. Unless…well, right now we don't."

My lungs are suddenly incapacitated. The silence in the cellar weighs dense and heavy around us as I wait for her response.

"Can I think about it?" she asks.

I nod, my throat feeling like I swallowed a whole grape.

"Okay. Well. It's nearly seven! I should go."

The back of my neck and shoulders tightens. I'm not ready for her to leave. "Stay for dinner."

She doesn't seem surprised by my impulsive invitation. She regards me thoughtfully.

"Can I tempt you with wine? I have a 2018 cab."

"A spectacular year," she murmurs, lips curving once again. "Tempting."

Oh, fuck yeah, I'm tempted.

"Okay," she says. "Thanks. I'll just call Rosa and let her know I won't be home for dinner." She pulls her phone out of a pocket in those indecent shorts. Speaking of temptation…

"They're probably busy doing the bone dance," she says as she makes the call.

I choke on a surprised laugh.

A moment later, she rolls her eyes at me as she leaves a voice mail. She ends the call and says, "See?" She waves a hand. "Okay, take me to the 2018 cab."

Chapter 7

Bianca

Should I be going to a surly stranger's home with him?

"I've been here before," I tell Jansen as we approach his ranch-style house. "It was years ago, though, when Rosa and Jake were dating."

I'm trusting my gut on this one. For one thing, he's friends with Millie and Ana and the guys. For another...he knew I was nervous on the Ferris wheel and tried to distract me. And I'm pretty sure he wasn't parked near me when we left the fair; he just made sure I got to my car safely.

He might be a little brusque on the outside, and he definitely looks tough, but my instincts are telling me he's got a soft interior. Soft-ish.

"I bet it hasn't changed since then." He jogs up the front steps and opens the front door. "It probably hasn't changed since the seventies."

"You're exaggerating."

"Probably. Maybe the eighties. I'm not really up on home décor. All I know is it's ugly."

We're greeted by unexpected barking, then whining. As I step inside the house, a brown and white dog charges at Jansen with excited yips and spins.

Jansen crouches down to pet the dog. "Hey buddy, yeah, I'm home. You don't need to make such a fuss, I wasn't gone that long."

I smile. "Who's this?"

"I call him Jack. I found him in the woods about a week ago, all skinny and matted and filthy. I took him to the vet and we've been trying to find his owner, but no luck."

"Ah. Poor guy." I crouch down, too, and Jack approaches me with bright eyes and sniffs. I hold out my hand palm down for him to check out. "He looks pretty handsome now, though." Although he's missing half an ear. Poor baby.

"Yeah, we cleaned him up. I don't know why I kept him here. I should have taken him to a shelter. I don't even like dogs."

My eyebrows shoot up. I look around at a bunch of dog toys strewn across the living room and a cozy dog bed near the fireplace. "Hmm. Well. That was nice of you."

Oh yeah. Definitely a soft interior.

"You like dogs," he states.

"Yeah. We had a dog when I was a kid. Rocky went with Nonna to live with Uncle Geno, and he died a couple of years after that. I was in college, but I still cried." My bottom lip pushes out.

"What kind of dog was Rocky?" Jansen asks gruffly.

"He was a golden retriever."

"Ah. I know what that is."

"He was a good boy.' I smile, determined to be upbeat. "I'm sure Jack is, too."

He grimaces. "I've never had a dog. He's a lot of work."

"Aw. Are you?" I rub his head again. "That's okay. He needs you."

"I don't need a dog."

"Everyone needs a dog. Dogs are unconditional love. All you have to do is feed and water them, play with them a bit, and be kind, and they'll love you no matter what."

We both stand and walk farther into the house, Jack prancing behind us. I'm not even sure why I'm here. I'd planned to go see Uncle Geno at Belmonte today, but when faced with a choice of looking at beautiful grapes with a handsome man or giving my uncle shit...I chose this.

Well, there was also business. I wanted to see his amazing lab. Because I already know my answer to his plea for help.

As I step down into the sunken living room, I look around. Eek. I do remember it from my teenage years, and he's right, it hasn't changed much. I catch my bottom lip between my teeth as I take in the orange and brown patterned carpet covering the floor. The massive stone fireplace fills one wall, and another wall is paneled with wood. "I see what you mean. That carpet is hideous. It has a great mid-century modern vibe, though. This house probably was probably built in the sixties. You could totally take advantage of that and have a really cool look."

"I don't know what mid-century modern is."

"Oh. Check out some pictures online. That teak paneling is amazing." I point at the living room wall. "The fireplace is a little...overwhelming. But I love the vaulted ceiling and the big windows..." I stop myself. "Sorry." I'm babbling. Now that I'm out of my element—the lab, the cellar—I'm freaking out.

This man unnerves me. He followed me around, watching me intently, making my skin hot and sensitive. I could focus on grapes and pH levels and tannins in the vineyard, and in the lab. But now, I'm in his house and I'm flustered, and how the hell is this man so fascinating? So appealing.

"The first thing I'm renovating is the kitchen," he says. "Come on."

I follow him into the kitchen. Jack's little nails click over the floor as he comes along with us. "I see what you mean." I drag my fingertips over the chipped green laminate counter and study the wood cabinets. "At least your appliances aren't avocado green."

His lips twitch.

"But there's lots of space to make it a dream kitchen. You could reconfigure it and have a big island and..." I stop again. "I probably watch too much HGTV."

He gives a little huff that might be amusement as he pauses in front of a wine rack and pulls out a bottle. He holds it up for my inspection.

I nod.

As he cuts off the foil and works the cork out of the bottle, I spy glasses on a shelf and I move to pick up two of them. "These are gorgeous glasses."

"Thanks. I don't know that much about wine, but I like drinking it out of nice glasses."

"Oh, me too! I love a nicely shaped glass. And a delicate stem." I trace my fingers over the glass, aware of his gaze following my motions. Which makes me aware that my nails are dirty. Shit. But when I look up at him, his eyes are hot. And so am I. "Are you still using corks?" I blurt.

"No." He clears his throat. "We've moved to screw caps."

I nod. "I approve."

"I was afraid you were going to give me shit for that." He pours the wine into the glasses.

I laugh. "Nah. I get the appeal of corks. The tradition. They're a renewable resource. But we have to be practical, too."

"Screw caps are much more affordable."

"Exactly."

He hands me a glass and picks up his own. Our eyes meet.

His attention dips to my mouth and lingers. My belly swoops and my thighs quiver. "To...perfectly ripened grapes," I say softly, lifting my glass.

He touches the rim of his glass to mine with a delicate ping. Again he watches me as I swirl and sniff. "Oh yeah. Black fruit and violet. The age gives it notes of cedar and eucalyptus."

A notch forms between his eyebrows. "I'm not sure if that sounds tasty."

I smile. "That's the nose." I take a sip. And savor it. Then I make a noise of delight. "Ohhhh. I think I just had a winegasm."

He grins. "A what now?"

Wow. That full on smile is...hot.

I give him a cheeky grin. "A winegasm. That little thrill you feel when you take your first sip of a really good wine."

His smile expands and he shakes his head.

I sip again. "Wow. Full-bodied. Vibrant acidity and smooth tannin."

Now he takes a sip, his eyes never leaving my face. "Black cherry."

I smile.

"Oak. Of course." He sips again. "Silky? That's not a taste."

"Mouth feel. That's a thing. And you're right, it is silky."

"There's something..." He sips again. "Is it cloves?"

I grin. "Yes, I taste that, too." I toast him, then drink more. "This is exceptional. Thank you for sharing it."

"Wine is better when it's shared."

I can't stop smiling. "Like a hockey game."

"Yeah."

A moment of shared recall stretches out.

"Taste is unique to everybody," I say. "What really matters is if you like it."

"Okay. Tell me how to make wine that everyone likes."

I laugh. "I went to university for four years to learn that, and it doesn't always work. I've had critics pan my best efforts."

"Well, fuck those idiots." He frowns.

I laugh again. "I make what *I* like. I can't try to please everybody."

"That makes sense." He drags his gaze away from me and looks around the kitchen. "I promised you dinner."

"Don't worry—"

"No, it's fine. I picked up some stuff at the farmers' market yesterday."

I lean against the counter. "Are you a good cook?"

"Mmm. I like what I cook. I don't know if that means it's good."

"Fair."

He goes to the fridge and starts pulling things out. "My plan is a sheet pan ratatouille with sausage." He pauses. "You're not vegetarian, are you?"

"I ate a corn dog last night."

"Right." He sets a package of sausages on the counter. "These looked really good. Handcrafted in Petaluma."

"Yum. What can I do?"

"Let's chop up the veg." He turns on the oven, then pulls out a couple of plastic cutting sheets.

I move to the sink and wash my hands. "My nails are filthy," I mutter.

"Here. A nail brush. And you can wash the eggplant and zucchini while you're there." He also hands over a yellow squash and a basket of cherry tomatoes, unbothered by my nasty nails. Occupational hazard. If I'm not dirty from the vineyard, I'm stained purple from grape juice.

It's easy to slice up all the veggies and the sausages. He tosses them with olive oil, salt, garlic, and fresh herbs, and slides the pan into the oven. "That'll take a while," he says. "I also bought polenta."

"I'm impressed."

"This couldn't be much easier."

His modesty turns my heart into a big swollen marshmallow. "You could serve me hot dogs," I say lightly. "And I wouldn't turn it down."

Not if I get to eat it with him.

He picks up the bottle of wine and refills our glasses. "We can go sit down while that cooks."

I trail him back into the living room. Obviously, the furniture is new. I curl up at one end of a massive charcoal sectional, shifting a cushion to a more comfortable position.

Jansen takes a seat on the other side of the sectional. Jack picks up a toy and brings it to Jansen. He absently grabs it and tugs. They get into a little back and forth, Jack growling ferociously.

"He's so cute." I smile at the pup.

"He needs a better name. I just called him Jack because he looks like he's part Jack Russell."

"Hmm. How about...Lucky? Because he's lucky you found him."

"Hmm."

"You could name him after a wine. Merlot. Zinny. Pinot."

"No."

I grin against the edge of my wine glass. "You come up with something then."

"Champ. Scout."

"Ugh. Who's your favorite hockey player?"

"Besides myself?"

I laugh. "Yes."

"Mark Messier."

"Okay, name him Mark."

"Or Mess."

I push my lips out. "That seems unfair."

"Moose. That was Messier's nickname."

"I love it!" I sit up straight. "Moose it is!" I look over at the dog, who in no way resembles a moose.

"I like it, too."

"Do you think pets have names for us, too?"

"Uh..."

I grin at his bewildered expression and lift my shoulders. "I think of weird stuff sometimes."

"Yeah." He shakes his head. "I'm sure they do have names for us. But...do we want to know them?"

I laugh again.

"Thank you for all your help, today. I appreciate it."

"I'm happy to help." I purse my lips. "To be honest, it's nice to be listened to."

His thick eyebrows launch up. "What does that mean? Nobody at your job listens to you?"

"Not at my job. Here at home." I smile and shrug. "There are some old-fashioned attitudes in my family. Plus, I was the middle kid. The one nobody noticed because Rosa was perfect and Allegra was always in trouble over something."

"Uh. You totalled your teacher's shed."

I press my fingertips to my smile. "That incident involving Mrs. Gerstenmayer was my one attempt to act out and get attention. I discovered I didn't like that kind of attention. Anyway, it was frustrating that I had all these ideas and dreams about making wine and nobody wanted to listen. So...that's why today was nice. Actually, Jake was listening to me earlier, too. He knows a lot but at least he didn't disregard my opinions. You know, I was kind of mad at him and I didn't like the idea that he's back and he and Rosa are together again, but he's really smart, and he loves her, and..." I stop. "Sorry. Sometimes I talk a lot."

One corner of his mouth jumps. "Why were you mad at him?"

"He deserted her! After graduation, he disappeared. I had to deal with a heartbroken Rosa, which was very disconcerting to me at age sixteen because she's always so unflappable. But she was flapped." I frown. "That doesn't work, does it."

One corner of his mouth hikes up. "I get what you mean. What about all those rumors people kept telling you about? About your winery."

"Wow, that was wild, wasn't it? I wonder if Uncle Geno started them? Or people are just making shit up. That happens in a small town. It's like that game of telephone—you know? Where the message gets repeated over and over until it's not even recognizable. We don't know how those started." I wave a hand but my stomach tightens in anticipation of confronting Uncle Geno about that. "Tell me more about what brings you here. You're not married, I take it? No kids?"

"No. No kids." He drops his gaze to his glass. "I'm divorced."

"Oh. I'm sorry."

He shrugs. "Shit happens. I retired from hockey and didn't know what to do with myself. Stephanie—my ex—still had her job. She owns a clothing boutique in Manhattan Beach, with one of her friends. She had all this other stuff going on, too—fitness classes, going to the spa, out for drinks with friends."

"You're young to be retired."

"Not in the hockey world. I'm thirty-six." He pauses, eying me as if he expects me to gasp with horror. I don't. I know how old he is after googling him late last night and watching videos of him playing hockey on YouTube. He won championships and medals and awards. Watching him play hockey was stupidly hot. Who knew?

"Anyway, I was trying to figure things out." He pauses. "Hockey pretty much consumed my life."

"I'm sure." I watch him over the rim of my glass as I sip.

"I still wanted to play," he says with a shrug that's trying for nonchalant. "It was hard to give it up. But it was time. All the injuries take a toll, and I wasn't producing like I used to."

Again, I feel like there's a lot going on beneath that careless shrug. After a moment of silence, I say, "Retirement can be hard."

"Eh." He drags up a smile. "I'm okay. And so far, I like it here. I feel like an outsider, but people are mostly friendly, and I enjoy a challenge."

"This is definitely a challenge. For *anybody*, never mind someone just starting out. But I give you credit for being open to advice and help from people who've been around."

An expression crosses his fast so fast, I almost miss it. Almost a flinch. "Yeah. I need to remember that I can't do it all myself."

"For sure. Wineries are run by a team." I grin. "You're a hockey player, so you know about teamwork."

He dips his chin, eyes thoughtful. "Yeah."

To be honest, I'm dying to help him. The wines I tasted today are miraculously lovely—clean, balanced, multi-dimensional. Most producers make blends that are cabernet sauvignon-dominant, and I could definitely see doing that. But I'm also imagining a blend reminiscent of wines I drank in Argentina, combining merlot, cabernet, syrah, and cabernet franc. Jansen has a magnificent syrah in his cellar that astonished me.

Blending is the craft of winemaking, and it excites me.

"Are you going to change the name of the vineyard?" I ask.

"Yeah. I want to. I haven't come up with anything, though."

The timer on the oven sounds.

We look at each other.

"You can help me brainstorm ideas over dinner." Jansen rises and heads back to the kitchen. "Since you helped so much with Jack. I mean, Moose."

I follow to see if I can help, with Moose again clicking along the floor behind me. Jansen asks me to set the table in the dining room off the kitchen, and I poke around and find plates and cutlery and set two places while he prepares the polenta to serve with the ratatouille.

With the last of the wine in our glasses, we sit down to eat. Moose sits quietly but hopefully beside Jansen's chair.

"This is fabulous," I say after a couple of bites.

"Like I said, really simple."

"You know, it's the fresh ingredients that make it so good. The local veggies, the craft sausage—it doesn't have to be fancy to be amazing." I fork up another chunk of eggplant.

"It is good," he agrees. "I like food."

I grin. "Me, too."

"I have to get back to healthy habits. I kind of got off track when I retired."

"You look great." I close my eyes briefly. *Sure, Bee, just admit you've checked him out. Repeatedly.*

That coaxes a smile from him. "Thanks. I feel better and I'm healthy, and that's what matters."

"Absolutely. Well, this is a healthy meal. I like food, but I do try to eat well. I mean, I love junk food, too. Burgers and fries? Yum. What's your biggest food weakness?"

"Potato chips. I'm not into sweets."

I nod. "Same! Although a little bit of really good chocolate is worth the calories."

Stop. Just shut up. Babbling about calories. That is *not* interesting dinner conversation. "Oh yeah! The new name for the winery."

"Right." He forks up a piece of sausage. "I'm not creative enough to come up with something good."

"Hmmm. I don't know if I am, either. Lots of names are already taken. Oak Creek, Redwoods, Olive Grove..." I heave a sigh. "What about something hockey themed? I know nothing about hockey, though."

"Hmmm. Five hole? That doesn't sound appealing. Hat Trick? Maybe. Top Shelf..."

"Taken."

"Of course." He purses his lips. "Body Check? Nope. Offside? Icing. Nah."

"What position did you play?"

"Right wing."

We look at each other. At the same time, we say, "Nope."

I laugh and his lips curve up into a half-smile.

Heat shimmies up my thighs and my heart flips.

Oh, sweet salty Jesus. I am in so much trouble.

"I know!" I bounce with excitement. "Bottle Jock!"

He stares at me blankly. "Huh?"

"Bottle Jock! Like the movie..."

More blankness.

"Bottle Shock," I say. "It's a true story about a California winery that thought their Chardonnay was ruined—bottle shock."

"I don't know what that is."

"It's when wine has a temporary loss of flavor from absorbing too much oxygen from excessive movement during transit. They thought their wine was ruined, but discovered it was just temporary and they went on to win a big award in France, beating out French wines."

"Uh huh."

"But Bottle Jock instead of Shock because…you're a jock." I gesture at him.

His expression is so vacant I start laughing. "Okay, I guess that's not going to work."

He shakes his head. "I mean…it's funny…if you know what it's about…"

"Never mind." I make a face. "It was really just a joke."

After a moment of silence, he says, "What about Bar Down?"

I cock my head. "Okay, now it's my turn to be lost. What does it mean?"

"It's a goal that hits the crossbar and goes down into the net."

"Hmmm. I like it!"

"Really?"

"Yes!" I lean forward. "You should totally make your brand about your hockey background."

"That's what the marketing woman I hired said. But hockey has nothing to do with wine. Although Wayne Gretzky's done it."

"There you go. Even I know who Wayne Gretzky is."

"There's hope for you."

"Wait." I eye him suspiciously. "Did you just make a joke?"

"Well, you're not laughing."

"Okay, it wasn't a laugh out loud joke. It was more like… teasing."

Our gazes lock. And hold.

"I may have been teasing you," he says, his voice low and sandpapery.

I swallow. "I may have liked it."

The air heats and swells around us, pressing on my skin.

His eyelids grow heavy, his focus drifting to my mouth, the pulse fluttering at my throat, my breasts. He wets his lips.

"I'm sorry I don't have dessert to offer you," he says about a year later.

"That's okay." I could imagine a different kind of dessert…

No. What am I thinking? This is not what I came home for. But wow. He's tempting.

Chapter 8

Jansen

I watch one of the tasting room associates fill a box with various bottles of wine. The customers are smiling and thrilled with their purchases after trying the wines here. I love that.

As I stroll behind the counter, Hanna rings up another purchase, and more customers wait in line. I don't know if it's the change in ownership, but business has been great.

I remember what Bianca said about making my brand about hockey. I have a branding professional working on that. She said kind of the same thing, but for her it was more about me—making the brand about me, as a hockey player. That doesn't thrill me, but if it gets people in the door, I guess I can see the benefit.

She had a lot of questions I couldn't answer, like, what is your vision? What style wine do you want to make? What is your voice? I felt like an idiot, but she suggested that I continue with the Take Flight wines, many of them named after birds, and gradually introduce my own.

I pause beside Hanna and greet the customers. "Seems you found some wines you like to take home."

"We did!" The young woman smiles. "You're Jansen Beck."

"That's me."

"We're big hockey fans," she says, gesturing to the man beside her, presumably her husband. "We used to live in Huntington Beach. We went to a lot of your games."

"Oh yeah? That's great."

We chat a bit more, then they step aside for the next customers.

"It's so cool to meet you," one man says. "I'll never forget that goal you scored against the Condors in overtime in the seventh game of the playoffs."

I grin. "That was a while ago."

"It was a great game, and beating the Condors was fantastic."

The Condors and my team, the Golden Eagles, have a long-standing rivalry.

"I enjoy beating them," I agree.

I spend a little more time chatting with customers. One couple wants to talk about wine rather than hockey, but I've been doing my homework on my wines and I can talk to them about Goldfinch, the small-production blend of cabernet sauvignon, petit verdot, and merlot.

"I really enjoyed it," the man says. "I think it'll be even better with more time in the cellar."

Huh. I file that away.

This is cool. I'm interested in the craft of making wine, but seeing your creations being consumed and enjoyed and talked about really brings it to life. Bianca talked about music. About how it should evoke emotion, and how wine is the same. How it should be a shared experience.

Yeah.

Maybe part of what I was missing after hockey was the fans —the passion and joy they have about hockey. The shared experience of being on the ice while the fans are cheering and losing their minds. And maybe I'm finding here a way to create joy for people in a completely different way.

Chapter 9

Bianca

"Jesus Jones."

I gaze around the space, mouth wide open.

I'm in the Caparelli cave a couple of days later.

It clearly hasn't been used in years, but the lights still work (some of them; we'll need a few more bulbs) and cobwebs stretch across shadowy corners, but the brick walls and floor are still amazing and beautiful. I shiver at the cool air and slowly walk farther into the cellar. Oak barrels line the walls—empty barrels—and I run a hand over the smooth old staves and hoops. They're in good shape, albeit dusty.

I haven't been in this cave for years. As kids, Rosa and Allegra thought it was creepy, but I was always fascinated by it. Nonna stopped using it years ago when new stainless-steel tanks were purchased for the cellar. This cave isn't a huge cellar, unlike other wineries in the area, but it's fascinating and full of history and character.

At the far end of the cave, I stop and stare. I narrow my eyes, unsure what I'm seeing. Rings in the brick floor encircle wooden lids. "Can this be real?" I step closer and pull up one lid to peer into the hole. "Oh my God." It's a huge terracotta vessel. "Qvevri tanks?"

I learned about these in school, the history of winemaking that utilized these huge pots to make wine. White grapes are poured into the container along with skins and stems, left to ferment with natural yeast, and then sealed to age. The wine produced has a deep color often referred to as orange.

"Wow." My mind is racing, possibilities bouncing around. This is something I don't have hands-on experience with but oh my God, it's so intriguing. I need to do some research into making orange wines. Could I do that here? I gaze around, wide-eyed, my blood fizzing with excitement.

But first I need to deal with Uncle Geno.

I find Rosa in her makeshift office in front of her computer.

"I'm going over to Belmonte," I tell her. "If I'm not back in an hour, call the cops."

She snorts. "Don't joke like that. I'm coming with you."

"You don't have to."

"Yes, I do." She stands. "We're a team."

I don't move for a second, my heart shifting in my chest.

Yeah. We're a team.

We drive down the road to Belmonte. Cars fill the parking lot there. My sunglasses and baseball cap shield me from the hot afternoon sun and our feet crunch on the gravel as we walk toward the tasting room. Voices from the patio on the other side of the building float on the soft air. No doubt the place is full of customers tasting (and buying) wine.

I want that, too. The tasting room may be Allegra's dream, but I do love that aspect of the business—watching people savor my creations. It's a wonderful feeling to bring joy into the world. Sure, it's great when we sell cases of wine to whole-salers, but you don't get that personal gratification of seeing people face to face getting pleasure from what you've produced. Maybe some day we'll have that at Caparelli. But will I be here to enjoy it?

We walk inside and stop at the reception counter.

"Hi, Rosa!" says the young girl working there. "How are you?"

"I'm great, thanks. You?"

"Busy!" She gestures at the indoor tasting room where people are gathered at the counter.

"This is my sister, Bianca." Rosa introduces us. "Bee, this is Arleth."

I smile. "Nice to meet you." I don't know why I expected the same people to be working here all these years later.

"We're looking for Geno," Rosa says.

"He's in the cellar with Vittorio."

"Okay, thanks." She leads the way through a "staff only" door and down to the cellar.

Uncle Geno and my cousin Vittorio are standing near the entrance talking. They look up as we walk in, surprise flashing on their faces.

"Hi, Uncle Geno! I'm back!" I open my arms for a hug. I mean, he's not an affectionate guy, but I'm his niece and he hasn't seen me for a while.

He frowns but moves toward me and gives me a perfunctory hug. "Bianca. I heard you're home."

"Of course you did." I roll my eyes, smiling. "Word travels fast here. Hi, Vitto."

"Hey, Bianca." We hug, too, his embrace a little warmer than my uncle's.

We make a little small talk, then Uncle Geno asks, "Why are you here?"

I give him a look, chin down. He actually grimaces.

"We have business to discuss with you. Do you want to talk here, or go to an office?" I gesture at the cellar rats—not literal rats; helpers in the cellar—moving around the space working.

"Let's go to my office," Uncle Geno says.

We follow him back upstairs. Rosa and I both know where his office is, directly behind the tasting room.

Vitto follows us, which I didn't expect, but I guess I should have. I've got Rosa here for backup, so he can support his dad.

We all take seats in the small space. Uncle Geno spends his money on the public-facing spaces; this room has old flooring, ancient furniture, and is windowless and stuffy. I study him where he sits behind his desk. His gray hair has thinned and receded over the years, revealing age spots on his brow from so much time in the sun. Creases line his forehead and his eyes.

"First of all, before we talk wine, I have to say something." I meet Uncle Geno's eyes steadily. "I've heard about the problems at Caparelli. The complaints to the sheriff's office. How hard it was to find workers. Someone messing with the equipment."

His eyes flicker but otherwise his face remains impassive.

"We *will* involve the police again if anything more happens." I make my gaze frosty, my chin lifted. "We won't stand for that kind of bullshit. We're *family*."

He narrows his eyes. "Are you accusing me of something?"

My eyebrows shoot up. "If the shoe fits..."

"Christ," Vitto mutters, scrubbing a hand over his face. "Nothing's going to happen."

I give him a long look. "Okay." Then I turn back to Uncle Geno. "Also, I heard about Rosa and Jake. Their marriage. And how you interfered with their marriage."

His mouth tightens.

"That was a terrible thing to do. Shameful. You separated them when they loved each other."

Rosa makes a soft noise next to me.

"Don't ever interfere in our personal lives again," I finish quietly.

"I'm your uncle. The only one left to look after you."

"You think trying to take away our inheritance is looking after us?" Outrage raises my voice and I take a breath to calm down.

"You girls need to come to your senses and realize you can't run a winery on your own,"

Although his tone is mild, the words offend me. That feeling of being brushed off floods back. He's never going to believe that I can be a great winemaker. But I'm not a little girl anymore; I'm an adult and I don't want or need his acceptance. I just need him to cooperate.

I fight back defensiveness and smile. "You make us sound like helpless children."

Uncle Geno rolls his eyes.

"That's not what Nonna thought of us," I continue. "Remember what her will said? Her wish was to rebuild the tradition of wine-making women. She obviously thought we're capable of doing that."

He frowns.

"Rosa has learned a lot about the business from working with you. I've learned a lot, at school and working at Castillo Lorenzo. And Allegra has been working in wineries in Europe." I grit my teeth a little, keeping my smile in place. "I'm sure she's learned a lot, too. There's no reason we can't do this." I pause and look at him, then Vitto. His expression is minutely softer than Uncle Geno's.

"Except..." I continue, sliding my gaze back to Uncle Geno. "Except for you."

Uncle Geno narrows his eyes. "Those grapes belong to me. I'm the one who cared for them for years."

"They belong to Caparelli," I say gently. "And Caparelli belongs to us." I look at Rosa. "We need those grapes."

Uncle Geno's mouth tightens.

"We also need our wine," I add staunchly.

His eyes widen. "Your wine? What are you talking about? You didn't grow and harvest those grapes. You didn't look after them while they were fermenting."

He has a point there. But I don't care. Nothing ventured, nothing gained. "Without wine, we have no way to make any money this season."

"Well, that's too bad. That's what happens when you start a business."

"Have you bottled the cabernet?" I ask.

Vitto shakes his head. "Not all of it."

"I want it."

Geno shakes his head sharply. "Absolutely not. We need it for the Carleo."

Vitto rubs between his eyebrows.

I knew this would be a hard sell. "Look. People are talking about us. I've heard rumors and I've only been back a few days. I've heard that we're supposedly going to sell Caparelli to you."

"As if I'd pay you for it. It should be mine." His words don't sound very determined, though.

"But it's not, and that's what Nonna wanted. I also heard that you're going to contest the will. Is that true?"

He hesitates. "I've talked to a lawyer about it."

Also not unequivocal. He may have talked to the lawyer, but he hasn't done anything. Yet. Maybe.

"People are talking about the family," Rosa says. "Calling it a feud. Do you really want that?"

I lean forward. "Remember what Mr. Davenport said. Nonna's greatest desire was that we remain a family, supporting each other, regardless of what happened with her will. She probably knew you wouldn't be happy about losing Caparelli. I think she was trying to tell you that we need to stay family, no matter what."

He says nothing.

"She's not wrong," Vitto says quietly to his dad.

I meet his eyes and dip my chin in thanks. That small amount of support encourages me. "We don't want everyone in the county talking about us. We have a reputation for quality wines. We don't want family drama to detract from that. Look what happened with the Mondavi family."

Uncle Geno's lips twist in acknowledgment.

I catch Rosa's quickly hidden smile.

"Will you think about it? We're working hard to make sure the grapes are healthy and harvested this season. We're going to work hard to make sure we offer quality wines. It would be generous and gracious of you to help us in that way. Even if that's the least you can do for us. For family."

"You could think about it, Dad," Vitto says. He looks back at me. "He'll think about it."

Uncle Geno just glowers.

I stand and glance at Rosa. She jumps to her feet.

"Thanks for your time this afternoon." I smile at Uncle Geno and Vitto.

And we leave.

We're quiet all the way along the paved pathway out front and across the parking lot. When we reach the car, Rosa turns to me. "Holy shit! You were amazing!"

Was I? I don't know. Hopefully I sounded strong, but inside I was shaking like that little girl I'm trying not to be anymore. I squeeze out a laugh. "Aw, thanks. But we'll see, I guess. I tried to appeal to his softer side. But I don't know if he even has a softer side anymore." I sigh.

"I think it's been hard on him," Rosa says musingly as we drive home. "He's been in charge of everything for a long time."

"I suppose. I guess I haven't given much thought to Uncle Geno's challenges. Still. He has the wine."

"Yep."

"And I'll let Jansen know that I have conditions for helping him. We'll see if he goes for it."

Rosa makes a face. "I have no idea. I don't know this guy."

"You will. He's our next-door neighbor." I pause. "You fell in love with the last guy who lived there."

She laughs. "I'm not going to fall for Jansen Beck."

I want to say the same. But falling for Jansen Beck seems like something entirely possible.

Chapter 10

Jansen

I'm driving into town when I get the call from my mom.

"Hey, Mom. How are you?"

"I'm great. How are you? How is that winery?"

"Things are moving along."

"I'm sure you're learning that there's a lot more to it than you expected."

I purse my lips. "Yeah, there's a lot to learn."

"Are you certain you're not in over your head?" Her tone takes on a fretful edge. "You spent a lot of money on that place."

"It's my money, Mom."

"I know, but you could invest your money in the stock market and make more money over the long term than by owning a winery. It's not a good investment."

"Buying stocks and bonds is boring. I want to do this. I want to make something." That sounds dumb. I know if I tell my mom more about that she'll be mortified. Hopes and dreams, fear and excitement are not things you talk about.

"Well, it's good that you're doing something again."

I wince. That's her way of telling me I was an unemployed bum who laid around all day drinking beer and doing nothing after I retired.

Okay, there's some truth to that. But I didn't get a lot of empathy from her about what I was going through. One day I told her that I thought I might be depressed, and she shut that down immediately. My dad was even worse. You don't talk about shit like that. You just suck it up and get on with things.

"Well, you know, I just sit around and drink wine all day. It's pretty great."

Silence.

Christ, I'm grouchy today.

I wanted to kiss Bianca last night.

I almost fucking did it, too. Jesus. What was I thinking?

"I think you're being sarcastic," Mom says, bringing me back to the present. "You sound out of sorts. Ever since you retired, you've been a big grouch."

She's not wrong.

"Sorry," I mutter.

"You made your decision, you have to live with it."

Yeah, yeah. *Control your emotions. Don't let them get to you. Toughen up.* "I'm doing fine, Mom."

"Are you making friends there? Dating anyone?"

"No. I mean, yeah, I've met a few people. I'm not interested in dating anyone. It's a small town, it's different here."

"I'm sure it is."

"Hey, I'm just on an errand. Can we talk later?" I pull up in front of the shoe store on Laurel Street.

After a brief silence, she says, "Of course.

"I'm fine. And things are going well here." More or less.

I end the call. Well. Some day I'll show them that this wasn't an epic mistake.

I hope.

I head inside to find new footwear, but I should have gone farther than Oak Creek Canyon to do this errand. As I'm trying on boots, Miles and Nolan walk in.

"Hey, Becky," Miles says with a big grin.

Becky. That's the nickname my teammates called me when I played hockey. I narrow my eyes at him.

"Uh...not cool?" He holds up his hands.

Am I the asshole here? Probably. My mom's right. "Becky's fine, Razor."

"Razor?"

I smile. "I worked with a guy named Raymond. We called him Razor."

"Ha," Nolan says. "That's good."

"Thank, Murrdawg."

They both laugh.

"What are you up to?" Nolan's gaze drops to my feet. "Boots. Yeah, you'll need those in the vineyard."

I stand to try out the new footwear. I take a few steps and assess the fit. They're pretty damn comfortable, actually.

"These are good for a lot of walking," the saleswoman says. "Especially outdoors."

"That's what I need." I look down at them. They don't look that much different than the athletic sneakers I wear when I'm working out. "I'll take them."

"Great!"

I sit and pull the boots off. The saleswoman takes them and places them back in the box.

"What are you two doing here?" I ask Miles and Nolan.

"I need new shoes for running," Miles says. "But I'm easy. I just get the same thing every time." He looks at the saleswoman. "I need a new pair of ASICS when you're done with Mr. Beck, here."

"Mr. Beck." I roll my eyes.

He laughs. "Kidding."

I slide my feet into my loafers and stand, pulling out my wallet.

"Those are nice shoes." Nolan nods at my feet.

"Thanks."

"They look expensive."

I purse my lips. "Uh. I guess they kinda were. They're Ferragamo."

"Huh." Nolan frowns. "Betty, you got any Ferragamo loafers?"

Betty snorts from behind the counter where she's ringing up my purchase. "Yeah, they're right behind the Christian Louboutin Oxfords."

"I know some people here wear Louboutins." Nolan shrugs. "I guess they go to San Francisco to buy them."

"Louboutins would get messed up working in the vineyard," Miles says.

I approach the counter and pull out my credit card to pay. Betty hands me a bag. "Here you go!"

"Thanks. I appreciate your help." I turn. "Nice to see you guys again.'

"Hold up, don't run off," Miles says. "We're going for a beer after this. Join us."

"Uh." I pause. Once again, I'm not used to this spontaneous sociability. I planned to buy my boots, go home, and jerk off thinking about Bianca in purple silk. I can't exactly tell them that. And I don't have any other excuse. I glance at the time. Nearly six. "Okay. Sure."

Betty brings Miles his sneakers. He tries them on, although they're exactly the same as the pair he's wearing, pronounces them good, and buys them.

"You must run a lot," I say as we walk out of the store.

"Yeah. I try for three or four times a week. About five miles."

"Shit. I need to start doing that again." I haven't been doing a lot of activity since I retired. I'd probably feel better if I started running again.

"Run with me," he says immediately. "I go at different times, depending on my shift, but I like doing it first thing in the morning if I can."

I used to like running in the morning, too. Only I ran by the ocean in Long Beach.

"I'm not that fast," he says. "You can probably outrun me, but that's okay."

"Yeah, I doubt that."

"Okay, tomorrow morning. Meet me at Oak Creek Park at seven. Bring water and wear sunscreen. A hat, too. There's no shade there. That's why I go early."

Great. No shade. Hot. Definitely not the Pacific Ocean.

We're walking down the sidewalk along Laurel Street. We pass the store with the purple silk slip in it. I glance at the window, but the display has changed to a pale pink lace garment with a silk and feathered robe. I swallow. "We're going out for beers and you plan to run at seven in the morning?"

He laughs. "Beer. One beer. Maybe."

"Miles can run a marathon the day after a bender." Nolan claps a hand on his buddy's shoulder. "He's famous for that."

I have to smile. "Okay, then."

"Great! It'll be good, not too hot at that time of day."

Oh. He thought I was agreeing. Ah, fuck.

We enter the Golden Cougar. This is the second time I've been here. It's dim and old and smells like beer.

Turns out the guys want food, too. They order burgers, I go for fish tacos. And a beer.

"So are you getting ready for harvest?" Nolan asks.

"Yeah. Yesterday Bianca came over and looked at the grapes. My viticulturist guy..." That still feels weird, saying that... "thinks we're nearly there, but he wanted another opinion."

"Bianca should know. She's been harvesting grapes since she was old enough to walk."

"Yeah. She knows a lot." I take a pull of my amber ale. I don't tell them that I want to hire her temporarily. That's between us. Until she makes a decision.

I was hoping I'd hear from her today, but I didn't. I won't take that as a no, though. She probably has her own things to worry about. Like finding people to help her harvest her own grapes.

Maybe I could help with that? We've got people and machinery lined up. Depending on the timing, maybe they could help her, too?

I'm probably being naïve. I don't know how this works.

There's no problem keeping a conversation going with Nolan, or Murrdawg here, who seems to never stop talking. We talk about harvest, running, and wedding plans for Miles and Millie.

"When's the wedding?" I ask.

"October. After harvest. Not that we're busy, but lots of our friends are, so it made sense to plan the wedding for after."

"Yeah."

"We're just about ready to send out invitations," Miles says. "I think they look really cool. They have sort of watercolor flowers on the top and the bottom—dark pink and light pink— which are the wedding colors. It was really hard picking out fonts. You need a couple of different fonts that complement each other—"

Nolan holds up a hand. "Enough. I can't handle all the wedding shit."

I press my lips together on a smile.

"He goes on about this stuff for hours," Nolan tells me.

I don't want to offend either of them so I just smile. I don't think I've ever met a guy who's so into wedding stuff.

"Fine," Miles grumbles. "Your invitation might get lost in the mail."

Nolan laughs. "I'm your fucking best man."

"Maybe." Then he laughs, too. "Sorry. I get carried away. Anyway, I was reading this article online you might be interested in *Murrdawg*. Sex positions for guys with a small penis."

Nolan and I both choke.

"What the fuck," Nolan says.

"Yeah, it said guys with a small penis can actually be better in bed because they make an effort."

"Fuck right off," Nolan says mildly and take a swallow of beer.

"Doggie style is apparently perfect. You can get really 'deep' penetration."

"Ana does love doggie style," Nolan says slowly.

"There you go." Miles lifts his beer.

"Asshole," Nolan says.

Their chirping almost makes me laugh. I miss this.

Our food arrives and we all dig in. The fish tacos are really good—grilled fish, fresh veggies, and a spicy sauce.

"I guess you've been through this," Nolan says to me. I've told them I'm divorced.

"Yeah." I make a face. "I wasn't much into the wedding planning. My ex did it, and it was really nice. We got married at a hotel in Dana Point. On a terrace in front of the ocean. Gourmet food, lots of champagne." I lift a shoulder. "It seemed fun at the time."

"I hate weddings." Nolan shoots Miles an apologetic glance. "Sorry, man. I'll be there."

"I know." Miles turns to me. "How long have you been divorced?"

"Almost two years."

"Not ready to tie the knot again?"

"I don't think I'll ever be." I swallow a mouthful of beer. "I don't need to get screwed over again. I had to pay her a shit ton of money."

I didn't really care about the money, but it's easier to be bitter about that than crying about her cheating on me. Less pathetic. Especially since she cheated on me with one of my teammates. And they're still together.

I didn't mention any of this to Bianca the other night. She's the last person I want to embarrass myself in front of.

"She took your money?" Nolan says. "Bitch."

I sigh inwardly. I can't let that go. "Nah, she's not a bitch. At least I was retired. If I'd still been playing, I probably would have had to pay her even more."

"Divorce laws." Miles shakes his head.

I shrug. "I get it. I get why it has to be fair."

They both regard me somberly.

"Eh, sorry. Didn't mean to drag the mood down. Hope you have a pre-nup." I manage a half-grin so they know I'm kidding and luckily they both laugh at my terrible joke. We need to move on from this ugly topic. "This food is good."

"Yeah, the food here's great. This place has been around forever."

"Did you both grow up here?" I ask.

"Yeah, or close by."

"I'm from San Francisco," Nolan says. "Moved here because of Ana. How are you liking it here?"

"I'm getting used to it," I say noncommittally. "I kind of miss the ocean and the beach, and there's definitely a small-town vibe here, but it's okay."

"You seem like a big city guy."

I nod. "Yeah. I grew up in Toronto. I played in Chicago for a couple of seasons, but the rest of my career was in Los Angeles."

"Well, it's not far to San Francisco. Or the beach," Nolan points out. "If you need a fix of night life or whatever."

"Women," Miles says. "He needs women."

"There are women here," Nolan says.

"Like who?" Miles raises his eyebrows in a challenge.

"Like, lots of women." He pauses. "Like Bianca."

"She's not staying," Miles says. "Millie says she's just here to help with harvest."

"Huh. Okay, then..." He squints. "Hell, I know there are single women here. Just can't think of any off the top of my head."

"It doesn't matter," I say. "Because I am definitely not looking for a woman."

Except I keep thinking about a woman. One specific woman.

And then I look up and there she is.

Bianca walks into the bar followed by a man—that jackhole she gave her number to at the fair. The old boyfriend.

I guess I shouldn't be surprised she's out with him. But I have to be honest—it bugs me.

She hasn't noticed me as they take a seat at a small table in the back corner. She smiles at him. Dammit. That smile. I'm an asshole. I want that smile for me.

What am I thinking? She's ten years younger than me. She's with a guy her age, young, someone she has a history with, someone from around here who knows her world. I'm an outsider, too old for her, and anyway I just finished telling these guys I'm not interested in a relationship, so clearly I'm just being a dick by being annoyed with her seeing that guy.

I'll just ignore them.

Chapter 11

Bianca

Mark takes another stool at the round table and pulls it around closer to me. He called this morning to invite me out for a drink and I agreed to meet him here. We had some good times when we were together, but we were kids. He was fun, maybe a little irresponsible but hey, a seventeen-year-old guy has a lot of growing up to do and I'm curious to see what kind of man he's turned out to be.

I got an uneasy feeling, though, when I met him on the sidewalk in front of the Golden Cougar, when he greeted me with a hug and I could smell the alcohol on his breath. He's already been drinking.

We look at the menu and make some small talk, but I'm studying him and the way he talks, which is loose and free-wheeling, his eyes a tiny bit unfocused. His face is more mature, his skin a bit more textured since I knew him in high school, his eyes creased at the corner, but he still seems like a happy, easy-going guy. He's wearing a pair of ripped and faded jeans, which is fine, and a nice button-down shirt with a small stain on the pocket.

I order a beer and he asks for a Jack and Coke, and adds, "Make it a double."

Oh boy.

Maybe he's nervous?

Nah.

"So." He smiles at me, hands resting on the table. "Is it good to be home?"

"Well. In some ways." I explain yet again why I'm here and for how long and that I wasn't entirely happy to leave my job in Argentina where things were going so well.

"But this is Napa," he interrupts me. "Can't beat Napa."

My smile tightens. "There is something special about Napa. How about you? What are you doing now?"

"I'm working at Espinoza's."

"Oh." That's his family-owned building supply company in Rocktram.

"I'm the yard manager," he says. "Well, sort of the manager. That's not my actual title, but I've worked there the longest and I basically run the yard. Looking after customers, unloading, loading, that kind of thing."

"Ah. That's interesting."

"It's hard work sometimes, but the pay's good, and it's steady work."

"And where are you living?"

"I still live with my parents. They're still in the house on Garden Road."

"Oh." *Don't judge him. Lots of people live with their parents longer these days.* "How are your parents?"

"They're good. Talking about retirement. They keep nagging me to get my own place so they can downsize and travel, but..." He shrugs and makes a face.

I smile and nod.

Our drinks arrive and Mark tosses back half of his at once. I pick up my beer and take a sip. That's when I spot Jansen across the room. He's with Miles and Nolan and they're all finishing up a meal, talking and looking relaxed.

He looks good.

He looks un-drunk. Unlike Mark.

I swallow a sigh.

As we talk more and Mark orders another drink, he starts to touch me. First my hand. Then my arm. My shoulder. He shifts closer. Then he says, "Remember the first time we did it?"

Uhhhhhh. I shift away from him. "Mark. Back off."

He blinks at me. "What?"

I frown at him. "Please stop touching me. And I don't want to talk about the first time we 'did it.'"

"Why not? It was so hot." He leans in and the fumes assail me.

I angle away from him. "I barely remember it, to be honest."

"What?" He scowls and stares. "How could you forget your first time?"

"We'd both been drinking. And it was a long time ago."

"I don't believe that."

I gaze at him, a little incredulous. "What? Are you calling me a liar?"

"You just don't want to admit how good it was." He smirks.

Holy shit. So far I'm not impressed with how Mark grew up. "Apparently it wasn't that memorable."

He frowns again. "Well, that's rude."

"This whole conversation is rude." I scoot my stool away from him. When I look up, I catch Jansen's eye. He's watching me.

I lift a hand in a brief wave to acknowledge him. He gives me a steely look.

"Maybe I should go," I say to Mark.

"We just got here!"

"Look, respect my boundaries," I tell him. "Or I'll leave."

"Boundaries? Oooh, you sound all fancy."

I grit my teeth. That's it. "I'm leaving." I pick up my purse and slide off the stool. I have to squeeze by Mark to get out, though, and he snakes an arm around my waist and pulls me closer.

"Aw, don't be like that, Bee."

"Let me go."

"Let's have one more drink." His other hand comes up, at first I think to touch my face, but he lays it over my throat. Panic flares inside me, heating my blood.

Then a big body appears next to us. "Let her go," Jansen growls.

Mark blinks at him.

"Let her go," Jansen repeats, his voice low and menacing.

If this is what he looked like to his opponents on the ice, I bet the other teams were scared spitless of him.

When Mark still doesn't move, Jansen grabs Mark's hand on my throat and forces it away, then pries his other arm away from me so I'm free. My blood is pumping fast, my breathing flimsy.

"Hey," Mark says loudly, standing. "Back off, bud."

"No." Jansen's voice is flinty. "You back off." With both hands on Mark's chest, he shoves him.

Mark stumbles a step backward and hits the wall. "Hey! What the fuck?"

I cringe at his raised voice and become excruciatingly aware of others in the bar watching us. It's happy hour and the place is nearly full. My skin prickles with heat and I wonder if this would be a good time to fling myself through the window.

"The lady said to let her go. You didn't let her go."

"It's okay, Jansen," I say. "All good."

He turns his hard gaze on me and his tone softens a bit. "Are you okay?"

"Yes, yes. I'm fine." I shoot Mark a disgusted look, then lay cool eyes on Jansen. "I could have handled this," I say in a low, terse tone. "There was no need to make a scene."

He rolls his right shoulder reflexively. "Uh. Sorry. I thought you needed help."

My mouth falls open. "What? Good lord." I exhale sharply. Who does he think he is? "I'm done here."

IN THE MORNING, I FEEL STUPID FOR HAVING GONE OUT with Mark. Millie and Ana said he was single again, like he was a potential partner. Why didn't they tell me he has... issues?

Nah, not their fault. Men!

Then Jansen got involved. I was embarrassed. And pissed. Also...a little impressed.

I didn't need Jansen to intervene. I could have handled Mark. He was so drunk I'm sure I could have knocked him off his stool if I poked him in the chest with one finger. What in the blueberry fuck muffins did he think he was doing?

I go downstairs and find Rosa and Jake in the kitchen, sitting at the big table eating cereal, steam probably coming out of my ears.

Rosa looks up from her phone. "What the hell happened last night?"

I gaze back at her. "Um...what do you mean?"

"At the Cougar. Apparently there was a big brawl."

"Oh, for fox sake." I shake my head, frowning, and move to

the fridge to get my overnight oats. "Not a brawl. Just a little... situation."

"That's not what everyone's saying on the town Facebook page. They're saying Jansen got in a knock down fight with Mark Overton. Some guys jumped to help Mark and then Miles and Nolan had to defend Jansen. Lots of broken glasses and there may have been blood."

"What!" I turn and gape at her. "That's ridiculous."

"Because of you," she adds with a repressed smile.

"I was there, yes. And Mark drank too much and got all handsy and gross and I told him to back off and then he grabbed me and—" I stop short. Do I want to mention Jansen's misguided rescue attempt?

"And Jansen punched him in the face!"

Okay, never mind, it's already out. "No, he didn't!" I pause. "He shoved him, but that was it. Then I left."

"So the brawl happened after you left."

"Oh my God." I sink onto a kitchen chair. "I can't believe this. I just thought it would be nice to see an old friend for a drink."

She wrinkles her nose. "I didn't know he was like that. He didn't used to be."

"And now everyone in town is pissed at Jansen," Jake adds. "What! Why?"

"He's the new guy. I mean, Mark's a bit of a screw up, but he's lived here his whole life and everyone loves his family. Of course they're going to support him over another stupid rich guy who thinks he can run a winery and who'll be gone before the year is over."

I pause. "Wow. Is that what you think of Jansen?"

His mouth thins. "Not me. That's what other people are saying."

I bite my lip as guilt pokes me in the chest. It's also what I thought, when I first met him. "Wait. How can everyone in town be mad at him? This just happened last night!"

"You know what this town is like."

Oh yeah, I know what this town is like. "He was defending me."

"I know that," Rosa says. "But rumors start."

"This is ridiculous. Nobody got hurt, right?"

"It sounds like Mark might have some bruises."

I cringe. "Yikes. I have to go talk to Jansen."

Rosa's eyebrows shoot up.

"I mean, I had to talk to him anyway," I say quickly. "Business. Wine business."

"Uh huh. Well, you can make sure he didn't break any bones."

"We need to talk about those barrels."

Rosa frowns. "I thought we did already."

Ordering new French oak barrels was part of our team meeting discussion with Allegra.

I haven't told Rosa about my discovery of the qvevris. I've been reading about making orange wine and I'm pretty sure I can do it. I just want to be sure before I broach the subject. We're already on different pages when it comes to barrels.

"We did, but I...think we're going to need more, and I prefer oak over stainless."

"They're expensive. You know we don't have a lot of money."

"But we have some. We just have to prioritize."

She rubs her forehead. "Okay, we can sit down and go over the budgets and see if there's somewhere we can cut."

I'd rather run through the streets of Oak Creek Canyon with my naked body smeared with bacon fat. But I have to make my case.

I finish my oatmeal. As I'm rinsing my bowl in the sink, I

gaze out the window at the clear blue sky, the sun blazing down on the ripening vines. Birds swoop and glide above the vineyard. Starlings.

I straighten to attention and watch more birds gather. "Look!" I point.

Rosa and Jake glance at each other. "What?"

"The birds!"

"Ah." Jake also peers out the window. "Yeah. We have to check the grapes."

"Let's get going."

As we hike to the vineyard, he fills me in on the blocks they've been checking and the samples they've gotten. He also tells me about the help they've lined up for the harvest. It's not a lot, but it's doable if we all pitch in. He's pretty darn knowledgeable. I'll feel okay leaving with him in charge of the vines here.

"We can start tonight," he says, and we make a plan.

"Okay. I'll be back. I have to go over to Jansen's and talk to him. Some of his vines are probably ready, too."

"Have you talked to him about your proposal?" Rosa asks.

"That's also what I need to talk to him about."

"Do you still think you can handle it all?" Her forehead puckers.

It's a lot. I'm not gonna lie. "We'll see!"

It sounds like Jansen's better prepared for harvest than we are, so he probably won't need my help as much.

As I cross the yard toward the path through the live oaks separating our properties, some of my anger and embarrassment from last night returns. I need to keep this about business.

I enter through the front entrance and pass the deserted wine tasting room, coming to a stop in front of Carol's office. Jansen's in there with her. "Hi."

They both look up at me.

"Hi, Bianca." Carol rises from her desk and comes toward me with arms outstretched. "I haven't seen you in so long!"

"I know!" I smile at her and we hug. She and my mom were friends when they were younger and she kind of checked in on us girls after Mama left.

"Have you heard anything from your mom?" she asks right on cue.

"I haven't heard from her for a while." I make a face. "They're busy with their winery, too."

"I suppose they are." She looks a little sad. "Will she come home for Maria's funeral?"

"I don't know. I hope so." In some ways, I feel like I don't have a mom. I look at Jansen. "Can I talk to you?"

He's watching me with a look of concern etched into his forehead. "Sure." He rises from the chair. "We can go to my office."

I follow him into the small room. There's a gorgeous new computer sitting on the desk but other than that, it's bare and spotless. On a shelf sit a few trophies which I assume are hockey related rather than wine awards.

He leans on the edge of his desk and gestures to a couple of chairs. "Have you made a decision?"

My anger about last night is still simmering, and despite my resolve to keep this business, I say, "Why the hell did you get in a fight with Mark last night?"

He lifts an eyebrow and crosses his arms. "You call that a fight? You've apparently never seen a hockey game."

I blink. "I heard there was a fight. After I left."

He gives me a what-the-fuck look.

"A bar brawl," I elaborate. "With broken bottles and blood and a bunch of people involved."

"Whoa." He shakes his head. "Um. That didn't happen."

"What?" I stare.

"There was no brawl. I had a few words with Mark." He says the name as if he's spitting out corked wine. "Then I finished my beer and came home."

"Oh, for the love of goats. The grapevine is working overtime here in Oak Creek Canyon. Word is out that there was a big brawl at the Cougar last night."

He gazes back at me with a crease between his eyebrows. "There was no brawl."

I sigh. "So you didn't punch him?"

"No, I did not punch him. Although I could have. Asshole."

I suck briefly on my bottom lip. My anger is fading in the face of his chivalry. That's an old-fashioned word. But I don't know a better one. It makes my heart beat in a funny rhythm that has me a tad breathless. "Okay. Wow. Apparently half the town is mad at you for beating him up."

"Jesus." He looks to the sky. "What am I doing here?"

"I wonder the same," I mutter. "I mean, me. Not you. I wonder what *I'm* doing here. Okay, we'll get Ana and Millie and the others on it to try to clear your name." I pause. "I wonder if Mark told people that?"

"If he did, he's an idiot. I wouldn't go around telling people I harassed a woman and got beat up for it."

I almost laugh. "I'm sure that's not how he'd frame it."

"Whatever. I don't have time for bullshit. Is that what you came here for?"

"Um. Actually, no. I came on business. I noticed the birds were really active over the vineyard this morning."

From the look on his face, I could have just told him I want to dip my feet in chocolate.

"The birds get more active over the vines when the grapes are ripe. They know."

"Ah."

"So we went through some blocks over at Caparelli and

we're starting to harvest tonight. I think we should go check out your grapes. Those sauvignon blanc were almost ready the other day."

"Okay." He straightens. "Does this mean you're going to help me?"

"Oh. Right." I nod in a businesslike manner. "I'll agree to help you, if you'll do something for me in return."

His lips twitch. "Sounds interesting."

I give him a chiding look. "I want to use your lab. Our equipment is old or gone and we're going to need to do testing."

"Damn." He feigns disappointment. "Hmmm. Well, apparently we're not really competitors, so I guess I'm okay with that."

I smile, relief sliding through my veins. "Thank you."

"I'll still pay you. I've been researching winemaker salaries and there's a range." He names some numbers.

"I'll only be working part time, since I have to also work at my own winery."

"Right. Okay. We'll take middle of the range and cut it in half."

"This is weird."

"What?"

"Negotiating salary with you."

"Then take my offer."

"Fine. Done."

The expression on his face is the happiest I've seen even though he's not really smiling. But the green and gold flecks in his hazel eyes light up and his face relaxes into satisfied softness. It's a good look on him and my belly flutters.

Business.

"Let's go. Where's Diego?"

"I think he's in the cellar with Antonio."

"Let's get him and check things out."

Chapter 12

Jansen

I meet Miles at Oak Creek Park as the sun is coming up. There's fog in lower areas and it's a nice temperature for running, though I do have a ball cap on. We've run together a few times now and it's been pretty good. The first run wasn't my best, but I kept up with Miles, and I feel better every time.

"Our dispatcher got a great call the other day," he says as we run along the path.

"Yeah?" He always has good stories from the sheriff's department.

"It was a lady. She said her friend is getting married and they're throwing her a bachelorette party."

I slide him a glance, grinning and waiting expectantly.

"And she asked if we could send out a couple of cops to the party to dance for them."

I bark out a laugh.

"And so Poppy says, I'm sorry, ma'am, police officers don't do that. And the woman said, yes, they do, haven't you seen them in movies? And Poppy says, ma'am, those aren't real police officers, they're strippers."

I'm chuckling as he talks.

"So the woman said, Really? Okay, fine, what about firefighters? Will they come dance for us?"

"Jesus." I bellow more laughter. "Maybe you guys *should* go dance at bachelorette parties. You could raise some extra cash for the department."

Miles guffaws. "Yeah, right."

The view here is spectacular. We're on an elevation overlooking a vineyard with mountains in the background. Beside the path, Spanish moss drips from live oak trees.

It's not the ocean, but it's growing on me.

We pass by a man in a straw hat and a young kid walking and give them waves. I huff out, "Morning."

As we approach a bench, Miles says, "Need a rest, old man?"

I snort. "Let's sprint." And I pick up my pace and leave him behind.

He laughs and catches up.

Then I skid to a halt. "Aaaaah!"

Miles stops dead, too, behind me, and peers over my shoulder.

"That's a snake," I say, unnecessarily, pointing at it.

"You are correct. It's a King snake."

We watch the black and white reptile wriggle its way across the path and disappear into the dry, ochre-colored grass.

I swipe at my forehead. "Jesus. And I was just thinking it's not so bad running here."

Miles laughs. "King snakes are harmless."

"No."

"Yes, they are. Nonvenomous."

"Do they have teeth? Yes? Then they can still bite."

He laughs again. "Okay, yeah."

Now I'm busy watching the path for snakes as I run.

We run alongside Oak Creek for a bit. Boulders line the edge of the creek and water burbles as it flows over and around them. Sunlight glints silver on the water where it filters through tree branches. This is the only shady point of the route and it's noticeably cooler here, although the sun isn't yet high in the sky.

I tell Miles that Bianca is going to help me with the harvest, with the things we need a winemaker for, and our deal that I'll let her use my lab for things she needs to do at Caparelli.

"Sounds like win-win," he says.

"Yeah." With the extra win that I'll get to see her again.

"Are you looking for a full-time winemaker?"

"Yeah, but I haven't had much interest. Maybe after harvest there'll be more people looking for new jobs. Or maybe nobody wants to work for a guy who knows nothing about making wine. I don't really know."

"Hey, you're learning. Have you met Bianca's uncle?"

"Yeah." My jaw clenches. "He showed up at Rosa's place when we were all there celebrating that they made it through that hailstorm. It was quite the scene. He kinda lost his shit because of Jake and Rosa being together."

"Yeah, that's pretty wild that they were actually married all that time. Geno's a hot head. When his mom was still alive, she used to keep him in line."

"Bianca's pretty sad about her grandma passing."

"No doubt. Maria was the polestar of that family."

I've never heard that term, but I get the meaning.

"Bianca takes after her," Miles continues. "Well, all three sisters do to a certain extent. But Bianca's got that winemaker talent that Maria had. Only Maria never got to really develop it. And to be honest, Bianca wasn't going to get that chance either, if she'd stayed here."

"Yeah, she alluded to that." I thought maybe that was just

her perception of her family, but I guess not. And having met Geno, I can see how dominant and single-minded he is.

Which only makes it understandable that she'd want to go back to her life in Argentina.

I'M FUCKING DEAD.

We've been picking grapes all day. After I ran just over four miles with Miles this morning. I have machines that are doing mechanical harvesting, but a bunch of us picked grapes manually as well. This is physical labor but, unlike working out in the gym, it's a lot more rewarding knowing that we're creating something magical.

And despite my bone-deep exhaustion, here I am, in the shower, jerking off thinking about Bianca.

Bianca is teaching me how to pick grapes while she's running back and forth between here and her place, directing the harvest and also supervising the crush pad. It was hot, sweaty, and sticky, with drunk bees buzzing around the crush pad, but I was completely drunk on Bianca. On her shiny dark hair sliding out of its ponytail, on sunburned cheeks and nose, on her long bare legs and slender arms. Mostly on her expertise —her knowledge, her efficiency, the easy way she directs everyone.

My fantasies involve her here in the shower with me so I can slide my hands through that silky hair, clean dirt and sweat and grape juice from her skin, taking my time on certain areas— her tits, between her legs, stroking her there until she comes in a shuddering orgasm that makes her feel so good. She deserves to feel so good.

That night at the Golden Cougar I lost my mind. That dipshit grabbed her. By the *throat*. He deserved to die. Or at least get punched in the face. I wanted to do that so fucking bad I could taste it, like when I used to inhale the acrid scent of smelling salts on the bench.

No one should ever do that to her.

On some level, I recognize that my reaction was over the top. Also, I don't care. I'd do it again to any asshole who touches her without her permission.

She's beautiful and smart and passionate. She deserves to feel good.

"Such a good girl," I groan as my hand moves faster on my shaft. "You should feel good. You should come on my fingers. My cock. Christ." My hand pumps harder, tension coiling up from the base of my spine, pleasure bursting, spreading through me. I let out a harsh shout, bracing myself against the shower wall with my other hand, gasping as the water pours down over me.

"Fuck." I drop my head forward. I'm tired, spent, and yet I'm still thinking of her. I'm still thinking of her as I dry off and stumble naked into my bed.

The alarm goes off early. I drag my ass down to the kitchen. While my coffee brews, I feed Moose and give him fresh water. It's still dark and when I step outside onto the deck, the morning air cloaks me, damp and chilly. I'm sipping my coffee when Bianca arrives, wearing another pair of short shorts with knee-high rubber boots and a thick sweatshirt with the hood tugged up over her head. I want to smile at the vision this creates—so far from sexy, but so goddamn charming.

Moose greets her with great excitement. She fusses over him with pets and compliments. Then she straightens and looks at me. "Morning."

"Have you had coffee?"

"No."

"I'll get you some. Have you had breakfast?"

"No."

"Jesus. You have to eat."

"I know. When I get all caught up in work, sometimes I forget about it."

"I was about to make myself some eggs. Sit. I'll make you some, too."

"You don't have to—"

"I know, but I don't want you to collapse from hunger in my vineyard."

"Okay. Thank you." She follows me into the kitchen. She's got her iPad and a bunch of samples from Caparelli. "I told Diego I'd meet him at six-thirty in the vineyard. We'll get the crew picking again. Make sure they're picking the right section, not picking any second crop, and leaving out other crap."

"Other crap?" I hand her a mug, then open the fridge.

"Leaves. Bugs. Snakes. Lizards."

"Jesus."

She grins then sips her coffee.

"They probably know what they're doing."

"Probably. But I don't know them and I'm a micro-manager."

"Ah." My lips twist into a smile at the interior of the fridge. I grab the egg carton.

"And we'll get samples to get the numbers."

Now I know what "numbers" she's talking about—the pH, Brix, and TA.

I whisk together eggs and melt butter in a pan.

"Then we can walk the rows and discuss what to pick next," she continues. "The forecast is for warm and sunny weather all week, so I expect things to keep ripening. But I think what we can do here is alternate days processing fruit and bottling. We can get busy bottling last year's wines."

"Okay, that sounds good." I can't help but watch her mouth as she talks. I could do that all day. Except I'd want to kiss that mouth.

"Have you cleaned out the old barrels?"

"Yeah."

"And you have new barrels?"

"Yep. And more on order."

"Great."

Her approval has warmth swelling in my chest. I remember my shower last night and my dick thickens in my briefs. I cough.

"I'm jealous," she continues. "Rosa won't let me order new barrels." She sighs.

"Why not?"

She holds up a hand a rubs thumb and forefingers together.

"Ah. Money."

"Unlike rich hockey players, we don't have a big bank account to get our winery going."

"My bank account is shrinking rapidly," I say dryly. "Don't tell my mom."

She smiles. "Why not?"

"She's afraid I'm blowing my entire savings on this crazy plan and won't be able to support myself."

Her eyebrows slide up. "Hmm."

"You think the same."

Her lips twist as she tries not to grin. "I may have thought that. But I'm learning more about you. Also, you have *me*."

"Haha. Yes."

You have me.

Fuck, I wish.

"I'd like to try blending some wines from different locations," she moves on. "The grapes on the hillsides often have a different feel—tannins that are tart and more rustic."

"Just growing them in a different location affects the taste." I do know that, but I'm interested to learn more.

"Yes. The soil type contributes to the grapes' flavors—whether it's clay or gravel or volcanic ground. Also the amount of sun exposure. They get less fog when they're higher up and more UV light gives the grapes thicker skins."

"It's pretty amazing."

She smiles and her eyes sparkle. "It is, isn't it? That's why I love it."

My eyes move over her face, my breath tightening in my chest. I nod. "I get it." I return my attention to the eggs in the pan. "Can you make some toast?"

"Sure." She moves to the counter where the bread sits. "You're okay with that?"

"With what?"

"The blending?"

"Oh. Yeah." I want to tell her to do whatever she wants. But it *is* my winery. "Are you talking about the Chardonnay grapes?"

"Yes."

"Okay. Yeah." I nod.

We eat our scrambled eggs and toast, then head out to the vineyard where the crew is assembled along with Diego, who's already got some samples to test. Bianca takes them to the lab to work on them, along with the ones she brought from Caparelli.

I start helping again, sore muscles protesting as I squat. Goddammit. I'd planned to find a gym in the area but there's no time right now. My runs with Miles are good, but I need some strength work. I'm a goddamn athlete, I'm not supposed to get sore from picking grapes.

Plus my bum shoulder is aching. Both shoulders have some

arthritis in them, but my right one is worse and I'm feeling it this morning. I try not to take too much medication for them because that stuff can eat away your gut, but this might be a day I need some.

This isn't what I envisioned when I thought of owning a winery. I'm not naïve or stupid; I knew there'd be work involved. But I kind of pictured myself walking the paths and sitting on a terrace drinking wine. I suppose I could just do that —I don't *have* to pick grapes. But I want to.

This place is mine. Its success depends on me. And I have to be successful.

I may feel old and cranky and horny, but I'm also determined. I can ignore a few sore muscles and a sexy winemaker and focus on grapes.

By eleven, I'm starving. Time for a lunch break. There's a shady spot in the yard with picnic tables the crew moves to with their lunch, which I assume is why that spot is there. I start past them, but Antonio waves at me. "Hey, boss! Come join us for lunch."

I halt. They want me to have lunch with them? "Um, okay, sure. I just have to check in with Bianca at the lab."

I find Antonio there but no Bianca.

"She went back to Caparelli," he tells me. "She said she'll check back later. I think they're a little short handed over there."

Right. Shit. She's probably working harder than I am.

Another thing to admire about her—she's definitely not lazy.

I go slap a handful of shaved ham between two slices of bread, add a little mustard, then carry it and a bottle of water back to the picnic tables. Antonio moves over to give me room to sit and I listen to the crew chat about all kinds of things— their kids, spouses, truck that needs a new muffler. Their camaraderie surprises me. I even answer some of their questions about hockey and my previous life.

After lunch, I have a brief huddle with Carol about delivery of the new barrels, then head back out to the crush pad. Trucks are dumping grapes from huge bins and we start the process of de-stemming and crushing the grapes to get white juice. It'll settle to reduce solids before we move it to tanks or barrels to ferment. Bianca has prepared yeast to inoculate the must—the unfermented juice—to start the fermentation process.

Bianca's back, waving away bees, sloshing around in rubber boots that are loose around her calves. When I catch sight of her face, my heart bumps. I corner her and frown. "What's wrong?"

Chapter 13

Bianca

Rosa and I are out in the yard talking about the capacitor for the forty-year-old press we're using, which has just broken down.

"Jake's trying to source one," I tell her. "But so far no luck. And they're not even expensive!"

"What's Jake trying to source?"

We both turn at the male voice behind us. Uncle Geno approaches, wearing his straw Panama hat.

"Hi, Uncle Geno," I say.

"Hi," Rosa adds.

He stops, waiting for us to answer him.

"The capacitor on our press is broken," I tell him reluctantly. The last thing I want to do is share our problems and challenges with him. He already thinks we can't do this.

Sure enough, he smirks. "Are you reconsidering your decision to keep this place? Since things don't seem to be going well."

"Things are going fine," I reply, resisting the urge to tell him to fuck off. "Just this one little problem."

"A new press is expensive," he says.

"We don't need a new press." Actually, we do. Forty years is ancient. I spare a brief, longing thought for the state-of-the art pneumatic press back at Castillo Lorenzo, with its touchscreen control and pre-programmed pressing cycles.

"You could always stomp the grapes yourselves," Uncle Geno says.

I narrow my eyes at him. "Why are you here, Uncle Geno?"

"Just checking in on you girls."

"To see if we need help?" I ask sweetly. "Do you have an extra capacitor?"

He laughs, but doesn't answer.

I fume, heat swirling in my gut. I glance at Rosa, her cheeks pinker than usual.

"We'll be fine, Uncle Geno," she says calmly. "Would you like a cup of coffee? I made banana bread this morning."

"I don't have time for coffee and banana bread. It's harvest."

"We know that," I say a little snidely. "Well, we should get back to work, then. Thanks for stopping by!" I grab Rosa's arm and drag her across the yard.

We both mutter under our breaths.

"I have to go over to Bar Down," I say.

"Okay. I'll let you know when Jake's back if he's been able to find something."

I walk over to the neighboring vineyard, still grumbling about Uncle Geno. He probably could have helped us, damn him.

I head straight to the crush pad to see how things are going here. Better than Caparelli. I've got my rubber boots on, my legs bare beneath the ragged hem of my cut-offs, and a stained

T-shirt that says winey bitch. I wave away a bee drifting in front of my face.

Jansen is just walking toward the crush pad and sees me. His steps quicken and he stops in front of me. "What's wrong?"

I stare up at him. "Nothing's wrong."

"Bullshit. Has that dipshit Mark been around again?"

My eyes widen, and then the corners of my mouth quirk up. "No. Although he did call the other day to apologize."

His jaw hardens. "Then what is it?"

I sigh. "Uncle Geno came by Caparelli a little while ago."

"What happened?"

"I was hoping maybe he'd given some thought to giving us some of their wine. But he said he hasn't had time. He wanted to check on us and see how we were doing. Like he was expecting us to be floundering."

"But you're not."

"Well." I bite my lip. "He did come just when Rosa and I were talking about the capacitor for our press breaking down." I fill him in. "Wait." My eyebrows snap together. "Is it possible... nah."

"What?"

"Is it possible he did something to our capacitor?"

"Jesus." Jansen's mouth sets in a thin line. "He wouldn't do that."

"I don't know. You wouldn't think he would pull all the workers from Caparelli, but he did. You wouldn't think he would spread rumors about us and tell people not to help us. You wouldn't think he would try to sabotage our vines by not watering them and then shutting off the irrigation system. But he did."

Jansen winces. "Yeah."

I sigh. "I wanted to tell him to fuck off."

He rubs a hand over his mouth. "I understand."

"He just makes me feel like I'm a kid again. Like I don't know what I'm doing."

"You do know what you're doing." His tone is assured.

I meet his eyes and he holds my gaze steadily. "Thank you."

"What can I do to help?"

I huff out a breath and smile. "Do you have an extra capacitor?"

"I have no idea. But I can ask someone."

"You don't," I say. "But thank you."

"You can use my crush machine."

"Your crush machine is busy." I wave a hand. My phone buzzes in my back pocket. I pull it out. "Rosa." I answer. "Hi."

"Jake's back," she says. "He's got a capacitor."

"Oh my God. How?"

"He went back to Dr. Armstrong at the college."

Dr. Armstrong is one of the top viticulture and enology experts in the field, and a former prof of Jake's. She helped him find workers for Caparelli.

"She came to the rescue again," Rosa continues. "She got hold of someone in the electronic engineering department. They made a capacitor!"

"Oh my God. That's amazing."

"Yeah! They're working on it right now."

I meet Jansen's eyes and smile. "Great. Let me know if you need me."

"Okay."

I end the call and shove my phone back in my pocket. I relate Rosa's call to him.

"Jake's a miracle worker."

I feel bad about being so hard on him. He's been amazing. "Okay, one problem solved. Now back to work."

"You're working too hard."

I give him an incredulous look. "It's harvest."

"Did you eat lunch?" He frowns.

One corner of my mouth lifts. "Yes, sir, I did eat."

"Good. Do you need help over at Caparelli? Because I can spare some people."

I cock my head. "We're okay. Millie and Miles and Nolan and Ana are there, and they put out the word that we need help so we have a bunch of volunteers. This community can drive me crazy, but also they're good people. And my ad for people wanting to get a true harvest experience got us a bunch more people. Tourists. They think it's fun." I grin.

"Genius."

"But thank you." I lay a purple-stained hand on his forearm and look up at him. "Seriously. That's kind of you."

After a beat, he nods brusquely. "If you're sure."

"We're good. Really."

Our eyes meet and we stand surrounded by equipment, grapes, and bees. His gaze drops to my throat where my pulse is fluttering wildly. My lips part involuntarily, my hand still on his arm. I swallow and step back.

"Okay," he says huskily.

Warmth curls deep inside me. I drag up a smile and scurry away toward the lab.

Later, I'm ready to go home and collapse onto my bed. I just need to check with Jansen about one more thing.

Carol has left for the day, but the tasting room is busy. I pause approvingly seeing the tasting room staff busy serving people who all seem to be enjoying themselves.

I do want to have that some day. I love seeing people coming together, tasting the wine, enjoying it.

I find Jansen in his office, working on his computer. "Hi," I say from the doorway.

He looks up and his eyes warm when he sees me. "Hey."

"Can I talk to you for a few minutes?"

"Of course. Come in."

His desk is built in along one wall, so he just has to swivel his chair to face me. I saunter in and take a seat. "What are you working on?"

"Uh." He swipes a hand down his face.

"Oh. Sorry. You don't have to tell me. I got a little presumptuous there."

"No, no, I can tell you. You might think it's weird."

I give him a curious smile.

"I'm reading up on what to do if ICE shows up."

I blink. "Oh."

"You mentioned it that day, and I've heard from a couple of other people about it. I want to know how to handle it and what my workers' rights are if it happens."

"Oh." I gaze at him, my heart slowly softening. "I see."

"I talked to Miles about it one day when we were running. He said they can come out and talk to the workers."

"Won't that scare them, if the cops show up?"

"It might," he agrees. "But they would assure the workers that the police don't have the power to arrest anyone for immigration violations."

I nod, taking this all in.

"They have a 'Know Your Rights' toolkit they can give out." Jansen goes on. "And a rapid response hotline number, and information about legal assistance."

"Wow."

"Yeah. That's good, right? I want everyone here to know we're looking out for them."

I suck on my bottom lip. "That's really great, Jansen. Do you know your own legal obligations?"

"Oh yeah. I know it's a felony to employ an illegal immigrant." He meets my eyes.

"Knowingly."

He smiles.

"I'm impressed. Maybe we need to talk to Deputy Romero again." Apparently he's been to Caparelli a few times because of the complaints that we assume came from Geno.

"Yeah. Miles says he's a good guy."

I can't even with this man. My heart is beating unevenly and I want to jump him and lay kisses all over his face for what he's doing. Highly inappropriate. I clear my throat. "Anyway. I wanted to ask you about new oak or old oak barrels for the pinot."

He purses his lips. "You should make that decision."

"It's your winery."

"You're the winemaker."

I grin. "Okay, here's what I'm thinking. Old oak over time becomes more neutral, but new oak imparts a lot of complexity. Pinot loves oak, but you still need to be careful. It's like seasoning food—too much salt or too much garlic can ruin a dish."

He nods attentively.

"I want to elevate the pinot but not impose too much taste of oak. I think new oak barrels will be too much, so I think we should use thirty percent new barrels."

He shakes his head, a hint of a smile touching his lips. "And you wanted me to weigh in on that?"

"I guess I want your blessing."

"Bianca. I trust you to make the right decisions. To make the best wine."

My chest fills with warmth. "Thank you. But some of these things are subjective. There are plenty of pinotphiles who love massively oaked pinot noir.'"

"But not you."

"No." I smile. "I like a soft, silky finish from oak, but not 'smoky, toasty oak with touches of charcoal.'"

He laughs. "Now I want to taste both and see what I think."

I push my lips out. "Really? Because we're ready—"

"I just mean out of curiosity. You go ahead and do what you think is best for those beautiful pinot grapes."

My face relaxes. "Okay! Good talk, boss."

He snorts as I rise and I walk out of his office with a huge smile on my face.

Chapter 14

Bianca

"What's wrong with the syrah you tasted yesterday?" Jansen shoves a hand into his thick hair. Those long, lean fingers slide through the silky strands in slow motion. I imagine the feel of his hair on my own fingers.

"Oh." I frown. "I found the tannins very harsh. But I've been thinking about it. I want to try blending it with some of the viognier."

He shifts in his chair to more fully face me in the Bar Down lab. "You want to blend white with red?"

"Yes. Don't look like that. It's actually quite common. Champagne, for example. It's chardonnay blended with pinot noir."

"Really?" His eyebrows elevate. "I didn't know that."

"Well, we're not making champagne."

"Obviously."

I smile. "I think the viognier will soften the rough edges of the syrah. It would have been better to co-ferment them, but we can do this now."

"What are the risks?"

I eye him approvingly. "Excellent question. Of course there's a risk it won't be good. But I'd say that's offset by the fact that the syrah as is won't be one of your better wines. It's drinkable, for sure. Just not great."

"I want it to be great."

My heart grows several sizes. "I know."

God. This man. I've watched him throw himself into work at the winery, getting his hands stained purple, ruining his beautiful leather brogues before he started wearing work boots, listening intently to everything I tell him. His absolute dedication and determination to getting things right makes my perfectionist winemaker's heart purr.

I put Jansen out of my mind to focus on work for the rest of the day. When I stumble into the kitchen at Caparelli at dinner time, Rosa and Jake are sitting at the table with empty plates in front of them.

"We didn't wait for you," Rosa says pointedly. "We've given up on that. You're working way too hard, Bee."

"It's harvest," I say, repeating what I told Jansen. When he said the same thing. I investigate the contents of a big pot on the stove. "Spaghetti?"

"Yes. I made Nonna's Bolognese sauce."

"Yum." I start dishing up. "I'm sorry. But yeah, don't wait for me if I'm not here."

She sighs. "You're running back and forth between here and Take Flight—"

"Bar Down," I correct her, licking sauce off my thumb. "Oh, garlic bread!"

"Whatever. My point is, you're exhausting yourself."

I carry my plate to the table and sit. At that moment, weariness rolls over me. Even my bones feel tired. She's right.

My days start at six in the morning. We have to clean the cellar before we can process the grapes and get the juice in the tanks, then I do my analysis and make adjustments and then we clean again. We have to punch down the reds every two hours. After lunch we spend a couple of hours tasting all the wines going through fermentation and talk about cap management technique. Then there's a conference call about grape picking and shipping logistics and a cellar meeting discussing tank logistics and the crew's schedule. I've been going back to the lab after supper to look over all the testing results, analyze the data, adjust tank temperatures, and create work orders.

"I'm fine." I summon up a smile and enough energy to eat.

She eyes me as if she sees through my act. "Bianca. You don't have to work this hard."

I frown at my spaghetti. "The work has to get done."

"I know, but you've taken on so much."

"I'm not here for long," I remind her, a little annoyed. "I'm doing what I have to."

She presses her lips together and glances at Jake. "We never see you."

"What? We see each other all the time!"

"Yeah, on the crush pad when you're yelling at us to be gentle with grapes or when we're all picking in different rows."

"Well, I'm sure you don't really want to see that much of me." I try for a smile to indicate I'm joking. Except I'm not really joking. "You two are busy with each other. And you've always had your own life."

For a moment she says nothing, and I twirl pasta around my fork.

"What does that mean?" she finally says.

I finish chewing and swallow, then take a gulp of water. "You're older than me. You always had your own life. You didn't have time for pesky little sisters." I smile and keep my expression pleasant. I'm not trying to start anything. "And that's totally normal." I keep telling myself that. Because I'm leaving again. My career and future and success as a wine-maker is somewhere else. And reconnecting with Rosa and Jake is fine, but getting too close to them will only make that harder.

Her forehead creases. "Really?"

I wave a hand. "It's okay. I have my own friends. And it's been great reconnecting with them. I'm thankful for their help."

"You don't think we're friends?"

I swallow a sigh. I really don't want to start anything. "We're sisters."

"And partners."

"Right. Partners in wine!" I chuckle at my own joke and eat more spaghetti, sucking in a strand through my lips.

Rosa doesn't laugh. Jake purses his lips.

"I'm going back to the lab for a while." I pause. "Oh. Do you want me to do the dishes? Since you cooked?"

"No. That's not the point. Bee—"

"Okay. Sorry I'm not around much. Let's make a point of dinner together Saturday, okay? See you later!"

I do still have some work to do in the lab, but I am, in fact, so, so tired. As I cross the yard and walk through the trees to Bar Down, my pace is that of a ninety-year-old woman with two artificial hips and arthritis in both knees. In the lab, I flick on the light and sink onto a stool at a counter.

I stare blearily at the binders of notes with color-coded tabs, charts, and piles of sticky notes tracking all the winemaking—press fractions, punchdown schedules, fermentation tempera-tures—and various logbooks. There's also a log tracking daily sanitation schedules, everything from scrubbing floors to sani-tizing empty tanks and steaming barrels.

I still need to transcribe my notes and log results, study the weather forecast, calculate grape tonnage and review the Brix charts, and then plan for tomorrow. We need to know which grapes are coming in to sort them, how much red and white we're getting, because there's a different press process for each.

I'm trying to move away from binders and sticky notes, so I open one of the spreadsheets I've set up on the computer and start transcribing the audio notes I recorded on my phone this morning. My head is bent and the lab is silent other than my own voice, so when the door opens, I shriek and nearly fall off my stool. I whirl around to see Jansen standing in the door.

"Oh God." I press a hand to my chest. "Sorry. What are you doing here?"

"What are *you* doing here?" He advances into the room, shutting the door behind him.

My voice is still droning from my phone and I reach for it and pause it. "Finishing up the stuff I didn't get done this afternoon."

He sighs. "Bianca. It's eight o'clock. Did you eat dinner?"

"Yes! I did! Spaghetti with Nonna's Bolognese sauce."

"Okay, good. Still. You need some rest."

I sigh. "Rosa says that, too."

He moves closer. Alone in this space, my skin tingles even more than it does when he's around. "Maybe because it's true."

I blow out a breath. "I just have to finish a few more things and then I'll go home and go to bed."

The air around us becomes charged at those words. I ignore it.

"Can you check the weather forecast?" I ask him.

"Sure." He knows what to do now. He pulls up the website on his phone and makes notes about temperature, winds, humidity. We briefly discuss that and the areas still to be harvested and I make notes for tomorrow on my iPad.

"What else can I do?" he asks quietly.

I want to tell him nothing, I can handle all this. But I'm tired. And he owns the winery. So I say, "Maybe you could finish transcribing my voice notes? I'll work on my plan for tomorrow."

"Sure."

We both focus on work for the next while. When he finishes and turns off my phone, he says, "Is all this absolutely necessary?"

"Yes." I give him a wry smile. "I know it seems like a lot. Like I'm being super persnickety."

"Persnickety." One corner of his mouth lifts.

I watch it, mesmerized. Then I say, "Yeah. I'm a bit of a perfectionist when it comes to this stuff, but you have to be. Harvest is a really busy time. If you don't keep good records and stay organized, the potential for major screw ups is huge. Plus we can learn from everything and do better."

He nods. "I guess I understand that. Were you like this in Argentina?"

"Of course." I did work hard there, but I also got out sometimes. We'd go horseback riding, hiking, or exploring Buenos Aires and Mendoza.

We go over the plan for tomorrow.

"Now I'll walk you home," he says, standing.

"You don't have to walk me home. It's next door."

"It's dark."

"I'm not afraid of the dark."

"What about bobcats? Are you afraid of bobcats?"

I laugh. "No. Because they never come here."

"They might. Also, you're so tired you might fall asleep on the way home and we'll find you snoring in the grass in the morning."

I snort.

"Come on."

I give up. We turn out the lights and lock the door, another thing I'm picky about for no good reason than it's better to be safe than sorry.

Tiny diamond stars stud the clear, dark sky, the moon a sliver of a gold coin. The temperature has dropped but it feels wonderful after the heat and sweat of the day, and I revel in the breeze stroking my hair back off my face as we walk across Jansen's yard toward the row of live oaks. The smell of grape juice hangs in the air, sweet, ripe, and full, and the chirrup of crickets surrounds us.

"I hate crickets."

He glances at me. "You do?"

"I do. They sound nice and as long as they're at a distance, that's fine, but when you come face to face with one, they are horrifying monsters."

He coughs. "They're high in protein."

"Aaaaah! I can't believe you said that! Ew, ew, ew."

He shrugs. "I'm sure they serve some other purpose."

"Yeah, probably. But I'm afraid of them."

"Hmm. Well, we all have our fears."

"What are you afraid of?"

He doesn't answer. Finally he says, "Apparently I don't like snakes."

I grin. "That's fair. Did you just discover this?"

"Yeah. Miles and I ran into a snake when we were running one day. I didn't encounter many snakes in Toronto or Los Angeles."

I grin. "That's hissssssterical."

He barks out a laugh.

"Oh my God! Did I make you laugh?" I stop walking, laughing, and move in front of him to face him. "Let me see! Are you really laughing?"

"What's the big deal? That was kinda funny. Bad, but funny."

"I'm always funny, but you've never laughed at me." I pause. "I mean, I don't want you to laugh *at* me. But when I make a joke, you know, a little polite chuckle or even a smile would be appreciated. Sometimes I think you're almost going to smile...the corners of your mouth tic up..." I lift my hand and touch my fingertips to the corner of his mouth. His eyes darken and the air thickens and heats around us. "But you never actually laugh," I finish breathlessly.

"You're not always funny." Our gazes connect, in the shadows of the live oaks, under blue and silver stars and the topaz crescent moon. I don't move my hand from where it touches his face.

"I-I'm not?"

"Sometimes you're sexy."

A warm slide of desire pools low inside me. We look into each other's eyes for a drawn out, laden moment.

I don't know what this is.

I've been attracted to men before. Of course I have. But I don't ever remember feeling like I'm going to die from wanting him, like my need for him is a powerful force I'm helpless against.

"Sometimes you're sweet." He curls his fingers around my hand and presses it to his cheek. His thick eyelashes sweep down and I know, I just *know* that he feels the same. He's feeling this overruling attraction, too. The way he looks at me— no man has ever looked at me like that, like he's drowning in lust. Like he's desperate for me.

I move closer. Heat radiates from him. He doesn't move. He's resisting. He thinks he can fight this. He thinks he's strong enough to hold out against it.

Maybe he is. I know he's strong. I know he's determined.

"But you're *always* fucking fascinating."

Oh God. My knees, no, my entire *legs*, have turned to oatmeal.

He lets go of my hand and cups my face in both hands. I let my fingers trail down over the scruff on his jaw and rest on his shoulder. We stare into each other's eyes, my body throbbing.

"I've tried so hard." His thumb brushes my lips. "So fucking hard."

I give a slow blink. "Tried what?"

"Tried to resist you."

"Why?"

He makes a noise in his throat. "Because you're young. Beautiful. Alive."

"Yes. I am alive." The sarcasm probably doesn't come across because my voice is a whisper.

But his lips quirk in that way I love, the way that excites me because I've almost, *almost* made him smile. I want to make him smile so badly. "I mean you're...full of life. Full of energy. You never stop."

I tip my head back and watch his mouth move as he talks. About me. As if he...likes me.

"I'm old and tired," he goes on, his gaze wandering over my face. "And probably an idiot. You deserve more."

"Oh my God." I close my eyes. How can he say that when he is so much? So strong, so determined, so kind. "I'm attracted to you, Jansen." That's not enough to describe how much I want him. "There's nothing wrong with that. With us wanting each other."

"I don't...I can't..." He stops.

My heart turns to ice in my chest. "Are you still in love with your wife?"

"No! Jesus." His instant, sincere reaction thaws my cardiac organ. "No."

"Then what is it?" I slip my arms over his shoulders and press closer still. "Are you worried because you're my boss and you don't want to abuse your power over me?"

"Uh..." His eyes widen.

"I'm kidding. And don't even think about the age difference between us. We're both adults."

"Okay, but...I'm not interested in marriage. Or a relationship. I want to focus on this winery. It's better if I'm alone."

"Hmm." I give a tiny nod. "Well, I'm not interested in a relationship either. I'm only here for another month or so. I have a job and a life in Argentina to go back to."

"So..."

"It's just an attraction." *Right.* "You're hot. I'm horny. We're both single. It's that easy."

"Well. When you put it that way..."

Chapter 15

Jansen

I'm weakening.

Maybe she's right. Maybe it is that easy. Maybe we can have a sexy fling without anybody getting hurt.

Or maybe I'm telling myself that because I want her so fucking bad I'm harder than a woodpecker's lips.

And yet...she's exhausted. Despite the glow in her eyes and the pout of her bottom lip, the way she's pressing into me with clear want and invitation, I can see it on her face.

"Okay," I murmur, kissing her forehead. "But not tonight."

"Whaaaaat?"

I nearly laugh at her whine. "You're exhausted. Tomorrow night. We'll do it right."

"Is there a wrong way?" she grumbles as I start leading her back to her place. "I don't think there is."

"There is if you fall asleep in the middle of it."

She huffs. "That's not saying much for your skills."

Lightness rises in my chest. Yeah, I'm horny as hell, but she amuses me. "Don't worry about my skills."

"Oh ho. Now my expectations are huge."

"I'll resist the obvious comeback."

She laughs. Her delighted giggle has that lightness expanding through me even more. "Now I'm even more disappointed."

"Patience, sweetheart."

We emerge from the trees onto her property. I know I don't need to walk her to the door, but I'm going to. She holds onto my arm as we cross the grounds and again, I can feel the fatigue in her sexy body.

We pause at the back door of the old Victorian house. I take in the peeling paint and overgrown weeds. Bianca and her sisters have their work cut out for them, bringing this place back to life. Emotion surges at how hard Bianca's been working, the load she's taken on, and especially what she's done for me given she has all this to worry about.

The outside light is on and it highlights the circles beneath her pretty eyes as I turn her into my arms. "Okay. Come to my place tomorrow night. I'll make you dinner again."

Her eyelids droop. "Dinner? Is that all?"

"No. That's not all." I bend my knees and dip my head to find her mouth with mine. She makes a soft noise in her throat and I pull her closer, right against me. Soft. She's soft and warm and she melts into me, like our bodies are made for each other. Her mouth opens for me and I'm gone. Jesus. My head spins as our tongues glide and taste and our lips cling.

Heat ripples over my skin and my balls draw up tight.

"More of that?"

"Jesus. Now that I've kissed you...now I know how sweet your mouth is...there's no way you're not getting fucked."

She whimpers.

I kiss her until I can't breathe, lift my mouth from hers to peer at her, then go in again. We kiss and kiss, luscious kisses, deep kisses, over and over. Then I catch her bottom lip in mine and suck gently. "Okay," I groan. "That's it. Or we're doing it right here on your back porch."

Eyes closed, she smiles.

"Good night, Bianca."

Her eyelids flutter open and she gazes at me dreamily. "I can't believe you're doing this. I mean not doing this."

"I can't either. Christ." My balls ache ferociously. I kiss her forehead and let her go. "Get some sleep."

I walk away but I turn and watch her enter the house and close the door behind her.

I take a few long, harsh breaths, sucking fresh night air into my lungs. Jesus. I've been jerking off to thoughts of her for weeks. How the fuck am I going to sleep now that I've actually tasted that soft mouth? Felt those sweet tits press against my chest...learned that she wants me, too.

Holy shit. I stare at Bianca as she stumbles into the pressing house the next morning. She looks...awful.

I head straight toward her. "Are you okay?"

She gazes at me with foggy eyes that are huge in her pale face. She looks...sweaty. "I'm fine."

"Jesus." I lift a hand and press it to her forehead. "No. You're not. You're sick."

"I have work to do."

"Fuck that. You need to be in bed."

"Jansen. I *can't*."

"Yes, you can. Come on." I try to steer her to the door but she digs in her heels. "Bianca. Now. Or I'll carry you out of here and I don't care who sees."

Her shoulders slump and I sense she gives in only because she feels like shit. Which is a little scary.

I take her home. Her house is empty, with both Rosa and Jake out working. I help her up the stairs and into her bedroom, where I've never been before. I get a quick impression of a few pieces of vintage furniture, an old-fashioned quilt on the bed, and sun pouring through gauzy curtains. I get Bianca onto the bed, pull off her boots and jeans.

Yeah, I'd like to be doing this for a different reason, but hell, she's in rough shape. I tuck her under the covers in her pink lace panties and T-shirt. Then I pull down the blind on the window to shut out the light and set out to find the bathroom.

It's a little weird, snooping through her drawers and cabinets. I find a washcloth that I soak in cold water. I search for a thermometer and come up empty, but I do find Advil. I run a glass of water and return to the bedroom. "Here." I hand over a pill and the water, and fold the cloth to lay it on her forehead.

"I'll be better in an hour," she croaks. "I just need a little more sleep."

"Sure." I don't believe that for a second.

"There's so much to do," she whines.

"It'll get done."

"By who?"

"By me," I reply firmly. "And the team."

"Nobody knows what to do," she mumbles.

A smile tugs my lips. "You are the boss," I agree. "But I think we can survive a day."

She looks like she's going to cry.

"It's okay," I soothe. "We got this. You need to rest."

I go down to the kitchen and find some juice for her. I send Rosa a text to let her know Bianca's sick.

When Bianca dozes off, I sit in a nearby chair and watch her. Her damp hair is flattened to her scalp and her skin is much paler than her usual golden tan. But she still looks beautiful. My eyes wander over the curve of her high cheekbones, the soft fullness of her lips, the dark crescents of her eyelashes.

I don't like seeing her like this. She's always so full of life. Unstoppable.

I rub my stomach, feeling like I just ate some bad shellfish.

I look around the room again in the dim light. There isn't a lot of Bianca's personal style, although I'm not sure what that is. I run a hand over the soft, well-washed quilt made of fabric squares in shades of green, pink, and cream. The rug next to the bed has similar colors. On the dresser sit a bottle of lotion, a hairbrush, a stack of folded towels and...a black and white bear. My gaze snags on the plush toy and stays there.

It's the panda I won at the fair that night. A slow smile tugs one corner of my lips up.

I get up to lay my hand gently on Bianca's forehead. Still warm. I go run the cloth under cold water, squeeze it out, and gently lay it on her forehead again. Then I sit on the edge of the chair, gnaw on my lip, and watch her more.

When Rosa shows up, her forehead creased with concern, I tell her that Bianca's had Advil and juice. "Jesus," I mutter, rubbing my mouth. "She looked terrible."

She gives me a strange look, then shoos me out. "I'll take care of her."

I stand at the bedroom door for one last look before I leave. I don't want to go, but there is work to be done.

I jog back to the lab. Bianca's a stickler for notes and I grab one of the binders where she makes plans. I quickly find the notes she made yesterday about what needs to be done today. Then I go find Antonio and we get busy.

"Which tank do you want to move this pinot noir to?" he asks me.

I almost panic.

No. I got this. I read Bianca's notes, and remember what she's said about the chardonnay. They're going to a stainless tank and with as much confidence as I can muster, I direct Antonio.

I keep checking my phone to see if Bianca's texted. By lunch time, I haven't heard anything, so I head back to her place. I knock before opening the door, and Jake appears.

"Hey," I say. "I came to check on Bianca."

"Rosa's with her," he says. "Come in."

"Can I go up?"

He gives me a crisp look, then shrugs. "Okay."

I take the stairs two at a time and knock on the bedroom door even though it's open. Bianca's still out flat on her back and Rosa, bless her, has a thermometer.

"She has quite a fever," she says to me.

"I thought so." I run a jerky hand through my hair and move closer. "Hey, beautiful."

Rosa gives me a pointed look not unlike Jake's. Right now, I don't care.

"Jansen." Bianca lifts a hand. "I'm sorry." Her bottom lip trembles.

"It's okay. I told you, we got this." I stroke her hair off her face.

"I called the doctor," Rosa says. "I think she has a UTI. She's had them before."

"Oh." I turn to Rosa, frowning.

"He's going to call a prescription in to the pharmacy."

Okay, good, good. "I'll go get it."

"That's okay, I can do it."

"Okay." I blow out a breath. "Medication will help, right?"

She smiles. "Yes. It should make her feel better pretty quickly."

"Whew." I look back at my girl. "You'll be better soon. You'll be back bossing everyone around in no time."

A smile ghosts over her lips.

I pick up her hand and kiss it. "Okay. I'll check back later."

Once again, I become aware of Rosa's acute regard. I lower Bianca's hand to the covers.

"Thank you," she whispers.

Back in the cellar, Antonio and I draw samples to taste. I've listened and learned from Bianca and I know that the TA decreases during fermentation. My tasting also tells me the wine should be more acidic, so I instruct Antonio to add tartaric acid in this tank.

When it's time for the cellar meeting to talk about the crew's schedule for tomorrow I'm again grateful for Bianca's detailed notes and the time I've spent with her, and with the input of Antonio and Diego, we draw up a plan for tomorrow.

I don't want to let her down, so I carefully make notes about everything we've done today, and then I hotfoot it back to her place to check on her.

She's better. Somewhat. She's sitting up in bed with pillows propped behind her, reading a book. Relief slides through my veins. "Hey. How're you doing?"

She looks up and smiles, still pale. "Better. A bit. I'm on antibiotics now."

"Yeah. That's good." I sit on the edge of the bed and feel her forehead. "Feels better."

"The Advil helped. Thank you."

I nod.

"So much for dinner tonight," she says. "And..."

I have to admit I'm disappointed. But I'm relieved she's okay. "Well, here you are in a bed..." I hoist an eyebrow and lift my hands to the buttons of my shirt.

She grins weakly. "You made a joke."

"Yeah." I reach out and smooth back her hair. "We have lots of time for...dinner."

Her eyes warm. "Okay. How did things go today?"

"Good. Don't worry about it."

"I'll be there tomorrow."

"Like hell you will."

"I'm sure I'll feel better."

Rather than argue, I say, "Let's play it by ear."

Again, she relents too easily, a sign of how ill she is.

"Are you hungry?" I ask.

"Mmm. Not really."

"Maybe some soup?"

She nods. "With crackers? Goldfish?" she adds hopefully.

I smile. "You got it, beautiful."

I don't know if they have Goldfish in their kitchen but I'll drive to San Francisco to get them if I have to, and then I will feed her the goddamn soup mouthful by mouthful to make sure she eats.

Chapter 16

Bianca

Afew days later, I'm much better. I'm not done the antibiotics, but I have to take all of them, I know. I feel well enough to be at work though, and I'm worried about what I'm going to find. Jake and Rosa update me on everything that's been done, and they've managed things fine, and over at Bar Down, I discover that Jansen has, too.

Wow. Things have gone smoothly. I review Jansen's notes, impressed.

"You did great," I tell him.

He dips his chin. "Thanks."

We're in the lab along with Antonio discussing punchdown schedules. I've been thinking about him for days. Okay, maybe not when I was really sick, but when I started feeling better, I remembered his kisses and how I melted inside and how good he tasted. And I remember his tenderness and concern when I was sick.

I study his stubble-shadowed jaw, sculped cheekbones, and firm lips. And I melt a little again.

Our eyes meet. He's burning me up with his eyes, and the tension that arcs between us has heat rippling in my belly.

Diego tromps in. "We have a problem."

I blink, yanked back to reality.

"Some of the grapes in block ten have black rot." He holds up a bunch of grapes. Most of the grapes are small, dark, and withered.

I stare at them, my stomach cramping. "Shit."

"Yeah."

"Cab sauv, right?"

"Yep."

"This doesn't sound good," Jansen says.

"Black rot is not good," I confirm.

"Some of the pickers discovered it this morning," Diego says.

"What did they do with the grapes?" I ask.

"They stopped picking right away and brought these to me."

"We should go have a look."

We leave Antonio in the cellar and Jansen, Diego, and I head out to block ten, a bit of a hike. Vineyards bigger than a few acres are partitioned into "blocks", which usually grow a single varietal, and also divide different soil types or take into account the grade of the land and things like roads, fences, or streams. Block ten is only two acres, with about two thousand vines, a smaller section.

I sense Jansen's worry as we tramp through the vines and we keep exchanging glances. I don't blame him. Black rot is a fungus that's a serious disease of both cultivated and wild grapes. It attacks all the green parts of the vine—leaves, shoots, stems, tendrils, and fruit. Obviously the most damaging consequence is to the grapes. It can result in complete crop losses.

I want to reach out and grab his hand and squeeze it. But I can't do that.

We still haven't had the "dinner" he promised me days ago. Every time we're together I think about what I missed and when it's going to happen and how good it's going to be. I've never wanted someone like this.

I've had boyfriends. I liked them. I was attracted to them. But I've never felt this eagerness to see him, like, every time I come over to Bar Down. I've never felt this desperate, intense need layered with affection and admiration.

I was thinking tonight might be the night...especially with how he was looking at me earlier...but now this.

We check out the vines. As I move up one aisle and down the other side, I find numerous infected plants.

"I don't know why I didn't notice this," Diego mutters. "I should have seen the lesions on the leaves."

I don't know what to say to him. Yeah, he should have. "You weren't here in the spring," I say, which is when the fungus should have been scouted for.

"What do we do?" Jansen forks his fingers into his hair, a frown etched into the sides of his mouth.

"It not great that we didn't notice until now," I say, staying calm. "But we did. Unfortunately, there's not much we can do this season."

"I guess we can't use any of these grapes?"

I suck in a breath. "Well. Studies have been done that show black rot of grapes doesn't cause health problems if it's incorporated into wine processing."

His brow creases skeptically.

"But infected grapes can lower the flavor and aroma qualities of the wine. Also, the government regulates the levels of volatile acidity in wines that's attributed to rot. You don't want your reputation impacted by producing lower quality wine, or worse, bad wine."

"Absolutely not."

"This block is to be hand harvested." I look around. "We need to talk to the workers and make sure they know about the fungus. *All* the workers, just in case."

"What do we tell them?" Jansen asks. "What do we do?"

"Sometimes we've left the grapes on the ground," Diego says. "I don't recommend that. The pathogens can overwinter and become active in the spring."

"Nope." Jansen shakes his head.

"We could have them separate the bad grapes from the good, and put the bad ones in cull buckets," Diego goes on. "But that's a lot of extra work."

"So..." Jansen lifts an eyebrow.

"It's probably best to leave the bad clusters on the vines. Then after harvest we can come back and deal with them, or prune them during the winter."

Jansen looks at me.

"Your call," I say softly.

"Fuck." He rubs his face. "Okay, leave them. Like you said, we'll deal with them after harvest."

Diego nods somberly. "Got it." He looks at Jansen. "I'm sorry, boss."

Jansen's mouth thins.

I sense their frustration. "Guys, neither of you were here in the spring," I remind them. "Things were in flux with the Wrights selling and you buying. It's not unexpected that something got overlooked. Let's be glad it's just this one block, and it's not a big block."

They both nod, but I don't know if I've convinced them. I can tell Jansen hates to lose. He's a determined competitor.

When we're alone, I grab his arm. "Hey. Talk to me."

His face is steely. "About what?"

"I know you're pissed about the black rot."

He gives one curt nod.

"Do you blame Diego?"

"No."

"You blame yourself." I pause. "Don't you?"

"I'm the owner," he says quietly. "Ultimately, I'm responsible."

"Don't beat yourself up about this."

"I'm not." His mouth is a thin line.

I gaze at him. He says nothing. "Yes, you are," I say gently. "Don't do that. There are going to be ups and downs. Successes and failures."

He looks away, then shoves a hand into his hair. "Yeah." He exhales a long breath. "One of my hockey coaches used to tell us, 'you either win or you learn.' I always tried to learn when we didn't win."

Something spins in my chest, warm and syrupy. "Yeah. That."

He gives me a reluctant smile. "Thanks."

I shrug. "You're the one with the pithy aphorism."

He barks out a laugh. "Okay."

I pause, waiting for...something. An invitation? Some kind of overture? Well. "I have to get back to Caparelli. Lots to do on the sauvignon blanc grapes. It looks like a great harvest. The Brix is exactly where we want it."

"Go." He smiles and waves his hands.

I call over my shoulder, "I'll be back later. I have to finish logging my data and work on the plan for tomorrow."

"Okay."

Over at Caparelli, I hunt down Jake to talk to him about the grosso grapes. We've started harvesting them and I think they're really good. Not good enough to use on their own, but perfect for blending.

"The warm weather has been good for them," Jake says.

"Yes. So, what do you think about blending them with the merlot? From my early tasting, it's very fruity this year."

He purses his lips. "We often combined merlot with cab sauv."

"I know. But I want to use the grosso grapes. They're not common and I think we could have something really unique."

"Like what?"

"Well, the classic Bordeaux blend is merlot, cabernet sauvignon, cabernet franc, petit verdot, and malbec."

"Petit verdot doesn't do well here. It needs more warmth."

"Right. But I'm thinking of using the grosso instead of it."

"Ahhhh."

"It'd be like a New World Old World wine."

He grins.

"The acidity and tannins from the grosso will add complexity to all the red fruit flavors from the malbec and the spice of the cabernet. The cabernet franc will add luscious aromatics."

"I like it."

Yay!

He updates me more about how harvest is going in the various blocks as we walk back to the crush pad. I spend some time there and then head back to the lab at Bar Down.

It's late. The tasting room is closed, most people have gone home. But Jansen's in his office with his laptop open, as he often is in the evening.

"I'm back."

He looks up at me and a slow spreads across his face, his eyes warm. "You are."

"I'll be in the lab for a while."

He nods. "Need any help?"

"Sure."

He rises and walks toward me. And my feet are glued in place as I watch him, with his athletic saunter and horny eyes. "Okay. Let's go."

I blink. That sounds hot.

Focus.

I head to the lab, aware of his big presence behind me.

"I have to test the juice from the chardonnay grapes that were harvested today," I tell him. "Our chardonnay. Also your sauvignon blanc."

"Double the work," he murmurs. "I really do appreciate what you're doing."

"I'm having fun," I say honestly.

"Even though you ended up sick in bed."

I scrunch up my face. "That was a freak thing."

We enter the lab.

"What are you testing for?" he asks me.

"A bunch of stuff. Brix, pH, titratable acidity. Yeast, malic acid concentration. Microbial stability."

"I love it when you talk science to me."

I laugh.

He knows what to do now and we both get busy. Haha, bad choice of words. I want to get busy with him so bad I'm sweating.

I log test results into my computer. Jansen checks the

weather forecast for tomorrow and he actually makes the plan for tomorrow's harvest for Bar Down while I work on Caparelli.

I'm sitting at the counter that runs along one wall, Jansen in another rolling chair next to me. I lean back and let out a long breath. "Okay. I think we're done."

Our eyes meet.

Warmth curls through me. I can't move. The air around us is electric and I gaze at him, transfixed. He watches me, too, eyes searching mine, and heat builds between us.

"I still owe you dinner," he says hoarsely, rolling his chair closer.

"Yes. You do."

His gaze drops to my mouth. Excitement flutters in my belly.

He curls his hands around the arms of my chair and drags me toward him until our knees are touching and his muscled arms box me in. "I can't stop thinking about you. It's been hell the last few days."

I let my head fall back to stare into his face. "I know. Me too."

"After I kissed you that night...Jesus."

The way he looks at me scorches me, making me feel so wanted. Heat slides through my veins, and my inner muscles low in my belly clench hard. My lips part, longing to feel his mouth on mine. "I'm sorry I got sick."

He closes his eyes, a sliver of a smile on his mouth. "Fuck, don't apologize for that." He opens his eyes and the corners crinkle up. "I'm glad you're feeling better."

"I'm feeling...like I might still have a fever."

His eyebrows twitch.

"Not really," I add quickly. "I'm just really...hot."

"Ah. Understandable. I am, too."

I can't help but let my eyes drop to the fly of his jeans. I roll my lips in, seeing the imposing bulge there. I let my gaze wander back up, over the thin cotton plaid shirt that drapes from his strong shoulders over his muscle-packed chest and flat abs. I linger at his throat. A pulse beats there and I want to lay my mouth there, breathe in the scent of his skin, and taste him.

Then I meet his eyes again. I remember the heat of his mouth and the feel of his body against mine and I want that again, so much. And more.

He leans closer, eyes going heavy-lidded, and presses his mouth to mine. Yes... He's warm and firm and I lean into the kiss, opening for him. A low groan rumbles in his chest and his tongue licks into my mouth.

That fever inside me flares up hotter. I need to be closer to him. A moan leaks from my lips.

His hands move from the arms of the chair to my bare thighs. I watch them, big and rough and tanned on my smoother skin. My skin immediately tingles everywhere, and heat gathers between my legs. Our kiss goes scorching, wilder, frenzied as we strain toward each other.

"God, Jansen." I let my head fall back as he drags his lips down my throat and sucks. "Please. I need..."

"Please what?" He licks my skin. "What do you need, Bianca?"

"You." I whimper. "I've been thinking about you, too. Dreaming about you."

"Yeah? Have you been masturbating thinking of me?"

My belly flips with excitement and I quiver.

"Because I've been thinking about you." He kisses the side of my neck, then nibbles at my ear lobe. Shivers flow down my spine, the aching need inside me torturous. "Jerking off every day in the shower thinking of you. Every night in my bed." His mouth slides over my cheek. "Imagining you."

"Y-yes. I have."

"Jesus." He growls out the word and jerks back. His chest is heaving and his eyes blaze at me. "Right now, Bianca. Right here."

My eyes widen and my pussy squeezes again. "We can't. Not here."

His eyes shift around the room. "You're right. This is a shit place. Come on." He pushes up out of his chair so fast it shoots across the floor, grabbing my hands and pulling me up, too. "Let's go."

He turns, still holding my hand, and tows me toward the door.

I scramble to keep up with him on rubbery legs. "Where?" I ask, my voice high and thin.

He doesn't answer, just strides out of the lab, down the hall, and into the dark reception area of the tasting room. Is he taking me to his place?

No. Apparently not. He stops at one of the leather couches in front of the big stone fireplace, and with his hands on my shoulders he pushes me down into it.

My eyelashes are fluttering wildly. "Here?"

"Yeah. I can't wait any longer." He bends and unbuttons my shorts, then pauses. He meets my eyes. "Okay?"

I blink. Swallow. Glance around the room.

It's beautiful here, with a thick rug on the stone floor, tall tropical plants in the corners, and leather couches and chairs, but it's also like an atrium, with glass walls and a high glass ceiling supported with beams. It's dark outside and it's dark in here, but...I bite my lip. "Someone could come."

"No one will come now." His low, steady voice sways me, and also turns me on even more.

"I don't want to wait either." I press a hand between my legs.

His eyes go darker and he draws in a sharp breath. "Are you aching there, sweetheart?"

"Yes. So bad. I need you."

He straightens and moves to the fireplace, picking up the remote sitting on the mantel. A push of a button has flames flickering to life, the only light in the room. It gilds his profile and outlines his body as he turns back to me, fingers working open the buttons of his shirt.

Ohhhhh. God.

I unzip my shorts and shimmy out of them and my panties.

"Jesus." He stops in front of me, then drops to a crouch. "Bianca."

My stomach swoops.

He pulls off my work boots and thick socks—so sexy! God, I should be wearing silk lingerie, not cut offs and work boots. Then every thought flies out of my head as he clasps my ankles and lifts them, setting my heels on the edge of the couch. I fall back into the cushions, revealed to him, spread wide and open. I can feel the beat of my heart right there, between my legs.

He stares at me for long moments, boldly, ravenously. Intimately. My mouth sags open, panting, watching his face.

"So beautiful," he growls. He lifts his head and grabs the hem of my T-shirt, lifting it. I help him pull it off over my head, both our hands frantic, and flick open the front clasp of my bra. It stays on, hanging at my sides, as his hands cover my breasts. "Good Christ. You are perfect." He cups my soft flesh, molds it in his palms, squeezes it firmly.

I swell into his hands, my head falling back. "Ohhhh God."

"Need a taste. Just a taste of these stunners. Shit, Bianca, your tits are gorgeous."

More shivers roll through me, hard, rocking me.

Kneeling on the floor, he leans in and closes his lips around one nipple. Sensation shoots to my pussy as he tugs and licks.

I'm burning up, pleasure rippling through me, the throb between my legs echoed in my wrists, my throat.

He sucks and nibbles on one breast, then the others, and then with a groan he kisses his way down my stomach. His rough hands glide over my thighs and butt as he kisses my pussy, then licks me. He lifts one of my feet and sets it on his shoulder, giving him more room, and he dives back in as if he's starving, his tongue sliding over my wet flesh in satiny licks, his lips pulling gently at me, his teeth grazing me.

I push a hand into his thick hair, my fingertips digging into his skull as he eats at me. Flames burn over me, heat spirals through me, swirling in my bloodstream, sensation lashing every nerve ending. Oh my God, he's good at this. So good.

I can't even think any more, just feel.

He shoves his fingers inside me, forcing a cry from my throat and then he lifts up over me to kiss me again while he finger fucks me, filling the air with wet, slick sounds, filling me with stunning flickers and flares and heat. "Tight," he murmurs. "Such a tight, tiny pussy."

He catches my lower lip in his teeth, sucks my tongue, and I can only whimper at this sextravaganza. I'm floating, coming apart, and I want this to go on forever, but I also want more.

He moves back, shoves my thighs back and up, and then buries his face again between my legs.

"Yes! Yes..." My head rolls from side to side, overcome as he licks me, parts my flesh and licks deeper, then sucks me. "Oh God. Oh God."

Sensation twists inside me, almost painfully, that fast. I thread my fingers into his hair. I want to tell him to stop. I want all of him, inside me, but it's too late and my orgasm submerges me, steals my words, my body convulsing against his lips and tongue.

"Please," I whimper, not even sure what I'm asking for now.

He straightens and my fingers fumble at the opening of his jeans. Watching my face, he opens them and is out of them in a heartbeat, and he's in front of me, naked, gorgeous, all muscles and sleek skin and oh yeah, his impressive erection. His cock is mouth wateringly beautiful, straining toward me, thick, engorged, dark with lust. I'm still panting, still blurry-eyed, but I want to study him and admire him.

"Look at me like that and you get fucked for sure," he growls.

"Oh God." Heat spirals straight to my pussy at his words, my belly fluttering. "That's what I want. Fuck me."

He makes a rough noise. He has a condom in his hand; he must have pulled it from his jeans pocket and I'm grateful in a distracted sort of way.

"W-will the condom fit on you?" I ask breathlessly.

He huffs a laugh, his mouth curving as he opens the package then rolls the latex over his length. It fits, but it's stretched tight and thin, and the empty ache inside me intensifies. I may never breathe normally again after this.

He circles an arm around my waist and lifts me, spinning me onto my back on the couch, and I stare up at him, startled. Then he comes down with me, parting my thighs, kneeling between them. "Okay?"

In the depths of my mind that aren't consumed by lust, I appreciate his check in and want him to know I am enthusiastically consenting. "Yes. Yes, please."

He doesn't take his eyes off my face as he positions himself, absorbing my reaction, the breathy sounds I make as he takes himself in hand and nudges at my entrance. "This might take some work."

"I'm ready."

He watches himself as he grips his cock at the base and slicks the head up and down through my wetness. "So wet," he rasps. "Wet everywhere. So beautiful. I'm dying, Bianca."

"Me, too. I need you inside me."

"I'm out of patience." His jaw tightens. "I don't want to hurt you."

"You won't. I don't care." He pushes into me, and yeah, there's a bite of pain, but then he fills me so lusciously, thickly, and it's magnificent. I'm glutted, stretched. He's so deep inside me, I press a hand to my stomach.

"Fuck," he grits out. He props himself on straight arms above me, his jaw clenched, eyes blazing. "I've wanted this for so fucking long."

"Me too," I whisper. I pet his back, now damp with sweat. I'm bursting, too full of sensation. I can't hold it in, and I'm making noises I've never made before as I squeeze around him.

"Fuck," he says again. "Jesus, Bianca." He starts to move his hips, slow, slow, then his caution turns to frenzy as he fully penetrates me. Fills me faster, harder, pistoning into me, watching my face, and it's so intimate and intense my chest is filling, expanding, and that twisting feeling inside me resumes, this time starting at a higher point and spiraling up fast.

I watch him too, the way his forehead pleats, the fullness of his bottom lip, the haze in his eyes. "Kiss me."

He kisses me again, hard, a little dirty, a lot desperate, plunging his tongue inside, sucking at me, tasting me so deeply. I link my arms around his neck and hook my ankles behind his back. "I love it. I love your cock inside me." I lick his jaw, then suck his ear lobe.

Noises slip from my mouth, I can't stop them as he fucks me. He makes noises, too, guttural, deep noises as we move together. I can't believe this is happening, but I'm swept up in it, in desire and excitement, lost in it all.

The sounds of our bodies slapping together fills the room along with our groans and whimpers and sighs. The light of the fireplace flickers and ripples around us. I grab onto the edge of the couch to brace myself as Jansen pounds into me.

"I'm close," he grits out. "Gonna come…"

I clench around him, letting that sweet coil inside me tighten and build. "Me too…"

I focus on it, wanting it, heat racing over my skin, my pelvis lifting against every thrust of his body. I just…need…a little more… I slip my hand between us, fingers finding my clit.

He grunts. "Yeah. Want you to come."

I circle my fingertips over the sensitive knot and sensation spirals up so hot and fast it steals my breath. I cry out as I shudder and press up into him, shattering, falling into a fiery ecstasy that consumes me.

I curl my fingers into his hair as his strokes quicken, his hips strong and powerful, his cock driving into me, and waves of pleasure draw out almost painfully. He buries his face in the side of my neck when he comes, his body going tight, his groin pressed against me, his breathing ragged. "Fuck," he groans. "Fuck. Bianca. Jesus."

I clasp his hips with my thighs and we ride it out together, such beautiful, shocking bliss.

Chapter 17

Jansen

Holy fuck.

I've had sex since my divorce, and it was always good because I love sex and women are amazing. But this... there are no words. Maybe because it's been a while, what with buying the winery and moving here and knowing no one. Yeah. That's it.

I'm still balls deep inside Bianca. My chest is heaving, my heart knocking so hard I feel like my whole body is pulsing. My brains are scrambled like fucking eggs. I don't want to move.

Her hands stroke up and down my damp back and gradually I regain enough consciousness to realize I'm crushing her. "Sorry," I mumble, shifting to the side.

"S'okay. You're heavy but I like it."

I shift her, too, so we're on our sides, her back to my front. I wrap my arms around her and she wriggles her perfect ass into my groin and clasps my arms, making a soft sound of contentment. Lust pulses in my balls again.

"You were right," she says.

"About what?"

173

"You told me not to worry about your sex skills. You were right. They're phenomenal."

I bark out a laugh at her unexpected humor. And I like the compliment.

"I agree that was phenomenal. But I can do even better in an actual bed." I kiss her shoulder.

"Really?" She sounds dubious. But then says, "Prove it."

I smile. "Okay. Let's go."

"Give me a minute. I'm pretty sure I can't walk."

"I'll carry you." But I don't move, because I'm pretty sure I can't walk either.

When we finally recover enough to move, I help her dress, tugging her panties and shorts up her legs while she slides the T-shirt over her head. I make a quick trip to the bathroom to dispose of the condom and when I return she watches me with avid eyes, forgetting about her socks and boots. The heavy weight between my legs thickens again and I have to be careful with my fly when I pull up my jeans..

"My place," I say.

She nods.

I turn off the fireplace and we lock up, then set out toward the house. I clasp her hand in mine as we cross the yard in the brisk darkness. "Are you hungry?"

"Oh yeah."

"I mean for food."

"That's what I meant." Her smile is sly.

We have to deal with Moose when we walk into the house. He's ecstatic to see Bianca. She always makes a fuss over him. I fucking love it.

I flick on lights and move to the fridge. "I have leftover enchilasagna I made yesterday." I pull it out and set it on the counter.

"Um, what?

"Enchilasagna. Like lasagna but made with enchilada sauce, also chicken and a lot of cheese."

"Mmm. Sounds good."

I step toward her and cup her face and kiss her. Her mouth fits to mine so perfectly. So sweetly. She wraps her arms around my neck and presses into me, and she has to feel my erection against her stomach. She makes a tiny whimper.

"How hungry are you?" I murmur.

"Starving. For you."

Fuck, yeah. Once more, I take her hand and this time I lead her into my bedroom. The blinds are closed but there's enough light to see each other in shadows. I stop beside the bed and kiss her again, finding that perfect angle, her tongue small and hot against mine as we open to each other. A groan rises in my chest.

She slides her fingers into my hair and sensation streams down my spine. My heart, already kicking, jolts harder.

"Fuck," I mutter. "Why do you have to be so goddamn sweet."

She moans against my mouth.

I push her down onto the bed, on her back, and kneel on the bed beside her. I study her, so fucking beautiful, her hair a mess, her lips swollen, her clothes wrinkled, then I move over her, and kiss her again. I want to kiss her like this forever. I never want to stop kissing her. We're grinding against each other, both of us live wires, desperate, frantic for each other again. Already.

A whine comes from beside the bed.

I go still, closing my eyes. "Jesus Christ." I rest my forehead against hers. "Go away, Moose."

I lift my head and meet her eyes. We both smile.

"Hang on." I roll off her and take Moose back out to the living room. "Sorry, buddy. You're gonna have to stay here for a while, okay." Back in the bedroom, I shut the door behind me. "Sorry about that."

"It's okay." She smiles leisurely. "How can you be mad at a cute little pupper?"

I pull in a breath. "A cute little cock blocker is what he is."

She giggles.

While I'm up I snag a condom from a drawer, then move back over her. This time I'm not so out of control. Now I can take my time exploring her, teasing her, making her feel good. I slide a hand up her thigh, her skin smooth and firm, on the way to absolute heaven. My dick hardens even more and I remove her jeans and those fucking miniscule purple panties that made me lose my mind earlier.

She watches me as I rise onto my knees and undo the buttons of my shirt. I toss it aside and shift to pull off my jeans. When I turn back to her she sits up and then we're kissing again, wrapped in each other's arms. I slide a hand into her hair, tangling in it and tugging. Her soft sound of pleasure is intoxicating. I grip the hem of her T-shirt and tug it up and over her head. Her bra is currently stuffed into a pocket of her jeans, and my gaze lingers hungrily on her perfect tits, her bare shoulders, and her narrow waist. I lean in again, slide one hand in her hair, and I cup her face with the other. Mouths biting and tongues sliding, she makes more delicious sounds.

"Jesus." Her nipples are hardened into tight points and I feast my gaze on them as I lower her back to the bed and stretch out between her legs. She glides her fingers over my neck, through my hair, and I find her mouth again, kissing hard and rough, catching her bottom lip in my teeth, then licking over it.

My dick is hard again, already, engorged and throbbing, and tingles simmer at the base of my spin. Hands holding her face, I lift my head and look down at her. We're locked into a cage of heat and hunger, and something shifts, slows. My eyelids drop, I lower my mouth to hers, and this kiss drifts slower. Consuming. Devastating.

Eventually I lift my mouth from hers and, eyes on hers, I kiss between her breasts. "So fucking gorgeous." I cup them, squeeze them, kiss the hard tips, then take quick sips, pulling one nipple into my mouth, then the other.

A cry spills from her lips and her body quivers.

"Are you sore?" I ask softly, brushing my fingertips over her bare mound.

"No. I mean, maybe a little. But I'm fine."

"Okay." I brush another kiss on her mouth while slapping a hand around on the bed for the condom packet. Quickly, I glove up and move between her legs. I lower myself to my elbows, lowering my face so we're nose to nose. Eye to eye. Gazes locked in an intimate connection. She reaches between us for my cock and guides it to her hot, wet opening. A groan rises in my chest, my eyes closing, and I rest my forehead on hers as I push into her. "Fuuuuck. You feel amazing."

This is pent-up lust and repressed craving and desperate, beautiful relief.

"Can you come again?" I whisper against her ear.

"I...think so..." She finds her clit, and with a few tight, slick circles... "Yessss..."

I thrust again and again, my balls tight, pressure building at my spine. Her pussy squeezes me, rippling around me, and I let out a mighty shout as exquisite pain rips through me. Sensation rocks me in waves and I go still, pulsing inside her, burying my face in the side of her neck and panting against her skin. She holds me with her arms and legs, her mouth on my shoulder.

"Jesus. Jesus Christ. Bianca."

"Mmmm."

Am I even still alive? I'm not sure. But if I've died, I've definitely gone to heaven.

"I HOPE THE ENCHILASAGNA IS OKAY BECAUSE I'M starving." Her voice is soft and drowsy.

"Yeah?" I roll toward her and prop my head on my elbow. "You sound like you want to go to sleep."

"Mmm. I always want to go to sleep after an orgasm. And that was *three* orgasms." Eyes still closed, her mouth curves into a satisfied smile.

I stroke hair back off her face. "Maybe you should sleep."

She cracks open an eye. "Are we back to me working too hard?"

One corner of my mouth lifts. "Maybe?"

Both eyes open and focus on me. "Can I eat first? Then sleep?"

"We can do that. Don't move." I shift away to get out of bed. "I'll be back."

Her eyes widen. "What are you doing?"

"Breakfast in bed is a thing. Why not dinner in bed?"

She smiles. "Why not."

I grab a pair of shorts and open the bedroom door. Moose is lying right outside it and he's shaking. "Oh no."

"What?" Bianca sits up.

I'm briefly distracted by her gorgeous tits. Giving my head a shake, I bend and scoop Moose up. "Moose, my man. What's wrong?"

"Is he okay?"

"He's shaking."

"Oh." After a beat, she adds, "Maybe we scared him."

I look over at her. She's not making a joke. "Do you think?"

She bites her lip. "We made a lot of noise. It was pretty, er, physical. Maybe he's...er, not used to that?"

"Well, no more sex for us then."

Her mouth drops open and then she catches my eye and bursts out laughing, flopping to her back.

A smile tugs at my lips, unfamiliar and yet so goddamn delightful.

"You made a joke," she wheezes, still giggling. "A good one. You said that with such a straight face I believed you."

Cuddling Moose to my chest, I walk over to her, bend, and kiss her smiling mouth. "After that, the only thing that'll stop me from having more sex with you is...well..." There's nothing. Other than if she said no. "Well, you."

Her eyes soften and her smile turns pensive. "I'm not going to stop you."

"Good." I straighten. "Come on, Moose, let's get dinner for this gorgeous woman."

"I can help!"

"That's okay. It's basically done."

I carry Moose to the kitchen but then I cross to the door onto the deck and hook him up to the tie out rope. "You're okay," I tell him. "We're okay. Sorry, little buddy." I give him a rub then let him go.

He pees on the deck.

"Damn. That's not how you do it, buddy." I take him to the grass, but of course it's too late this time. He's been doing so well with going outside. Maybe he's mad at us. Are dogs that smart?

I leave him out there to sniff around and return to the kitchen. I throw the enchilasagna into the microwave, toss the salad together, just a packaged one from the grocery store, fix two plates on a tray, then grab a bottle of wine and glasses.

Moose appears at the sliding door and I let him in. "Better now? Maybe you just had to pee."

I guess a good dog dad would keep that in mind. This dog dad, however, lost his mind.

I can't regret it.

Holy shit.

Exhaling a hot air balloon's volume of gas, I carry the tray to the bedroom.

My steps halt as I walk in, taking in the sight of Bianca in my bed. She turned on the lamp beside the bed. Her dark hair is a tousled mess, shining in the light, the skin of her shoulders smooth and tawny from time in the sun. She's curled on her side under the covers and looks like she's asleep, her face relaxed and wearing that perpetual smile, but when she hears me she opens her eyes and her smile deepens.

"Oh, wow. You weren't kidding."

"Nope."

She pushes herself up to sit and I don't miss the lingering sweep of her gaze over my bare chest and arms. She sinks her teeth briefly into her bottom lip and her eyes heat.

She likes what she sees.

Fuck, yeah.

I never worried about that before, but getting rejected, cheated on, giving up the sport I love, and putting on weight apparently impacted my confidence. Under her admiring gaze, I stride over and set the tray on the end of the bed.

Moose jumps up to inspect it.

Bianca laughs.

"Hey, get down. You're not allowed on the bed," I tell him.

"He's not?" Bianca widens big dark eyes at me.

"Not while we're eating." I pause. "Or fucking."

She laughs.

"Or maybe ever. I don't know. I don't know anything about

dogs." I round the bed and sit back down. "He peed on the deck. I think he did it to be a little asshole."

She giggles. "Oh well. You can hose it off."

"Yeah, but I have to train him not to do that."

"It's okay. We got this."

We got this.

My heart gives a sharp twist in my chest.

We get ourselves settled with plates on our laps and glass of wine on the tray between us. Bianca picks up a fork and cuts off a piece of the casserole. "Yum! This is so good!"

Moose is not cooperating. He's dancing around on the bed, sniffing our plates, pawing at us.

"Back off," I tell him sternly. He gives me the same puppy dog eyes Bianca did. With his one ear, he's adorably lopsided. I lift my plate higher so he can't stick his nose in it. For a moment, he lies down and watches us, but then he's up again, nudging at Bianca's arm.

She drops a piece of salad on the bed. "Oh no!" But she's laughing. "Moose, you can't do that!"

"I should take him out of here."

"It's okay. Moose, sit." She holds up a tiny piece of lasagna noodle.

Moose does not sit. He jumps for the noodle...and lands on the tray. Our glasses tip and the bottle falls over and red wine sprays everywhere.

Bianca shrieks. I curse. Moose disappears with a flash of his white tail.

Smart guy.

Chapter 18

Jansen

I look at Bianca and our eyes meet. My annoyance fades in the face of her dancing eyes and the laughter she's trying to hold back.

"How to impress a woman," I deadpan.

Her laugher bursts free, and I fucking love that sound.

"You have wine on your chest."

She glances down. "So I do."

I set my plate on the nightstand and lean over to her. "This is a fantasy come true." And, surrounded by grape carnage, I drag my tongue between her breasts, licking up red wine. "Licking wine off your naked body."

"I-it is?" She tosses her plate onto the nightstand.

"Of course. You make wine." I lick again, lower, then around her navel where wine has pooled. "What could be better?"

"You fantasize about me?"

I groan, licking back up to one nipple. "Oh fuck, yeah." I slide my tongue over to the other one. They taste amazing even without the wine. "Every goddamn night. I fantasize about you wearing a purple silk slip."

"Ohhhhh."

As I suck her nipple into my mouth, she gives a full-body shiver.

I draw back to inspect my clean up. Her round breasts are wet, shining in the light, her tight nipples the color of merlot. My dick is hardening into a thick spike. "Beautiful."

She gazes at me with melting eyes.

"We should clean this up," I say reluctantly.

"Yes." She lets out a hearty sigh.

I move away and she slides out of bed. I enjoy this view as she helps me pull the duvet cover off the bed. The white top sheet is stained with spots of purple, but the fitted sheet is unscathed.

"I have another quilt." I go out to the hall and retrieve it from the closet along with a clean sheet.

We make the bed together, both of us eying the other. I'm wearing shorts, but my hard on is evident beneath the gray cotton and when her eyes drift there and she smiles, I get even harder.

"I love gray sweatpants on men," she remarks. "Or shorts."

"Yeah?"

"Mmmm."

Sweatpants and shorts were a staple of my wardrobe when I was playing. Maybe I should wear them all the time. "I like what you're wearing, too."

"I'm not wearing anything!"

"Exactly."

We each pick up a corner of the clean quilt and lay it over the bed. Moose jumps up into the middle of it.

"Maybe dinner in bed wasn't such a good idea." I purse my lips regretfully.

"It was a *great* idea." She leans over and rubs Moose's head. "Just not with this little stinker here."

"Here." I turn and grab a T-shirt out of my dresser. I hand it to her. "You can wear this."

"Thanks." She takes it and slides it on over her head. It's huge on her, of course, but her tits push the fabric out, showing off her hard nipples, and the hem ends mid-thigh. I swallow.

"Let's go sit in the kitchen."

Bianca picks up the wine bottle. "Oh hey! It didn't all spill. Lucky, because we broke the rule."

"What rule?"

"Always drink responsibly. As in, don't spill."

A laugh rises in my throat. Jesus. What's happening to me? I feel so relaxed. So loose. Free.

We eat at the kitchen table while Moose sits at our feet, much better behaved out here. Bianca fills clean glasses and we finish the wine as we eat, and talk.

"How's harvest going at Caparelli?" I ask.

She filles me in on some details, mostly positive. I'm still blown away by the fact that so many people came to help them pick grapes. Between her and Rosa, they know everyone in town and apparently people like them enough to support their new venture. The small community where everyone knows each other has its downsides—that story about the bar brawl being one of them—but also advantages, too.

The only one not helping them is her uncle. And cousins, I guess. I can see how that bothers her.

"You'll show them," I say.

She lifts her chin. "We will. It's just kind of disheartening, you know? I don't think Nonna would like this. Family was so important to her."

I nod.

"What about *your* family?" she asks. "You haven't said much about them."

"My parents are great. They were always supportive of my hockey career. A little *too* supportive at times." I grimace.

She sets down her fork and rests her chin on her hand, watching me. "They pushed you to play?"

"They did, but I also loved it. They were convinced from the time I laced up a pair of skates that I was going to be a superstar."

"Ah. That's nice."

"Yeah. They did a lot for me, that's for sure. Made a lot of sacrifices. They're a little concerned about my mental health, not to mention my investment portfolio at the moment."

She smiles. "Because of buying the winery."

"Yeah. They didn't want me to retire in the first place. To them, that was giving up. Never mind that I'd had a pretty good run—twelve years in the NHL. Then they tried to talk me out of buying a winery. And if I *was* going to buy a winery, they thought I should at least buy one close to home, like Niagara-on-the-Lake."

"Where do they live?"

"Toronto."

"Ah. Is that where you grew up?"

"Yep. Until I was fifteen. Then I moved to Ottawa to play major junior hockey."

She purses her lips, a small indent appearing between her eyebrows. "Did your whole family move there for you?"

"No. Just me. I was billeted with a family. Both my parents worked and they couldn't just up and move. But they were still really involved."

"That's really young to leave home."

"It is. Thank God for billet families. I landed a really good one."

"Do you have siblings?"

"No. Only child."

She nods. "So hockey was really a huge part of your life."

"It was my *whole* life." I meet her eyes and give a thin smile. "In retrospect, it probably shouldn't have been. That may be why my marriage flatlined."

She tilts her head, and her focus on me and open expression make me feel like I matter. "Really?"

I shrug. I shouldn't have said that. I tried to make it sound flippant. I don't want to talk about my failed marriage

"Well." Bianca stands, takes two steps over to me, and sits on my lap. She slides her fingers around the back of my neck, her face inches away from mine. Her skin is so pure, the texture of her lips so inviting, her shaggy hair a messy temptation. I close one hand around her waist and rest the other on her smooth thigh. "I have thoughts."

"Oh yeah?" I glide my hand up, up, under the hem of my shirt.

"Yeah. I think you're hot."

My lips quirk. "Go on."

"That's it." She smirks.

"That's only one thought."

"I'm kidding. I have lots of thoughts." She traces her fingertips over my bottom lip. "You're hot. You don't say a lot, but what you say is worth listening to." Now her fingers play with my hair. "You work hard, you're determined. I think you're hard on yourself—harder than you need to be, and I think that right here..." She presses a hand to my chest. "Your heart is big. You just protect it. You took in a dog. You care about the people who work for you." She pauses. "I know that night at the fair you didn't park near me. You just wanted to make sure I got to my car safely."

Busted.

She tips her head and closes the distance between us to kiss me. Her mouth moves on mine softly.

Her words sink into my consciousness while I kiss her back, drinking in her sweetness. I feel like I don't deserve those words, like I've screwed up so much and I'm probably going to screw up more. In spite of that, I love what she said...what she thinks about me. It makes me feel like maybe I'm not a total loser.

"Do you miss hockey?" she asks.

"Yeah." I stroke her shoulder. "I thought about things I could do to stay involved with the sport. But I'm not a coach. I'm not a talker. Had to figure out something else."

"You couldn't get much farther away from hockey than buying a winery in Napa."

"I know."

"Is that why you did it?"

"Nah. I was interested in making wine, that's all."

"Tell me what you loved about hockey."

"Ah. Everything. I love skating. I love puck handling. Shooting. I love competing and winning." Wistfulness tightens my chest for a moment. I do miss all that. With my marriage imploding soon after retiring, I really haven't acknowledged how much I miss it.

"I watched you on YouTube. You're pretty famous."

I'm a little startled, but I shrug. "I guess."

"So modest. From what I saw online, you'd have every right to be full of yourself. You're really good. Not that I know anything about hockey, but the guys talking about it in those videos seemed impressed with you."

I laugh. I'm surprisingly moved by her praise. I was a good player; I knew that. But hearing her say it feels important. "Thanks." I kiss her shoulder. "I also miss the guys." I pause, my throat squeezing briefly thinking about Stephanie with

Austin. "We were all so close. They were like my family." Before one of my family betrayed me with my wife.

She studies my face and I guess she can see how wound up I am. "Do you keep in touch?"

I taste acid at the back of my throat and I swallow. "With a couple of them, yeah. My buddies. They came here and visited me right after I moved here, to check out the place."

"You should invite them back."

"The hockey season is just getting started. They probably don't have time."

"You could check with them. It's good to keep people we care about in our lives."

"Did you do that when you left here?"

She pouts and her eyelids lower. "Ouch."

"Sorry."

She huffs out a breath. "No. I didn't. I wanted out of here, and I wasn't really thinking about the relationships, you know? My friends. My sisters. The rest of the family." She traces her fingers over my chest. "I'm lucky my friends were better about staying in touch even though I never came back to visit. I regret that I wasn't here when Nonna died. I thought she'd always be here." Her voice thickens. "And I wonder if some of the problems with Uncle Geno and the boys are because I wasn't here."

"You can't blame yourself for that." I fucking hate how her family is reacting to her and her sisters inheriting Caparelli. Family should support each other. They should be doing everything they can to make sure the sisters are successful. Instead, her jackass uncle is trying to make things worse. That pisses me off.

"No, I'm not. But I have been thinking about family and how we support each other and I...haven't really been here. For any of them. I don't know what the hell Allegra is up to in Europe, or how Rosa really managed these past years, especially now Nonna is gone. Nonna was the glue...the one who kept us girls, the Martinellis, joined with the Lambertis. Three girls, three boys...when we were little we all played together. Went to school together. We were all friends. And now..." She clears her throat. "I don't even know Gianni and Vittorio and Leo anymore."

"Is it too late? I don't think it's too late." I move strands of hair off her neck. I like hearing her talk, although not when she criticizes herself.

"I guess not." She goes pensive. "I've just been so busy with harvest. That's all I've been able to focus on."

"I know. And I asked even more of you."

She tilts her head back. "But I love it. You know I do. Yes, it's hard work, but there's so much satisfaction when I taste something that I helped create."

"Yeah. I don't contribute much, but I like feeling like I helped create something, too."

"You do contribute!"

"Not like you."

"Well, Mother Nature does most of the work; I'm just trying to bottle it. It's like bottling the wind, the sun, the rain. Even the soil. And if I'm lucky...a little magic."

My chest tightens hearing her words. I entered into this thinking I understood what I was doing, but Bianca is both an artist and a scientist. Her connection to wine goes so deep and it's an incredible, beautiful thing. *She's* incredible and beautiful.

"But the best thing about winemaking..." She lifts her head and regards me with twinkling eyes. "Is that I get to use the word bunghole."

A laugh bursts from my chest. My arms tighten around her reflexively, an unfamiliar lightness rising up inside me.

Christ. What is happening to me? She convinced me that a

little hot sex isn't a problem because neither of us are looking for more, but now I'm worried that might not be exactly true. After having her, after feeling her come around me, after tasting her, after talking to her and her stroking my ego with compliments and greedy eyes, and now her making me laugh, in bed for fuck's sake, my world is shook. Somehow more than my dick is involved in this situation now. I'm starting to wonder how I can ever live without her in my life.

That's fucking dangerous thinking.

If I open up to the wrong person, trust the wrong person again, I'll be screwed with a capital F. Again. I can't do that.

And yet, if she got up to leave right now, I'd stop her.

This internal conflict of wanting her beyond anything and yet being terrified out of my mind by that is really inconvenient.

Well, since I'm not going to kick her out of bed, might as well make the best of it.

Chapter 19

I'm obsessed with orange wine.

Also with Jansen Beck. But I'm trying not to think of him. I can't afford to be obsessed with anything besides wine right now.

I can do this. I can have sexy shenanigans with a hot hockey player, and then leave when it's time. I did that with Tomás.

I can do it again.

Back to the wine. I need to talk to Rosa about it. She's meeting me here in the pressing house in a few minutes and I'm prepared for the discussion.

She walks in and drops into one of the ancient chairs. "What's up?"

"I want to talk to you about what we're going to do with the viognier."

"Sure."

"I want to make orange wine."

She frowns. "What?"

"You have to have heard of it. It's getting more popular."

"I don't know anyone who's making orange wines. What is it? Do we mix white wine with orange juice? Or...?"

"No, no."

"Because our brand isn't fruity wines like peach Moscato or those strawberry flavored wines. Ugh."

"It's not that. Some wineries in Argentina were making them. One thing about Argentina is that they're not governed by Denominations of Origin."

She nods. "Like Champagne."

"Yeah. So we had more freedom to try new things. And I found some qvevris in our cave."

She gives me a blank look. Okay, Rosa knows a lot about wine, obviously, but this is a bit obscure.

"They're terra cotta vessels that wine is fermented in. I think they've been there a long time. Probably they were there when we were kids but they're in the ground so we didn't realize. I want to clean them up and put some Viognier grapes in there to ferment."

"That sounds...weird. Terra cotta?"

"Yeah."

"I don't know, Bee..."

I clamp my bottom lip between my teeth briefly. "I want them to ferment a year. Then age another year."

She frowns. "I thought we were going to make wines that we can drink sooner."

"I know. That's why I'm talking to you about this. I won't use all the viognier grapes. But it will be a longer process."

She makes an annoyed sound. "Bee. We need to start making money as soon as we can."

"I know! Believe me, I know. I'm just...I found those qvevris and it seems like a sign. And I've been doing a ton of research and I think we'd be getting in early on a growing trend."

"We're not a family who jumps on trends."

"This is *our* winery. *Our* vineyard. We don't have to stick to Lamberti traditions. We can make it what we want."

I can't tell her how much I want this. How much I need to do this, to make my *own* history in this family. "In fact, I think we should change our name."

Her eyes fly open. "What? Change the name? From Caparelli?"

"Yes. It hasn't really been Caparelli for years anyway; with Geno running it, all the wines have been Belmonte wines."

"But...it's always been Caparelli."

"Think about it, okay? It's an idea. We can talk to Allegra about it, too."

"If she ever shows up," Rosa mutters.

"I know." I sigh. "So back to the orange wine. It's another way for us to differentiate ourselves from Belmonte. To make our own name." *To show what I can do.*

"The whites are ready to drink sooner," she says slowly. "Do you have to use white grapes?"

"Yes. That's what orange wine is. It's making wine using white grapes as though they are red. With the skins and seeds in contact with the juice. I tracked down a few bottles—one from Australia, a couple from Italy. Would you try them and see what you think?"

She tilts her head. "You're really set on this."

"Yeah." I eye her expectantly.

She gives me a long, appraising look.

"What?" I run a hand through my hair.

"I'll try them," she says. "But I'm still not sure."

"Fair. But we do have to make a decision. The viognier grapes are coming in soon."

She nods. "Okay."

She leaves and I sit back in my chair.

She doubts me.

Never mind Uncle Geno, Rosa doesn't even trust me.

My mouth twists and I sigh.

This is why I stayed in Argentina. This is why I need to go back. They believe in me there. They give me opportunities and the freedom to show what I can do.

Coming back has messed up my head. I was doing great in Argentina. Now I have all these hopes and dreams and desires and I shouldn't, because my family is never going to let me do the things I want to.

And now I'm getting involved with Jansen, another risk. God, if I hadn't promised, if it wasn't the middle of harvest, I'd leave right now and run back to my mentor Milenko and Castillo Lorenzo where I'm appreciated and respected.

But I can't do that.

So. I'm here. But I can't care. I have to just do my job. Just make wine. And I have to make sure that this romp with Jansen is just a romp...short, sweet, and casual.

OUR PICNIC THE FOLLOWING SUNDAY IS NOT SHORT. IT starts sweet but quickly gets dirty. And it doesn't feel very casual.

After helping with the harvests, we're at a point where we can't pick any more grapes right now, so Jansen and I are escaping for a little relaxation time. Jansen packed a late lunch/early dinner in a cooler bag and I brought a couple bottles of wine. I lead him and Moose down to the creek the town is named after, a small but burbling stream of water. Moose is in heaven with all the new sniffs.

There's a place we used to hang out and play when I was a

kid, and I hope it's as nice as I remember. After a short hike through the woods, we arrive at the wooden foot bridge, which thankfully appears well-maintained. We cross it and I pause to lean on the railing and peer down at the water bubbling over boulders.

"Cute," Jansen says, standing so close our shoulders touch.

"Isn't it?"

On the other side of the creek there's a grassy, shady area dappled with sunlight, and we spread out our blanket and stretch out on the ground. It's peaceful and quiet and I inhale a big breath of the fresh air scented by trees—a mix of pine needles, citrus, and herbs.

Jansen ties Moose's long leash to a nearby sapling. Moose does a few circles on the blanket, then curls up near our feet.

Both of us lying on our backs looking up at the oak branches, Jansen lets out a sigh. "This is nice."

"It is. I'm glad it's still here."

He lets out another sigh, which tells me he's been holding a lot of stress. Well, that makes two of us. This is a nice break.

"What color is the sound of silence?" I ask.

I feel his amusement. "Hmm. I'd say blue."

"Why?"

"I have no idea. Because of the sky? It's big and silent."

"That's good. I'd say green."

"Why?"

"Because it's green here. But...it's not *completely* silent. The wind rustles the leaves. There are birds. So maybe your answer is right."

"I don't think there's actually a right or wrong answer to that."

I smile. "Fair point."

He takes my hand and curls his fingers around mine. His hand is strength and warmth and assurance. He's been there every step of the way, doing whatever I ask of him and more, taking it all in, reassuring me that we can do this. And by we, I mean all of us—my sister, Jake, him, me. His belief in me is unhesitating. His trust in my winemaker skills means so much to me. He's honest and hard-working and he does what he says he'll do. I admire that so much and it makes me want to hold onto him. My fingers tighten involuntarily on his.

I've also seen a different side of him. He's not such a grumpy bear. He has a sense of humor, and he's showing it more and more. I feel like he's happier than he was when I first met him, despite working his ass off. For some reason that creates a happy bubble in my chest, too. I like it when he's happy. I like it when he's laughing. I also like it when he's kissing me, and touching me...

Because not only do I admire him and like him, I'm hot for him.

Dammit, we're lying here in the woods having a picnic and I've talked myself into a buzz of arousal.

I roll toward him and he shifts too, so we're lying on our sides facing each other.

He brushes his fingertips over my face, studying me with soft, warm eyes. "You're so beautiful."

My lips lift. "Thank you," I whisper. "I think you are, too."

"Beautiful?" One corner of his mouth quirks.

"Yes. I love your throat."

He chokes out a chuckle. "My *throat*?"

"Yes." I trail a finger over it. "It's perfect. Your whole neck is. Strong. I like to imagine kissing you there. Sucking on your skin."

His eyes darken. "Ah."

"I also like your forearms. Also strong. The way the veins stand out." I lift his arm away from me to study it. "So hot. Well, you're hot everywhere."

His smile is a full-on smile and as always, it does things to my girl parts.

"I think you're hot, too."

We're staring into each other's eyes, smiling goofily, and the breeze shifts the leaves into a moving pattern of sunlight and shadow on us. His eyelids drift lower and he leans over to kiss me.

His mouth on mine is...everything. I want him so much. The softness of his lips, the slide of his tongue, the low growl he makes in his throat...God. I kiss him back, trying to devour his kisses like I'm starving.

"I want to kiss you forever," I mumble. "I love kissing you."

"Christ." He rolls over me, pinning me to the blanket, gazing down at me with lust-blown eyes. His body is solid and strong on mine, and I'm soft and yielding, thrilling in the hardness of his erection against me. "More."

He kisses me again, and again, and then kissing's not enough. I'm aching deep in my core and my hips lift against his. I want everything from him. His hand molds my breast through my T-shirt, grips my waist, slides over my hip. He nips at my bottom lip then sucks it and a moan leaks from my lips.

His hands move slowly on me, our mouths cling and lift, and I hold onto his big shoulders and cradle him between my thighs. The breeze sweeps away the sounds we make, the soft gurgle of the creek a gentle soundtrack to our making out.

He slips a hand under the hem of my shorts, finding the tender skin of my hip and groin. He pushes his thick cock into my softness. He's wearing similar shorts and I'm not sure he has underwear on. I glide my hands down his back and under the elastic waistband and find his bare ass. "Commando," I whisper.

His lips curve against mine. "Is that a problem?"

"God no."

"I thought we might go skinny dipping in the creek."

Smiling, I push at his shorts.

"We're doing this here?" His mouth is on the side of my neck and I shiver.

"There's no one around."

"I feel obligated to point out that that could change at any moment, but honestly, if I can't fuck you right now I'm gonna cry."

I smile too and he goes up onto his knees to shove his shorts down, freeing his beautiful cock. I'm admiring it when he reaches for my shorts and whisks them down my legs along with my panties. He pushes up my T-shirt but doesn't take it off, just exposes my mesh and lace bralette. He brushes fingertips over my nipples, visible through the sheer fabric. "So pretty."

"So handsome." I curl my fingers around his shaft. "You're beautiful here, too. Please. I want to kiss you here." I rub my thumb over the head. "Taste you."

His groan rumbles in his chest and he moves, straddling my torso, and holy angels singing, he's right there in front of my mouth and I'm dying for him. Holding him, I slide my tongue over wet, silky skin, swirl it around the defined rim, then close my lips over him.

"Fuuuuck."

He towers above me, feeding me his cock, rocking his hips in restrained pulses so he slides slowly deeper. And deeper. I suck and lick and taste him, his skin thin and delicate over hard rock. I make ecstatic noises in my throat, reveling in the feel of him in my mouth, so solid and virile, my lips stretched around his girth. I seek his balls with my fingers, cupping them, and he makes another animal noise that has my pussy clenching hard.

Then he pulls away.

Panting, I gaze up at him.

He glares back at me, not in anger, but self-control, his chest rising and falling. "So close," he grits out. "Wanna be inside you."

"Yes."

He gropes around for his shorts and pulls out a condom and I grin with delight as he rips it open and rolls it on his straining cock.

Eyes fastened on mine, he moves back between my legs. Inside me. Slowly. Thickly. I can't breathe and all I can see is him against a background of blurred green and gold, the perfect V shape of his torso, the opposite V shape of his meaty thighs spread wide between my legs, his firm stomach. His eyes—green and gold and brown like the trees, pulling me into their depths until I'm lost in another world, a fog, a dream.

"Jansen."

He takes my hands and threads our fingers together, and we move in a rhythm we create together ours, new and yet familiar.

"I can't stop thinking about you," he rasps. "I can't stop wanting you."

"I know." The drag of his cock over sensitive nerve endings sparks and catches fire, a hot coil of flame building. "I know."

Everything inside me expands, too fast, too hot, and I can't go slow because I'm desperate, dying. I whine and lift my hips and he smiles tightly, letting go of one hand so he can find my clit with his thumb. I gasp and lose my mind, staring up at the sky then my eyes falling closed as he drives into me, harder, grunting and gulping in his own rapture. Pleasure rips through me and I shudder and quake and he drops over me, elbows on the ground, his face in my neck, pushing into me in urgent thrusts. He groans, and I clench around him as he comes, milking him, holding onto him with everything I have. And I never want to let go.

I'm exquisitely aware that I want him with me, next to me,

always. I'm fascinated with him. I'm infatuated with him. I want to live inside him and keep him.

We doze off in each other's arms, a second blanket tossed over us in case someone comes by, but we're alone in the woods. The sun warms us and I'm so cozy and sleepy I might never move, drifting on a haze of sexual satisfaction and happiness, with Moose curled up at our feet.

We both wake up at the same time, stirring, slowly surfacing. We smile at each other.

"This is a first for me," he says.

"What is?"

"Sex in the woods."

"City boy," I scoff, sliding my fingers through the hair at his temple.

"I'm not opposed to it. It just never happened."

"Well, I'll be honest. I've never had sex here before either."

His eyes crinkle up. "Good."

I want him again, with an urgency that's out of place with the fact that I'm still here in his arms. When he moves to pull his shorts back on, I want to grab him and hold on. But I let him go. I find my own shorts, straighten my bra and my top, and run my hands through my hair.

Jansen reaches over and pulls a piece of grass from my hair with a smile. "Hungry?"

"Famished."

We open the cooler bag, which interests Moose, and spend the next while slowly eating a tomato salad, an assortment of charcuterie, cheeses and crackers, and fresh fruit. I pour us glasses of the wine I brought and we sip the zinfandel sitting with our knees touching, the breeze nudging my hair.

"Do you think—"

He makes a choking sound.

I give him a chiding look. "Wait! Hear me out."

He rolls his lips in on a smile and nods, feeding Moose a little piece of salami.

"Do you think our future selves are watching us right now through memories?"

His mouth relaxes. He sips his wine and looks over my shoulder. Then he nods. "Yeah," he says slowly. "I think so. And this...this is a good memory. My future self will love this memory."

My heart throbs. "Yeah. For me too. We should have memories that make us happy, right?"

"That's all we ever really have, in the end."

Yeah. He's right. His words move me and give me a glimpse into his character. And I like it.

"Not all memories are good, though," he adds. "Shit happens."

I grin. "True. I'd definitely rather forget that I destroyed Mrs. Gerstenmayer's shed."

His lips quirk but his eyes are shadowy.

"I know there are worse memories than that," I say quietly. "My dad dying. My mom leaving. I was only thirteen. One time Zoe Mayberry told me my mom left because she didn't love me."

"Fuck."

"It was true, though." I lift a shoulder. "How could she have left us like that if she loved us? I've come to terms with it now, but it was hard."

"Of course it was hard. I can't say I understand that, a parent abandoning her kids."

"Nobody did. Nonna tried to tell us that Mama wasn't herself because of the heartbreak of losing Daddy, but she left with a man and she's still with him and she hasn't come back, so I guess she *is* herself. That's who she is."

"It's not a reflection on you."

"It's hard not to feel that way. That you're lacking somehow. How else could a mother do that?"

He doesn't reply, his gaze going blurred again. "I'm sorry your mom left. You lost both parents and you were young."

"Thank you."

Jansen pulls out the wine bottle and tops up our glasses.

"What's something you can't do that you wish you could?" I ask.

He holds out a morsel of cheese to Moose and thinks. "Speak another language."

"Oh, me too! I wish I could speak Italian. I know a few words from Nonna, but we always spoke English."

"I took French in school for a few years. But I wasn't good at it. Now I regret not trying harder."

"There are apps you can use to learn a language. We could both join and do challenges together."

"We could."

"You don't sound enthused."

"How about after harvest is done?"

"Okay." Except I'll be gone. But we could still do language challenges long distance.

Wow. That's sad.

A sudden feeling of being swamped, of drowning, not being able to breath rises in my chest. I gulp my wine. "I'm obsessed with orange wine."

He blinks at the rapid change of subject. "Orange wine?"

I tell him of my discovery in the wine cellar and my research into orange wines.

"What makes them orange?" he asks

"We leave the skin and seeds in contact with the juice."

"Like red wine, but with white grapes."

"Exactly." I beam at my favorite student. "It's all about the skin contact."

"I like skin contact."

He says it so seriously I almost don't get it. Then I see the gleam in his eyes and I crack up. "Well, to be honest, I do too. But I'm talking about grapes."

"Right." His lips twitch.

"Rosa agreed to taste some, but she's not enthusiastic about the idea." I make a face. "She wants wines that are ready more quickly so we can start making money."

"That's practical."

"I guess. I feel like she doesn't trust my winemaking abilities, though."

He inclines his head. "Really? I'm sure she knows what a great winemaker you are."

I snort. "I don't know if anyone here in Napa knows that. Especially Uncle Geno."

"And that matters to you."

"I don't care what they think."

The corners of his mouth deepen. "Sure."

My mouth pinches. "Okay, okay, it's a tiny little chip on my shoulder."

He smiles.

"I think it's practical to try this new wine, because I think it's growing in popularity. It's something new and different and people will be intrigued. Especially if it's good."

"Of course it will be good. Bianca Martinelli is making it."

His belief in me pulls at my heart and warmth spreads through my chest. "Thank you."

Chapter 20

Jansen

We drink a bottle of wine. We talk about lots of things. We get into the creek and splash around in the water until I slip on the rocks and fall in. Bianca finds this hilarious and helps me out of the water, laughing so hard she almost falls in herself. And I'm laughing, too, even though my right shoulder is now throbbing.

We take Moose in the water, too. I don't know if he can swim, but Bianca assures me all dogs know instinctively. We crack up when I lower him closer to the water and his little legs start paddling in the air.

"I think he knows what he's doing," I say, letting him go in the water.

He paddles straight to the bank of the creek, climbs out, and shakes himself.

Since there's still nobody else here, I take off my shorts and shirt and hang them on a bush in the sun to dry. And without any pants on, it's hard to hide my dick (yeah pun intended) when it eagerly thickens at Bianca's heated gaze.

So we have more outdoor rolling in the hay. Grass. Whatever.

This time it's different. We're both a little drunk and laughing and it's messy and hot and the most fun I've had in… well, forever, I think.

When we're sweaty and wasted from wine and orgasms, lying slack on the blanket again, Bianca says, "What's wrong with your shoulder?"

Ugh. A reminder of how old I am. "Arthritis."

She lifts her head to peer at me. "Really?"

"Yeah. Both shoulders. The right is worse. They get sore sometimes."

Instead of being repelled, she leans down and presses her mouth to my shoulder in a long, warm kiss. "I'm sorry. I think you worked your body hard playing hockey."

"Yeah."

She snuggles in beside me. "What's your favorite sex position?"

The questions are killing me. Killing me with amusement. I don't know what to say most of the time. But this one's easy. "Missionary. And don't tell me I'm boring."

"Wow, you didn't even have to think about that one."

"Nope. I like being face to face." I roll my head to look at her. "Especially with you. I like watching you. Your cheeks get pink and your eyes get hazy." I touch her bottom lip. "Your lips open and you look like you're dying for it."

"I am." Her voice is a trace of sound. "For you."

Oh yeah. "And I like watching you when you come."

"Oh God. My O face is probably terrible."

"It's not. It's real." I pause, searching for words. "It's open and unguarded. I love it."

She nibbles her bottom lip, gazing back at me. "That's the best answer."

"What's *your* favorite position?"

"The butter churner."

I give her side-eye.

I can tell she's trying not to laugh. "I think some people call it the pile driver. I call it the butter churner. So I'm on my back, with my legs in the air and you stand over me—"

"Stop." Now I'm laughing. "I am not doing that."

"What? Why not? If I like it, you should try it."

"You don't like it. You're bullshitting me."

She giggles. "Okay, I am. I used to subscribe to a newsletter that sent out new sex positions and that one was in it. I think it's only done in porn movies."

"You might be right."

"Then there's the snow angel. It looked okay for me—on my back, but you on top facing away."

I squint, trying to picture it. "I can't...the mechanics..."

"I know. I think it's dangerous for the guy. You could break your penis. And we don't want that."

"We definitely don't want that," I reply fervently.

"I like your penis."

"He likes you, too."

She laughs again. "I noticed that!"

This is silly and probably illegal, but Christ, I'm having fun. My chest is filled with a lightness I haven't felt for a long time and I think I could do anything right now. Catch light in a box. Slay zombies. Time travel. I don't feel like a failure. I feel like I've won the Stanley Cup and solved climate change and the rise of fascism.

I fucking love feeling like this. And I fucking love being with the woman who does that for me.

On the way home, Bianca lays a hand on my arm. "Can I show you something?"

"You already did." I smirk.

She giggles. "No. The cave."

"Right. Yeah, I want to see it."

She takes me to the Caparelli buildings and leads me through an old oak door and down a flight of stone stairs. She flicks on a light and a few dusty old bulbs flare to life and illuminate the space.

"Wow." I look around, taking in the arched ceiling, the old bricks, and all the barrels. "I had no idea this was here."

"I know." She moves farther into the space. "It hasn't been used for a long time. We came down here as kids but it was kind of creepy. I was fascinated by it, though. And look at this..." She walks down to the end of the cave. "These are the qvevris."

She told me about her dream and hope to make the orange wine using these. It seems...dubious to me, but what do I know? I just loved listening to her talk about it with so much passion.

"I've been coming down here sometimes to think." She gestures around. "It's a nice, quiet place."

"Except for the spiders."

"Can you imagine what this would look like all cleaned up? I've dusted things a bit, but I think it would be gorgeous with the brick and the barrels cleaned and better lighting."

"Oh yeah. It would be cool."

"I'm sure this is another thing Rosa and I will disagree on."

"You haven't talked to her about it yet?"

"No." I wrinkle my nose. "I know what she'll say. We don't have money to do anything with this. But I'm not saying we have to do it tomorrow! We don't have any wine yet. I know what our priorities have to be. But this could be amazing in the future."

He nods thoughtfully.

"We could have special events down here—it's not huge, so not big weddings or anything, but special wine tasting events or private dinners."

"That would be amazing."

"I picture a round table...over here...with lots of candles, maybe white flowers, beautiful wine glasses. Moody lighting. Instead of those old bulbs, we could put sconces on the walls. And we could fill wine bottles with strings of little white lights! That would be awesome."

His eyes crinkle up at the corners listening to me.

"The elegant tables with white linens and silver and glass would contrast with the rough bricks walls and floors. And we could serve amazing wines and food. People would love it."

"You need to be around to make that happen."

My stomach drops. Right. I won't even be here. I turn back to him, then make a face. "Yeah. It's silly for me to have these visions when I won't even be here."

"But you'll still be a part owner. You're entitled to have visions for what you want it to be."

I sigh. "We need to make money first. I know that."

He moves closer to me, sets his hands on my hips, and pulls me against him. "I bet if you talked to Rosa about it, she has visions, too."

I meet his eyes. "You think?"

"I think...I never had visions about a winery, until I moved here. Now I find myself thinking about it all the time. Ways to improve the winery, things we could do to bring in more visitors."

I smile at him. "The jock is also a visionary."

His lips curve upwards in response. "How can you not be? Think about it. Lowly grape juice is turned into art. Liquid art."

I beam at him, a glow spreading through my chest. "Yes!"

"And it does so many things. I think the most important is that it brings people together."

My heart flutters as I gaze at him. "You really get it," I whisper.

"I'm learning."

I give one last wistful look around the cave. "Maybe some day those dreams will come true. But right now—it's already a dream come true, owning a winery. Having this opportunity. I want it to be amazing."

He brushes his mouth over mine. "It will be."

Chapter 21

Bianca

"It's okay, buddy." Jansen rubs Moose's head. "You don't need those bro globes."

I spit out my coffee. "Those *what?*"

"Bro globes." Jansen gives me a "come on" look.

He's about to take Moose to the vet to be neutered. I think it's more worrying to Jansen than to Moose. Well, Moose has no idea.

"Don't tell him that. He doesn't know what's going to happen."

"He should know. He's going to lose his manhood."

"He's a dog. They'll put him to sleep and he'll wake up and—"

"He'll be without his bo-jangles."

I walk up to Jansen and slide my arms around his waist, tipping my head back. "Do you want to hear a joke about testicles?"

He looks at me doubtfully.

"Never mind. It's scrotally unacceptaball." I crack up laughing.

His body is stiff but one corner of his mouth drags upward. "That's terrible."

"Oh, come on. That was hilarious." I look up at him. "I think you're more worried about your own bo-jangles. Don't worry, honey. It's not *you* getting castrated."

He winces. "Neutered."

"It'll be fine." I squeeze him.

"I know." He gives a crooked smile. "I'm just empathetic to what he's going through."

He loves that dog. If all the toys and treats scattered around Jansen's house didn't tell me that, taking him to get neutered definitely does. He already took Moose for his shots, but this is a major admission that he's keeping Moose. Moose will also have a chip implanted while he's under because Jansen doesn't want him to get lost again. Even though he still says he's not really his dog.

"What is this?" I pick up a card from his kitchen counter.

Jansen glances over at me. "It's an invitation."

"I see that."

"Then why'd you ask, Bianca?"

I repress a smile. His humor is dry, but I'm getting it. "It's an invitation that *I* didn't get."

"Ah." He moves closer and peers over my shoulder at it, sliding his arms around my waist from behind. "It's from Belmonte Winery."

"Yeah. I can't believe this." I look over my shoulder at him. "Every year, Belmonte hosts this harvest dinner in the vineyard —a four-course meal with music, lights strung through the trees, and of course wine."

"You have to buy tickets, so it's not really an invitation," he points out. "I assume anyone can buy tickets."

I nod slowly. "But you specifically got a notice about it.

There are limited numbers of tickets. We should be part of that, as family. We never used to need an invitation."

"How about this? I'll buy two tickets and you can come as my date."

I turn in his arms to face him. "We're not dating."

We've been spending time together but mostly at his place, making dinner together, training Moose, and banging. We haven't said anything to anyone, not even to Rosa, and during work we keep our distance other than when we need to discuss something.

"We can go to a business dinner together."

Thoughts flit through my head. We agreed this was casual. What would people think if we show up together? But who cares? It *could* be a business dinner.

I lift my chin. "Okay. Sure. Let's do it."

He heads out with Moose, who I make a fuss over before he leaves even though he doesn't know what's going on, and then I go back to Caparelli.

Jake and Rosa are at the crush pad.

"Hi," I greet them. "How are things going here?"

"You were gone all night," Rosa says.

"I was." I'm not going to be embarrassed about it, but I guess it's time to come clean. "I was at Jansen's."

"Shock," Jake mutters.

I widen my eyes at him.

He shrugs.

"What's going on with you two?" Rosa asks in a low voice.

"We're just, uh, intimate neighbors."

They both choke.

"Oh my God," Rosa says. "What does that even mean?"

"You know what it means."

"I think we get it," Jake says. He eyes me with concern.

"We're adults," I say quietly. "It's fine. You know I'm only here for a short time, and he's...not looking for anything either. So it's just casual."

She eyes me thoughtfully. "When you were sick, it didn't look casual. He looked like he was terrified that you were on your death bed."

I blink. "Well. He was probably worried, sure."

Rosa scrunches her face up.

"What are you worried about?"

She doesn't answer right away. "I don't want you to get hurt."

"Neither do I." I give her a big smile. "That's why we're not getting serious."

"Oh, little sister." She pats my shoulder.

I frown. "What does that mean?"

"You think you can have a fling with him or whatever you want to call it without catching feelings?"

"Of course I can." Something shifts in my belly. I ignore it. "I was with Tomás for months and neither of us ever got serious."

She studies my face, glances at Jake, then looks back at me. "Okay. You're right. You're an adult."

I smile and nod. "Thanks."

My phone buzzes in the back pocket of my shorts. I pull it out. "Ah! It's Milenko!"

My boss at Castillo Lorenzo. I answer the call. "Hi, Milenko!"

"Hello, Bianca. ¿Cómo estás?"

I grin. "Estoy bien, gracias." I learned a little Spanish while there, but Milenko speaks perfect English.

"Good, good. I am glad to hear it. How is your harvest going?"

I smile at Rosa and Jake and take a few steps away. I fill him in on how things are going at Caparelli, and also Bar Down.

Then he says, "I'm calling with news."

"What kind of news?"

"Good news." I hear the smile in his voice. "It's about the Star Winemaker Awards."

I blink. "What about them?"

"You, my dear, have been nominated for an award."

I go statue still. I blink several more times. "I have? Really? What award?"

It can't be a Star Winemakers Award. Those are top awards, celebrating the best winemakers of the year as judged by Elite Global Winemakers, a huge wine publication.

"Best cabernet franc."

I shake my head in disbelief, then laugh out loud. "Are you shitting me?"

"I am not shitting you, as you so charmingly put it."

"That's crazy!"

"It is well deserved. I knew it was a remarkable wine."

"I can't believe this!"

"The awards will be given out in a black-tie event in Paris," he says. "In January."

"Wow." I press my fingers to my mouth briefly. "This is wild."

"Congratulations."

"Thank you."

"When are you coming back?"

"Oh. Jeez. I'm not sure. In a few weeks, I guess."

"Okay. Let me know. We'll talk about a promotion and pay raise."

My eyebrows shoot up. "Oh. Okay."

I end the call and tip my head back to gaze up at cotton ball clouds in the blue sky. This is amazing!

"What's up?" Rosa asks, approaching. "Is everything okay?"

I grin at her. "Yes! Everything is fucking fantastic!"

She laughs, eyes widening, and I tell her about the award nomination.

"Oh my God! That's incredible!" She throws her arms around me and squeezes and for a moment, we sway back and forth, both of us laughing. Then she turns and calls out to everyone in hearing distance, "My sister is nominated for a big winemaker award!"

Everyone gathers around, cheering, congratulating me, hugging me.

I'm in a daze. Drunk on celebration. I want to tell Jansen.

I stop myself from rushing over to Bar Down. He's probably not even back from dropping off Moose. I'll see him at some point today. I can tell him then. I don't need to make a big thing of it.

Even though I'm jumping up and down with excitement.

I can't stop myself from bouncing up to Jansen over at Bar Down later. He's in the cellar talking to Antonio and I hop across the floor to him, a smile stretching across my face.

He looks up and grins in response. "Hi. You look happy."

"I'm so happy!" I squeal. I want to throw myself into his arms, but Antonio and others are around so I bounce on my toes in front of him. "I have news!"

"Yeah?" His smile is so warm and affectionate, my heart somersaults in my chest.

I tell him about the award, which of course he knows

nothing about. I show him the website listing all the nominations on my phone. "There's my name!"

Antonio and others congratulate me, and so does Jansen, but I can tell he's holding back, too. We need to be alone to celebrate this properly.

"Come over later," he says in a low voice. "We'll have a little celebration party."

More excitement fizzes in my veins. "Okay."

When I get to his place later, he has a dopey Moose snoozing in his bed and a bottle of Billecart-Salmon Brut Réserve chilling. I clap my hands. "Oh my God. I love that wine."

"I've never had it, but it came highly recommended."

I hurry over to Moose to give him gentle cuddles before he attempts to jump all over me and hurts himself. "Are you okay, little buddy?" I stroke his back. "You're a brave boy, aren't you? Good boy."

Jansen pops the cork rather expertly, then pours wine into pretty egg-shaped champagne glasses. He hands me one, picks up the other, and says, "Congratulations, beautiful. This is just the start of an amazing journey for you, I'm sure."

His words touch me and make my heart trip. "Thank you."

Our eyes meet and hold as we touch our glasses together then sip the sparkling wine.

"Mmmm." I hold the glass up. "Fizzy. Citric."

His lips tip up with amusement. "Light bodied."

"Yes." God, I...like him. So much. I take a big breath. "My boss says we'll talk about a promotion and a raise when I get back."

Jansen's expression doesn't waver, although his eyes dim slightly. "Good for you. Congratulations on that, too."

"Thanks."

I've known all along I have to go back to Argentina. Maybe I've had fleeting thoughts about what it would be like to stay here. To be truly involved in Caparelli. And see Bar Down flourish. But those were just musings. Not real. And now...I have even more reason to go back.

Chapter 22

The harvest dinner at Belmonte isn't super fancy, but I think I should wear something nicer than cut-offs or jeans. I'm not exactly a fancy person and I have exactly one dress here with me—a cotton sundress. Maybe this is a good excuse to buy something new?

There are a couple of small shops in town, but this warrants a trip to Napa where there's more selection. When I ask Ana and Millie for advice on where to go, they want to come with me. So we're going to do lunch and a little shopping.

"Okay, so what's going on with you and the hockey player?" Ana asks.

"Jansen."

"Right." She grins.

"He and Miles have been running together," Millie says, which I already know. "Miles thinks he's a great guy."

So do I.

"It's just a fling thing," I say, though the words feel hollow.

Millie's driving and she parks in a parking garage in downtown Napa. We stroll down the street and around a corner and she leads us into a women's wear boutique. I look around. It's cute! Kind of funky, with a couple of purple velvet couches, bright pink pedestal tables, plants, and wicker-shaded pendant lamps.

I'm distracted by a display of jeans and sweaters, but Ana gently pushes me away from them and toward the rack of dresses Millie is already rifling through.

"Long or short?" she asks.

"I don't know."

"With sleeves? Or no?"

I throw up my hands. "I have no idea!"

"No sleeves," Ana says. "Like this one." She plucks a dress from the rack—strapless and form fitting in a black and white pattern.

I nod. "That's okay."

"How about this?" Millie holds up a dress. "Completely different."

Yes. It's hot pink, very short with a poufy skirt, spaghetti straps, and big bows on the bodice.

I look up at her. "Do you know me at all?"

She laughs.

"I am not a pink poufy girl," I say.

"But you have such great legs, this would look amazing." She pouts. "What color are you, then?"

"Deep colors," Anna says. "Jewel tones."

I give her a skeptical look.

"Here we go." She shows me a long, slender dress with a halter neckline. The silky fabric is in shades of navy, deep green, and dark red.

"I like that." I touch the fabric with my fingertips.

"Okay! One to try on. What else?'

"I only need one dress."

"You have to try on more than one!"

I say a firm no to a sequin and feathers number, and to a black ruffled chiffon dress that's pretty but too fancy for the harvest dinner.

They load me up with other options and then lock me into a dressing room. I wrinkle my nose at all the garments hanging there. Trying on clothes is not my idea of fun.

The first one I try on is a purple one that caught my attention. I love purple. It matches the stains on my fingers. Haha!

Okay, it's a purple print, flowers in shades of mauve, plum, and periwinkle. It's also a halter style, but different with a plunging neckline and ruched and fitted around the waist.

Eeek. I study myself in the mirror. Holy cleavage, batman. I tug at the small ruffle on the edge of the neckline.

It's a long dress but it has a slit. I flutter the skirt and do a twirl. That slit is high.

"Let's see!" Ana calls.

I suck in a breath and open the door.

"Ohhh. Nice."

I pluck at the bodice again. "It's really low."

"Sexy." Millie nods approvingly. "Jansen will love it."

Well, that's all she has to say and I'm sold. But truthfully, I love it too. The fabric is my dream. So I'll go along with the revealing style.

I do like the idea of Jansen loving it.

"But try the others!" Millie urges.

"Do I have to?" I whine. "I like this one."

They exchange a look.

"Fine," Ana says. "More time for cocktails at lunch."

As I head to the counter to pay for the dress, Millie asks, "What do you have for shoes?"

"Uh...flip flops?"

Her head rears back and her eyes pop open. "No."

"Shoes are in that corner." The sales associate points with a smile. "I'll hold the dress here."

Great. Now I have to buy shoes, too.

Immediately Ana picks up a pair of sandals that are nothing but two tiny straps and a stiletto heel.

"I can't walk in those," I object. "Especially not in the yard. Those heels will sink into the ground."

"Okay, you have a point. How about flat sandals?"

Millie finds a pair of slides crusted with pearls.

I study them doubtfully. "Those are pretty elaborate."

"They're cute."

"I could use some new Birkenstocks."

They look at me like I just said I want to go to the dinner naked.

I survey the shelves. "Oh, here. These." I pick up a pair of tan sandals with thin leather straps. "I like these."

"I guess they'll do," Millie says.

I peer at the price tag. "Jesus. We should have gone to Old Navy."

They both crack up at that.

"I like Old Navy!" I protest.

"We know." Millie pats my shoulder. "I like it too. But not for a date with a handsome hockey player."

"It's a business date."

They both snort.

With my purchases bagged up, we emerge back outside to bright fall sunshine. "Okay, I'm starving," I say. "Where to?"

"Riverside Grill," Ana says. "This way."

We elect to sit outside on the patio with a view of the river. It's peaceful and pleasant and I let out a long sigh as I relax into my chair. "This is lovely." I pick up the wine menu and peruse it.

"Order a bottle," Millie says. "Whatever you like. We'll share."

I pick out a cabernet from Paso Robles and order a crab enchilada that sounds amazing.

Of course we have to hear wedding details, it's coming so close now. Millie doesn't seem stressed at all, though. And we all catch up on our jobs and families.

"You only came to one yoga class," Ana says to me.

I wince. "I know. Sorry. It's been so busy. Things are starting to settle down..."

"But you're leaving," she finishes.

I push my lips out. "Yeah. But I really need to work out. It's good for stress."

"It is." Millie nods.

"I always meet my step count." I hold up my arm with the fitness tracker on my wrist.

"Oh, that's good."

"Apparently new studies show only five minutes of vigorous exercise a day helps your heath," Ana says.

"No, no," Millie interjects. "That was for people who don't exercise at all. If they started doing five minutes a day, it had an effect on their heart health."

"Oh." Ana frowns. "It's hard to stay on top of all the latest news."

I make a face. I don't have a hard time, because I don't even try. But I should. My life has been so insular while I've been here. Maybe everyone is right—I've been working too hard. I worked hard in Argentina, too, but at least I got out sometimes, hiking, horseback riding...things that are all available here, too. In fact, now that I think of it, the things I liked about Mendoza —the blend of urban and rural, the rustic ambience combined with the magic of wine—are here as well.

"Thanks for keeping it real," I say to my friends. "I've been kind of isolated in the wine world."

"But you love it." Ana smiles at me.

"I do. But there's more to life than wine."

"There's sex," Millie says.

I give her a look.

She grins. "You've been doing that, too."

I have to laugh. "Okay, yeah." There's been quite a lot of that, actually. And top tier, five star, first class sex.

"There are lots of health benefits from sex," she points out.

"Now I don't feel so bad." I give them a naughty smile.

I study my new dress in the mirror, ready for the harvest dinner, then go downstairs to the kitchen. Rosa's there with her laptop on the table.

"I can't believe you're going to that dinner," she says. "We should be boycotting it, since they didn't even invite us."

"We're part of the family. And part of the community. They can't exclude us like this."

"True." Her bottom lip drops into a brief pout. "It kind of hurts."

"I know. I was pissed when I saw that invitation." I drop onto a chair at the table.

Rosa's focused on her computer screen. "Why didn't you tell me about you and Jansen?"

"I...I don't know. It's personal."

"We're sisters. We can share personal stuff."

Is she...hurt? I study her face.

She looks up. "Is this about what you said before? About how you felt like I didn't have time for you?"

My insides all tighten up. Is it? Am I letting old hurts impact my relationship with Rosa now? "Maybe?"

"I know you're a private person. I know you have other friends. But we're sisters."

I nod slowly. "It's not just that I'm private. It's..." Oh God. I swallow, my throat constricted. "It's easier to not get too close to people. Then it doesn't hurt as much when they leave, or when they let me down."

She nods, her face solemn. "I understand that. I'm just sad that you feel that way about me."

"I'm sorry." I blink at the sting in the corners of my eyes. "You're right. Our childhood was a long time ago. We're adults now. I shouldn't be living in the past like that. And you've never really let me down. Other than that time you wouldn't let me go to the movies with you and Sasha."

"What?" Her mouth sags open.

"I'm kidding."

"Are you, though?" she asks slowly.

My heart twists. I look away and suck my lower lip between my teeth. "I mean, it hurt at the time. I was just a kid, though." A lump of air catches in my chest.

"I never meant to hurt you."

"I know. But...I've spent literally half my life wondering what I could have done to make Mama leave. So I was probably oversensitive about stuff like that."

"Oh, Bee." Her voice is strangled.

"I'm over it," I assure her, lifting my chin.

There's a knock at the back door, startling us. Jansen. I go to let him in.

He looks gorgeous as always, his beard stubble trimmed, hair combed back off his face. He's wearing beige chinos, a navy blue shirt fitted to his muscled body with the sleeves rolled back on his strong forearms, and...my gaze drops to his feet... expensive-looking loafers. I'm a little shaky from the conversation I just had, and he looks so strong, so safe...so precious.

I go very still as I'm flooded with feelings of desire and affection and...I close my eyes on a rush of fierce, complex emotions. Love. I'm in love with him.

I love to be with Jansen. I love being in bed with him... having our hot little fling...but I like just being with him. Working. Having a picnic. Trying to get Moose to sit. Just hanging out. I like talking to him. Making him laugh. Also rubbing my hands all over him. He is becoming one of my favorite people.

Oh shit.

"What's wrong?" he asks, his brow muscles bunching low.

I blink. I want to throw myself into his arms and feel him wrap me up in his strength and comfort. But I restrain myself and dig up a stiff smile. "Nothing!"

His frown eases and his eyes grow hot as he takes in the low-cut neckline and the high-cut slit of my dress. "Wow. You look gorgeous."

My heart cartwheels behind my ribs. "Thank you. You look gorgeous, too."

"Hey, Jansen," Rosa calls from the kitchen.

He pokes his head around the door. "Hi, Rosa. Would you like to join us?"

She screws up her face. "I don't have a ticket. Damn them."

"You could crash the party with us." He grins.

"Tempting," she says. "You go and give them hell."

Jansen and I step back outside where the low sun casts long shadows across the yard and road. Jansen drives us to Belmonte in his truck. I try to act normal. Like I haven't just snorted several lines of coke. Or zip lined through the redwoods near Sonoma. Like my heart isn't racing like a squirrel on crack.

"This dinner is a Belmonte tradition," I babble mindlessly. "Uncle Geno will have invited friends and prominent members of the community like the mayor and council, and owners of the bigger businesses in not only Oak Creek Canyon, but Napa and St. Helena."

"I'm actually looking forward to this."

"You are?"

"Yeah. I don't get out much. It's been so busy. So it's good to meet other people here in the community. Also...I want to give them hell."

I stare at him. "Give who hell?"

"Your family." He glances sideways at me. "They make you sad."

I blink. He's not wrong. His assessment of that and his plan to give them hell has my heart swelling up so big I can't breathe. Oh God. I'm in so much trouble.

We park in the already crowded lot and stroll toward the yard. Round tables covered in white cloths are arranged under the trees, small flower arrangements on each table, with simple wooden folding chairs. Guests mingle, their laughter floating on the air along with the cool jazz tune playing and the clink of glasses. A couple of men in white shirts pour wine at the bar.

Jansen gestures to the bar. "We need some of that."

"Oh, hell yeah." I breathe out and start toward the bar.

I take a sip of the Belmonte cab sauv served to me and nod. "I would say this wine pairs well with difficult family members."

He chokes on a laugh.

We find our table where a few people stand around talking. They smile at us and Jansen introduces himself. "Hi, I'm Jansen Beck. I'm the new owner of Take Flight. Now called Bar Down."

One man shakes his hand. "Oh hey, good to meet you. I'm Tyler Borhek and this is my wife, Zoe."

"Bianca Martinelli!" the woman says. "Oh my gosh, we went to school together in middle school."

"Zoe! Of course. How are you?" Ack. She's the one who told me my mom left because she didn't love me. It's so much fun, coming home.

Jansen glances at me. He remembers. Is he going to give her hell, too? When our eyes meet, his glint with amusement. But instead of saying anything, he moves closer to me, slides an arm around my waist, and kisses my temple.

He's showing Zoe that I'm loved.

Except, I'm not. I've fallen in love with a man who has renounced relationships.

I stick a smile on my face and make small talk with Zoe and Tyler and the other couples there. Of course we talk about wine and harvest—they all work in local wineries as well.

We're joined by other guests and we mingle through the crowd with our wine. Jansen's watching me as much as he looks at the other guests, setting a hand on the small of my back, brushing my shoulder, sliding his arm around my waist. We called it a "business dinner," but this doesn't feel like business.

It feels good. So good. I sense his support and approval for how I'm working the room. Er, the yard. It's so tempting to believe it's real. That he has feelings for me, too.

We run into my cousins. Seeing all three of them together, I'm struck with how handsome they all are. They all give me hugs and I start to introduce them to Jansen, but they remind me they've already met.

"I know it's a crazy time of year," I say to them. "But I was thinking that you guys should come over to Caparelli one night for dinner. Rosa makes Nonna's Bolognese sauce just as well as Nonna did."

"Impossible," Gianni says with a grin.

I smile too. "Okay, it's pretty close. And I'm getting pretty good at making her garlic bread. Anyway, we could have some spaghetti and wine and talk about old times, and catch up, just us cousins."

"That'd be great," Vitto says with unexpected enthusiasm.

"Good! Where's Uncle Geno?"

"I think he's still inside with our congressman," Leo says. "They're talking about that new AI Sommelier technology."

I frown. "Is someone actually doing that here?"

"In Santa Barbara."

"That's ridiculous."

Leo shrugs. "They say it takes the complexity out of choosing the perfect wine."

"What's wrong with people doing that?" I ask peevishly.

"You can't have sommeliers everywhere. This way people can go online and get comparisons, tasting notes. Pairing suggestions."

"Hmmm," Jansen says.

I give him a narrow-eyed look. "You're not thinking about that."

He grins. "Maybe we need to get with the times."

"I don't like it."

"Oh hey, there's Uncle Geno. Hey, Uncle Geno, look who's here." Leo waves.

Uncle Geno looks up, nods, frowns at seeing me, then says a few words to the people he's with before starting across the lawn toward us.

"Bianca," he says, ignoring everyone else. From his tone I expect something different than, "So nice to see you."

"You too, Uncle Geno." I smile at him, showing my teeth. "It's a lovely evening. I have so many memories of the harvest dinners."

"It's a tradition," he agrees. Is he going to call me out on not having an invitation? But he turns to Jansen. "Hello, Jansen."

"Hi, Mr. Lamberti." Jansen extends a casual hand. "Good to see you again."

Uncle Geno's face tightens. Apparently the night he met Jansen he had a total melt down over Rosa and Jake's marriage. "So you've taken over Take Flight."

"That's right. Now called Bar Down."

"I hear you're a hockey player."

Jansen smiles. "Yep. I retired a couple of years ago. I played for the Long Beach Golden Eagles."

Uncle Geno shrugs. "I don't know much about hockey."

"That's okay. I don't know much about wine." Jansen gives a charming, self-deprecating smile.

Uncle Geo doesn't smile back. "There seem to be a lot of people with no knowledge or experience trying to run wineries."

Oh yeah. I felt that burn. My teeth grind together.

"Actually, I'm really lucky I have Bianca helping me," Jansen says. "She's incredible. So knowledgeable and smart. She's had a bunch of great ideas for me to get my brand off the ground. I'm learning a lot from her."

Gianni, Leo, and Vitto all bite back grins. Vitto gives him a nod of appreciation.

And I'm once again having a moment where I'm falling a little deeper into love with him.

Uncle Geno frowns at me. "I thought you were working at Caparelli."

"I am. But I've been helping Jansen, too. I'm sure you know that Randall retired when the Wrights sold. And this isn't a good time of year to be looking for a new winemaker."

Uncle Geno appears nonplussed by this.

"Did you hear about Bianca's award nomination?" Jansen asks.

Their faces all wear surprised expressions.

I'm struggling with more affection and gratitude to this man.

"Award?" Geno asks.

"Yeah." Jensen smiles easily. "Everyone's so proud of her. Nominated for the Star Winemakers Award for best cabernet franc."

"Holy shit," Vitto says. "That's amazing."

I smile tentatively. I'm not sure how happy he is for me.

But he breaks into a face-splitting grin. "Seriously! That is a high honor."

"Thank you."

They all congratulate me, even Uncle Geno, although I think he looks puzzled. I guess because it's me. Ugh.

At that moment, Aunt Janet joins us, slipping her arm through Uncle Geno's. "Hello Bianca. And Jansen. So nice to see you." She looks at Uncle Geno, her forehead puckered. "I thought...well." She shakes her head. "It's just about dinner time. We should all take our seats."

"Oh, I'm looking forward to the meal," I say brightly.

Jansen and I return to the table and join the others sitting there who we met earlier. As the sun sets, the lights strung through the walnut trees come on, creating a fairy-tale atmosphere. Servers bring the first course—grilled artichokes with parmesan truffle aioli—and pour the paired wine.

"Artichokes are difficult to pair with wine," I say. "I'm curious about this."

"It's a sauvignon blanc," the server tells me.

I nod and wait until everyone has wine in their glasses to take a sip.

"How is it?" Zoe asks. "We need to hear from the winemaker."

I look at Jansen. "What do you think?"

I smile slowly. "Dry. Some citrus, I think, and no oak."

"Bone dry," I confirm with a smile. "Light and crisp. I think it's a good choice for artichokes."

"I've been so immersed in harvest and learning technicalities about wine production, there's been no time for sampling good food and matched wines," Jensen says to the table.

"What about our picnic," I whisper to him.

He grins. "Oh yeah. Fine dining."

I burst out laughing and lean my head briefly on his shoulder.

Ooops. This is supposed to be a business dinner. I'm getting all sentimental and soppy.

The next course is a Caesar salad and the wine a chardonnay. An oaky chardonnay.

"What do you think?" I ask Jansen again.

"I think the acidity cuts through the creaminess of the salad dressing. And the full body complements the richness."

"I agree. It's perfect."

The next course isn't so successful for me. The pan roasted half chicken accompanied by asparagus, wild mushrooms, peas, and chicken au jus is delicious. The wine? A merlot.

"I think it works," Jansen says.

"It's fine. But this chicken is simple—no creamy or spicy sauce. I think the merlot's a bit overpowering. But you know what *would* be perfect?"

"What?"

"An orange wine."

He grins. "I need to taste this magical orange wine."

"I have some. We can try it later."

Also not very boss/employee talk, if anyone's listening to us. Oh well.

I drink more wine.

"Did you say orange wine?" Zoe asks, leaning forward.

"I did."

I'm happy to talk about that, sharing my new knowledge.

"Is it a secret?" Jansen leans in to ask quietly.

"Mmm. Not exactly. I just don't want to tell the whole world about it and then it turns out to taste like Alka seltzer."

He chokes on a laugh. "Fair. But I don't think that'll happen."

"Did I hear that you used to play hockey?" the man across the table from us asks Jansen. Tucker Diaz.

"That's right."

"I know another guy who was a professional player. Lewis York."

Jansen nods.

"I think he played in the AHL," Tucker says. "Anyway, he runs a youth hockey organization in Kirkmont, about forty minutes from here. They have a bunch of teams for girls and boys. One of the boys who played here when he was younger just got drafted into the NHL."

"No way." Jansen's interest is piqued.

"Truth. He's a pretty talented kid."

"That's awesome."

"I don't know if you're into coaching but Lewis is always looking for help. He's about your age, has a couple of kids that play now."

Jansen cocks his head and nods slowly.

"It's called Bobcats hockey," Tucker continues. "You can find it online. Next time I see Lewis I'll tell him we have a pro hockey player living here now. He'll be thrilled, and I know he'd love to hear from you."

"Yeah. That would be great. Thanks."

Is he thinking of doing that? I know he misses hockey. Maybe this would be a good thing for him, to find a way to bring the sport he loves back into his life.

Dessert arrives, strawberry shortcake accompanied by a sparkling chenin blanc. I smile with delight when I taste the wine. "Nice. A little acidic bite cuts through the cream, and the peach and citrus complement the strawberries."

"It's fantastic," Jansen agrees. "Now I want to make sparkling wines."

I smile. "We can talk about that for the future."

After dinner, guests start mingling again. Vitto and Leo join us.

"So, Jansen," Vitto says. "What are your intentions toward Bianca?"

I nearly spew chardonnay all over everyone. "Vitto!"

"What?" He turns back to Jansen and tilts his head.

Jansen seems amused. "That's a bit old-fashioned. Why aren't you asking Bianca what her intentions are toward *me*?"

I freakin' love that, but holy shit, I can't handle this right now. "Good point." I shake my head. "It's just business."

They all give me skeptical looks. "It doesn't look like just business," Gianni says pointedly, his gaze dropping to Jansen's hand on my hip.

I slide my tongue over my bottom lip, then say, "Okay, fine. I'm using him for sex."

Now everyone else chokes, including Jansen. I give him a look that says, *right?*

"You asked," I tell my cousins.

"True." Vitto shakes his head. "Okay, then. Are you married, Jansen?"

I roll my eyes.

Jansen laughs. "Not anymore."

"Ah. Divorced?" Leo arches an eyebrow. "What happened with your marriage?"

"Leo! That's personal!" I can't believe they're doing this!

"She cheated on me," Jansen says, deadpan.

I gasp, then slap my hand over my mouth. Is that true? I did not know that!

"Oh man. That sucks." Vitto slaps a hand on Jansen's shoulder. "Sorry to hear that."

"Yeah." Leo shakes his head. "You have any kids?"

"Nope." He lifts his wineglass to his lips, not looking at me.

His wife cheated on him? Why didn't he tell me that? I tune out the conversation as I mull all this over, my stomach squeezing. We've talked about so many things. I feel stupid that I didn't know that. I also feel...hurt.

I guess I shouldn't. We're not in a serious relationship. He doesn't have to tell me everything. We've both been honest about that. Except...I've fallen in love with him. And I *do* feel hurt. And, well, sad.

The truth is—he doesn't really tell me anything about his past life. He told me retirement was hard, but that's it. He told me he's divorced, but that's it. And I've been open with him about so much. Damn. Am I not good enough for him to tell me those kinds of personal things?

We've been sleeping together and I thought I could do it without catching feelings. I know better than to let someone in like that, someone who's going to let me down. But I can't deny the ache in my chest.

I also feel unreasonably pissed at Jansens' ex-wife. Who would do that to him? She's clearly an evil bitch and I hurt for Jansen.

People are leaving and I need to focus and find Uncle Geno. I ask Leo where he is and he points toward the fountain where he and Aunt Janet are talking to a couple.

"I'm going to talk to him," I say to Jansen in a low voice.

"Want me to come with you?"

"No. That's okay. I can do this."

Feeling twitchy and irritated, I straighten my shoulders and march across the grass toward him. In perfect timing, he says goodnight to the guests and I pounce. "Uncle Geno."

He turns, eyebrows raised.

I keep my voice low so others don't hear us. "Why didn't you invite us to this dinner?"

He seems surprised that I've been so direct. His mouth opens, then closes.

Aunt Janet casts him a worried look.

"You don't have a good reason, do you? It was just to exclude us."

His lips thin. "You seem to not want to be part of the Lamberti family anymore."

"What? That's ridiculous. Why would you say that?"

"If you were part of the family, you'd let us keep the wineries together. We'd all work for Belmonte."

I stare at him, then shake my head. "I wouldn't be working for Belmonte, though. You wouldn't hire me as a winemaker. Would you?"

"We have a winemaker. Vittorio is doing very well."

"Exactly." Old hurt and resentment rises up inside me on top of my already irked state, a pressure building in my chest. "I'd be working as a cellar rat forever if we kept the wineries together and I stayed here."

He says nothing.

"That's not what I want," I tell him, the words coming out in a rush. "And that's not what Nonna wanted. And you know that."

His face tightens.

"You can't believe I've been nominated for such a prestigious award, can you?" I demand. "You've never taken me seriously. You brushed off my ideas, and my attempts to create wines. You never bothered to see if I had any talent." I raise my chin and hold his gaze. "Well, news flash. I do have talent. My boss in Argentina believed in me. I have opportunities there that I would never have here at Belmonte."

"Or at Caparelli," he points out.

My ire flares even hotter. "Why not Caparelli? Just because we're basically starting over, doesn't mean we can't be successful with it. You keep making that mistake. And it's really pissing me off."

His chin jerks down and his forehead turns frowny.

"Bianca," Aunt Janet says, clearly ill at ease.

I look at my aunt. She's a nice lady, but she'll always support her husband. "Well, thanks for a lovely evening," I say crisply. "Even though you didn't invite me."

And I turn back to Jansen.

He frowns as I storm up to him. "Uh oh."

My cousins have moved away to talk to other guests, so it's just him and me.

"Yeah," I snap. "Uh oh. Let's go."

"Okay." He takes my hand and we start walking toward the driveway. "What happened?"

I shake off his touch. "I lost my shit."

"Oh."

"He pisses me off! Argh. I tried to be calm and unemotional and ask what was going on with leaving us out of this party, but he insulted us again, and..." I sigh. "I think I made things worse."

We walk toward his truck in silence, other than the sound of our steps on the road and crickets in the grass.

Once in the truck, buckled up, I ask, "Why didn't you tell me your wife cheated on you?"

There's a beat, and then he says, "Because it doesn't matter."

"I think something like that matters."

"I mean, it doesn't matter to us. It's done. It was a long time ago."

"Hmmm." My chest is spinning with emotion and thoughts are jumbled inside my head. I don't know what to think right now, but I do know I'm worked up. I need to figure things out.

When we arrive at the road to Caparelli, he looks over at me. "Come to my place?"

I gaze at him, emotions still churning inside me. Sex is a great distraction, but...maybe I'm getting too close to Jansen. Clearly, he sees me as a fuck buddy and nothing more. Which is what we both want! I press my lips together and shake my head. "Not tonight."

The air in the truck turns thick.

"Okay." He pulls in at Caparelli and stops.

I jump out. "Good night. Thanks for taking me to the dinner."

I turn and march toward Caparelli, knots coiled in my belly, my chin trembling.

Chapter 23

Jansen

I'm in the lab with Bianca and Antonio, trying to focus on malolactic conversion. I've been feeling unsettled since the night of the harvest dinner. There's a stiffness between Bianca and me, and I hate it. I miss her. We haven't had time to talk since then, when she got upset at her uncle. And basically brushed me off. I'm worried he said something that hurt her. If he hurt her, I'll shove his teeth so far down his throat he'll be smiling with his ass.

"What's so funny?" Bianca frowns at me.

"Uh...nothing." *Focus, man.*

She's still acting weird. Distant. I don't like it.

I start when my phone chimes with a call. I check the call display. It's the vet clinic. What's up with that? Frowning, I answer. Are they checking up on Moose after his little snip snip?

"Hi, Jansen. It's Ana. We just got a call from someone about their lost dog."

My heart drops to my feet like a stone. "Oh."

"I didn't give them your number," she says. "But they gave

238

me theirs. Can you call them and set up a time for them to see, uh, Moose? They said they can come to you."

No. No, I can't. "Sure," I manage to say. "What's the number?"

She gives me a name and number. I grab a pen and paper on the counter and scribble it down. "Okay, thanks."

"Who was that?" Bianca asks.

I tell her.

She turns wide eyes on me. "Oh no." She pauses. "I mean..." She closes her eyes and her mouth compresses. "Oh no."

"I'm sure they're excited to have found him." I swallow, my throat feeling thick and rough. My numb fingers tap in the digits on my phone. I speak to the guy named Chris and we arrange for him and his wife to come pick up Moose tomorrow afternoon.

Bianca watches me with a notch between her eyebrows, sucking on her bottom lip. She looks so sad.

I'm already stressed, and now this happens. I try to keep my emotions under control. "They saw the notice at the pet store in Napa. They've been looking for him for weeks." I ignore the iron bands tightening around my chest.

"Oh my God. Oh, Jansen."

"It's fine." I shrug. Her sympathy rankles me. "We always knew this would happen."

She gives me a bewildered look. "They're coming to get him?"

I nod again.

"Let's go. We can grab him and make a run for it."

I choke out a laugh. "What? Where are we going?"

"Mexico. We'll take Moose with us."

"That's pretty far." It does sound appealing, though.

"I don't care."

Antonio looks back and forth between us with raised eyebrows.

"I have to give him back, Bee."

"I know." She sniffs. "But how hard could they have looked for him? I don't know if they deserve him."

"He's their dog. They're his people. Hey, there's no point in crying about it. I knew this could happen."

She tilts her head, looking at me curiously. "I know, but..."

I shrug. "It is what it is." I change the subject to work stuff. "So do we need to inoculate the wine?"

"I don't think so. We just need to make sure the temperature is right."

Later, at home, being greeted ecstatically by Moose makes me feel even worse. I walk into the living room and sit on the floor, back against the couch, and let him climb onto my lap and frantically lick my face everywhere. I don't deserve this.

Which is why he's being taken away from me tomorrow, probably.

Fuck, that makes my eyes burn. I hold his little head and look into his eyes, a stabbing sensation piercing my chest. "You're a good dog. Even though you pee on the deck and freak out about adult fun times."

He licks my chin more.

I stroke his fur and talk to him. "I don't want to give you back. I want to keep you. But they probably love you as much as I do, and you need to be with them. I'm going to miss you. You're always so happy to see me, and you follow me around. Bianca was right. Dogs love you no matter what. Even when you're a dick."

Moose nuzzles my chest and I hug him. A weird, hard feeling climbs from my chest into my throat.

"I don't know what I'm doing. What am I doing, Moose?" I gaze into his brown eyes. "I came here to start over and get my life back, and now I feel like I've lost even more." I have a new life here, sure, with new friends, but now Moose is leaving, and Bianca is mad at me for something, and she's going to leave, too.

My heart feels shredded.

I am so fucked up.

Chapter 24

Bianca

Rosa and I spend the latter part of an afternoon cooking together, re-creating Nonna's homemade ravioli stuffed with beef, marinara sauce, and a radicchio salad for a family dinner. All the cousins are coming.

"I got Castelvetrano olives for the salad at the market," I tell her. "Just like Nonna."

"I can't believe I didn't think of doing this," Rosa says. "It's not like we're enemies now. Although it kind of feels like it."

"I know. And I hate that. They're family, and Nonna would hate it." I pause. "I wish I hadn't lost my temper that night at the harvest dinner. I know we need to be nicer to Uncle Geno. Especially if we want his wine."

I'm also uncomfortable with how I ended things with Jansen that night. We've barely talked the last few days, other than when he got the call about Moose. My stomach clenches again, thinking about Jansen losing him.

"I don't think he's ever going to help us," Rosa says quietly. "I think we're on our own."

I look at her. "Yeah. I think you're right. But we can do it!"

"Yes, we can!"

"Never mind Uncle Geno and whatever climbed up his butt crack. The younger generation can still be friends."

Gianni, Vitto, and Leo arrive bearing wine, of course, and—sweetly—flowers. Rosa takes them and finds a vase for them, setting the arrangement of autumn-colored sunflowers and chrysanthemums on the dining table we've already set for seven.

Jake is joining us. The three cousins are all single, although apparently Gianni is seeing someone but it's not serious so he didn't invite her. And I...sadly didn't invite Jansen.

I tried to talk to him about his wife cheating on him and it was clear that he really doesn't take our relationship seriously. Which is fine! That's what we agreed to.

Except I was crushed by his dismissal. Dammit! Rosa had a point about catching feelings.

After my mom left, I learned to keep a fence around my heart. I'm not doing well at that and I'm going to end up going back to Argentina with a bruised heart.

So it's better if Jansen and I cool things a bit.

We all sit around the table for hours, first nibbling on salami, mortadella, prosciutto, cheeses, bread, and warmed marinated olives while we drink delicious wine. A lot of the talk is about wine at first, naturally. It's something we all share, including Jake. Vitto is now making wine at Belmonte, and we have that in common. There's lots of laughter, more food, more wine.

"I think we should change the name from Caparelli to something else," I tell them, slightly tipsy. "Rosa's not so sure."

"I like tradition," she admits.

The three cousins exchange looks.

"Okay," I say. "Let's just get it out there. Are you pissed at us that Nonna left us Caparelli?"

They don't answer right away. Then Gianni says, "No. How could we be pissed at you about what she did?"

I tip my head. "Are you mad at *her*?"

"We were shocked, at first," Vitto admits. "Nobody had any clue she would do that. And the two wineries have been run as one for years."

Rosa and I nod. "Understandable."

"But we've talked about it," Vitto says. "And it's actually pretty cool that she did that. To continue the Martinelli tradition of wine-making women."

I suck briefly on my bottom lip, emotion tightening my chest. It means so much to hear that from my cousins. Maybe they do think I can make good wines.

I mean, *we*. All three of us are involved in this winery. Well, so far, two of us. I mentally roll my eyes again at Allegra's absence.

"That's what you could name the winery," Leo says. "Three sisters. Or le tre sorelle."

"That's what Nonna used to call us," I say wistfully, turning my wine glass in my fingers. I like that idea. I glance at Rosa to gauge her reaction. She looks thoughtful. "Well, it's something to think about."

The conversation shifts to memories of Nonna and our childhoods.

"I wish Allegra was here," I say with a pout.

"Yeah." Everyone agrees.

"Remember that science fair where she made a tasting box?" Vitto says with a grin.

My eyes widen. "Oh yeah! She put all these essential oils into little bottles to teach people how to taste them in the wine."

"Like that movie?" Jansen asks. "French Kiss."

"Exactly!" Leo laughs. "Where do you think she got the idea?"

"It was a great idea, but one of the oils was hemlock." I make a yikes face at Jansen.

"Hemlock? As in...poison?"

"Yep."

"I'm still not sure she wasn't trying to poison her science teacher," Rosa says with a grin.

"People were only sniffing it!" I say with a laugh.

"Remember the time you were going to Evan Rivera's place to do homework?" Gianni asks me. "And we all followed you to make sure you were okay?"

"Aaah! You stood outside the house yelling! I was mortified!"

Everyone is laughing at the memory. "How about the time you and Vitto dared Leo to moon cars passing by on the road?" I say to him.

"Oh, Jesus." Leo swipes a hand over his face.

"You did it," Rosa reminds him, grinning.

"People were lucky to see my perfect ass."

We all crack up laughing again. "How old were you? I think your ass was pretty scrawny," Vitto says. "You probably traumatized people."

"How about that time Rosa punched Harvey Clark," Gianni says.

Jake's head whips around to stare at Rosa. "What?"

"He was picking on me," Gianni continues. "He was a mean kid, he liked to bully people. She came to my rescue and hit him right in the chops. He never bothered me again."

Jake grins. "I love that."

I get up to fetch another bottle of wine. Vitto follows me to the kitchen. "Tell me more about Argentina," he says, setting his empty glass on the counter. "The wines you were making."

I fill his glass, then mine, and lean on the counter. "Castillo Lorenzo is in the Luján de Cuyo region of Mendoza. The wines are very terroir-driven." I give him a saucy smile. "There are four secrets of the Andes."

"Are they top secret? Or can you tell me?"

I laugh. "The first is the dry weather and sunlight." I don't have to explain to him how that helps concentrate colors, aromas, and flavors. "The second is the soils. They're actually very poor, but well drained. The third is water and irrigation. They don't get much rain there so they have to irrigate. But the melting snow from the Andes is amazing."

"Oh, yeah."

"And fourth is the altitude."

"Yeah, I've heard that."

I nod. "The different elevations make a whole range of weather. Perfect conditions for malbec."

He nods. He knows exactly what I'm talking about.

"So it's exciting working with grapes that have that kind of concentrated flavors and balanced acidity."

"All malbec? No, wait. Your award is for cabernet franc."

"Yes!" I'm still excited about that. "But we're mostly known for the malbec. The unique terroir makes it really powerful and robust."

"It's different focusing on bringing out the attributes of the region rather than a varietal-first approach."

"Yes!" Passion for wine, also the glasses of wine I've consumed and having someone like-minded to talk to loosen my tongue, and Vitto and I get it into it.

"Congratulations again on that award nomination," he says a while later with a sincere smile. "It really is impressive. I hope you win."

"Even being nominated is amazing. Wait, that's a cliché, isn't it?" I laugh. "But it's true."

"I'd love to try new things like that," Vitto says, lifting his glass to his lips, sounding a little wistful.

I tilt my head thoughtfully. "You're happy working here, though? Right?"

"Oh yeah. A little envious of you, though, I have to admit."

I can only blink. Oh.

"Belmonte's been doing the same things forever," he says. "Tradition is really important to Dad."

"But you're the winemaker. You should have a say in what you make."

"Have you met Dad?" he asks with a rueful smile. "Also, he still makes the Carleo. He won't let anyone else touch it."

I make a face. "And it's not even that great." Then I slap my hand to my mouth.

Vitto chuckles. "Don't worry, I agree. But Dad's so attached to it, he won't hear about trying to make it better, or trying something new."

"Ugh. Rosa and I have disagreements, too."

"Of course you do. You're the winemaker."

I smile but my eyebrows pull down. "Yeah..."

"And she's not," he goes on matter-of-factly. "When you aren't as invested in the fundamental qualities of the wine you produce, it's easier to make business decisions."

"She cares," I object.

"Sure, but not like you do."

I slowly lower and raise my chin.

"That's why good winemakers don't usually make good CEOs of wine businesses, and good CEOs usually aren't good winemakers. The businessperson wants to keep things simple. To compromise. But good winemakers are really bad at compromising."

I let that all sink in.

I'm about to tell him about my idea of making orange wine when Rosa appears. "Hey. I thought you came to get more wine."

"Ooops." I flash a smile at Vitto. "We got talking shop."

"Of course you did." Rosa comes over and picks up the bottle. Holding it aloft, she shakes her head. "You've already drank most of it."

"We were carried away," Vitto says, grinning. "Thanks, Bee. It's fun talking to you about that stuff. I love hearing about what you've been doing, and you have great ideas."

My heart kicks against my ribs. I stare at him as he follows Rosa back to the living room. Hearing that from one of my cousins is...touching. Significant. His interest and respect for my experience and opinions means so much to me. My eyes actually water a bit, and I blink back tears. Damn.

"How did you end up working at Bar Down?" Leo asks as I rejoin the group with another bottle of Cabernet.

"Ana and Millie introduced me to Jansen." I open the wine. "They said he needed help because he didn't know anything about wine."

"So you just jumped in to help a stranger? When you have a winery here you're trying to get up and running?"

"Basically, yeah." I shrug and pour wine into his glass then mine. "Although I did have an ulterior motive."

"What's that?" Leo frowns.

"We don't have a lab here. Jansen has a beautiful lab. I agreed to help him in exchange for using his lab."

One corner of Leo's mouth hikes, and Vitto hoots. "Ha! Good job, Bee."

"It still seems like a lot," Vitto says.

"That's what we've been trying to tell her," Rosa says.

I'm getting an overprotective vibe from the room. "I'm fine. It's fine."

"At the harvest dinner, you two looked pretty friendly," Gianni says.

The other cousins nod.

Rosa gives me a look.

"Are you going to stay here, then?" Leo asks.

"No." I shake my head and sip my wine. "I need to go back to Castillo Lorenzo."

"So you're just going to abandon Caparelli," Gianni says. "And your sisters."

"I'm not abandoning them!" I glance at Rosa. Even as I protest, guilt pinches in my chest. "I'll still do what I can to help. I can come home sometimes."

They all make noises like "huh" and shake their heads.

It's midnight by the time everyone leaves, and Rosa and I survey the damage in the kitchen. Neither of us can leave it till morning, though, and Jake helps, too, as we store leftovers and clean up and haul an embarrassing number of wine bottles to the recycling.

"That was fun," Rosa says. "I'm so glad you did that."

"Me, too. I'm glad we talked things out. A little."

"Yeah. And I'm sure Uncle Geno will come around, too."

I'm not so sure. Hearing that Uncle Geno hasn't even given Vitto the freedom he needs to create his own wines kind of pisses me off.

This puts things in a different light than I've always seen them. In my head, my cousins were the same as Uncle Geno— set in his ways, traditional, a little chauvinistic. But now I'm seeing that Vitto faces challenges, too. I wanted to come home and do my duty, help my sisters. Then when I got here, I was sucked into the magic of Caparelli—the history, the mythos— and memories of Nonna made me want to do this for her. And now, I feel like a lot of my resentment and feelings of being overlooked and unworthy were maybe a me problem. Like I said to Rosa...maybe it's time to let my youthful insecurities go. Because I didn't feel like that tonight with the cousins. Vitto was interested in what I had to say. He asked me questions and we shared experiences. We all have a history together and I felt part of that. Part of the legacy. The heritage. Part of the family.

Chapter 25

Jansen

"They're coming at one o'clock. I have to go pack up his stuff."

"Do you want me to come with you?" Bianca asks.

I shake my head. "Nah, it's fine." It's better she's not there if I break into tears when they take Moose away.

I don't even like dogs.

"You're going to give them all his stuff?"

"Of course. What am I going to do with it?"

She bites her lip.

I rub my forehead. "Sorry," I mutter. "I better go."

"Could I come say goodbye to him?" Her voice is small.

I glance at her and see the sadness in her eyes. She probably loves the little dude more than I do. "Sure," I say gruffly.

When we walk in, Moose greets us with his usual ecstasy. Bianca sits on the floor and hugs him tightly, her face pressed to his fur. "I'm going to miss you, buddy."

The air in my lungs is burning. He's almost like *our* dog. I feel as bad for Bianca as I do for myself. Maybe worse. I fucking hate seeing her sad.

When he wriggles away from her, she swipes at her cheeks. "You okay?"

"No," she says in a "duh" tone. "I'm *sad.*"

Without thinking, I reach for her hand and pull her to her feet, then wrap my arms around her. We stand like that for a few minutes, my eyes stinging, tension vibrating in my body. I just want Bianca to feel better.

Eventually we pull apart. She looks up at me, and I force a calm, reassuring smile. "It'll be okay."

She just gazes at me, then helps me gather up toys from every corner of the house, a big bag of dog food I just bought, and a several kinds of treats.

"These ones are his favorite." I shake a package of soft cookies. "I'll have to tell them that."

We hear a car door and voices. I move to the door before they ring the bell, and Bianca scoops Moose...er, Benny, I guess...into my arms. His leash is on the table near the door.

I open the door. "Hi."

A man and a woman stand there. The man says, "Hi. Are you Jansen?"

"That's me." I move to the side so they can step in. "And this is...Benny. We named him Moose, but I'm sure he'll remember Benny."

They walk inside.

Moose cocks his head.

The woman takes a step closer, smiling, hand outstretched. Then she stops. "That's not Benny."

I swear to God time stops. Totally freezes.

I stare at her.

"It's not," the man confirms, disappointment tugging his lips down. He peers closer at Moose. "That white on his head... this is just a spot. Benny's white was a stripe that went all the way back."

"The picture looked just like him," the woman says brokenly.

My heart is thrashing in my chest like a wild animal. "It's not your dog," I repeat.

"No." The woman's eyes fill with tears. "Oh my God. I thought we'd found him."

"I'm sorry," I croak, not sure what else to say.

The man comforts the woman. "It's okay, honey. We'll keep looking."

She sniffles. "I'm sorry. Thank you anyway."

My head is a dry, forsaken desert. Relief has my legs feeling like overripe bananas. I don't think I can move. "I hope you find Benny," I manage to say as they leave. I close the door and stand there facing it, my eyes prickling, my arms tightening on Moose to the point he grunts.

I swallow and set him down. He prances to one of the bags and pulls out a toy. He has no idea what just happened.

"Hey." Bianca takes a step toward me. "Are you okay?"

I nod and pull my lips back from my teeth in a smile. "Oh yeah. I'm just disappointed. I was going to ask them to repay me for all the vet bills."

Her eyes widen. "Jansen!"

I shrug.

She watches me with a notch between her eyebrows. "I'm so relieved," she says on an exhalation. "Although I do feel sorry for those folks. I hope they find their dog."

"Yeah." I walk past her toward the kitchen. "Better get back to work. Come on. We have grapes to crush."

She stops me with a hand on my arm. "Are you sure you're okay?" She moves closer and lays her hand on my chest. It feels...so good. So good. "It's okay to feel relieved. I know those people are disappointed, but you can feel bad for them and happy for yourself at the same time."

I smile. "I'm fine. I'll keep the little guy a while longer."

"Jansen." She shakes her head. "Talk to me."

His forehead bunches low. "About what?"

"About how you're feeling. About Moose."

I study her beautiful face. She looks at me across the counter, her warm brown eyes steady and brimming with... something.

Apprehension? Worry? Pity?

"Talk to me," she says softly. "Please, Jansen." She pauses. "I love you."

Her words crash over me. My throat goes dry. And yet, I'm not surprised. Words bounce around in my head for about an hour. My heart goes feral in my chest and I feel an urge to run, adrenaline flooding my veins. Finally, all I can say is, "But you're leaving."

She closes her eyes briefly, as if that hurts. And nods.

No. That can't happen.

But what can I do? My head feels stuffed with wool. I can't think.

Then the scariest thought of all jumps into my head. The riskiest thing. Opening myself wide to rejection. "What if... what if I asked you to stay?"

Her eyes fly open. She stares at me, then inhales a shaky breath. "Jansen."

My heart is a fist punching inside my chest. I don't look away. "I know this isn't what you planned. But you could stay."

"You..." She stops. Her throat works. "Why?"

I frown. "Why?"

"Why do you want me to stay?"

I gaze back at her. "I..." Jesus. I feel like I'm back on that Ferris wheel with my stomach swooping on the up swing. I want to throw myself at her feet and hold onto her and never let her go. I've never had this feeling before. I'm terrified.

I won't beg her to stay. My lips feel numb as I manage to say, "I don't want you to leave."

Her eyes flatten and she presses trembling lips together, nodding. For a long moment she gazes at me and I feel it like a knife gutting me. "I can't stay."

My heart drops, right to the soles of my feet.

She pulls in a breath and lifts her chin, giving me a mouth-only smile. "I have that award happening. Maybe a promotion, a raise. Wines to work on. I can be myself there." She gives a firm nod.

She said she loves me. That filled me with exhilaration and exultation, and yeah, okay, panic. Desperation to keep her here. I asked her to stay.

She doesn't love me enough to stay.

"I think I'll leave this weekend," she says calmly. "You have interviews for winemakers next week. Things are pretty solid here."

I don't even nod, just watch her face with my chest squeezing so hard I can't breathe. I watch her stand and move to the door. Watch her leave.

My heart lodges in my throat, throbbing, stopping my breath. I'm stiff, frozen in place. As if he knows, Moose comes over and puts his front paws on my leg, staring at me.

Like with him, I have to let Bianca go, if that's what she wants.

Chapter 26

Bianca

"I'm a woman. I have needs." I beckon. "Pass me the wine."

Ana picks up the bottle of zinfandel. "Empty."

"We need more."

"I'll get it." Millie rises and heads to Ana's little kitchen.

We're sitting in Ana's living room in her townhouse condo in Napa. It's an older complex but she's made her little place cute with funky furniture and art. I'm snuggled into one end of the putty-colored sectional with squishy cushions. Ana's at the other end. Millie returns with a bottle of merlot and sits on the fringed pouf next to the low table, which is an old farm table with the legs cut down.

Millie pours more wine into my glass. "Okay, tell us what's going on."

I sigh. "The other night when we went to the harvest dinner at Belmonte, I found out that the reason Jansen got divorced was because his wife cheated on him."

Ana gives me an *and...?* look.

"He didn't tell me that himself. He told my cousins."

"Oh."

"Ohhh," Millie says.

"Yeah." My heart weighs about a hundred pounds. "He told me about the divorce, but he didn't tell me that. And then he just blurted it out to strangers. So...I asked him why he didn't tell me, and he said it's not important."

They both wrinkle their noses.

"But I felt like...I wasn't good enough for him to open up to. I've told him so many things...about Papa dying, Mama leaving. Our crazy family. And I realized that he hasn't really told me a lot about himself. I mean, basics, of course. I tried to get him talk to me and it didn't go so well. It was after we discovered that Moose isn't Benny."

"I was so relieved about that!" Ana says.

"I know, me too! But Jansen was...weird about it. Like he didn't care. But I know he loves that dog." I pause. "He never really talks about his feelings."

"Lots of guys are like that," Millie says with a sigh.

"But Miles tells you he loves you, right?"

"Oh yeah."

I nod, bowing my head. "I told Jansen I'm in love with him."

They both make small noises.

"And then...he asked me to stay."

"Aaaah!" Millie bounces in her seat. "So what's the problem?"

"He didn't say he loves me." I press my lips together and rub the knuckle of my index finger at the outer corner of my eye. "I even asked him why he wanted me to stay. And he just s-said...he said he doesn't want me to leave."

They both gaze back at me with distressed expressions. "After you said the L word to him."

"Yeah." I nod miserably. "So I told him I'm leaving this weekend. I've booked a flight."

"Whaaaat!" They both shout the word at the same time.

"Bee! You can't!" Ana says.

I give them a frustrated look. "I didn't come home to stay here. And now I've been nominated for that award, I really have to go back."

"You won't get the award if you don't go back?" Millie's brow furrows.

"No, that's not it. I feel like I owe them. Especially Milenko. And he's given me so much. The chance to make amazing wines like the cabernet franc, wines that are recognized globally." I drink more wine. "It's the chance to *be* someone. Not just a Martinelli relying on the Lambertis."

"That is not the case," Millie says firmly. "At least, not anymore. Your grandma left you the winery. She obviously had faith in you."

"She gave you the chance to 'be' someone..." Ana adds. "*Here.*"

I let those words sink in. "True. But...I can't stay. I told Jansen I'm in love with him and he doesn't feel the same. That's beyond awkward."

"Wow." Millie shakes her head. "I would have sworn Jansen feels the same about you."

"Me, too," Ana says. "The way you two look at each other. Touch each other. It's absolutely adorable."

I suck my bottom lip. "Really?"

"Oh yeah," Millie confirms. "And Miles says when they run, Jansen doesn't stop talking about you. He's crazy about you."

I shake my head sadly. "No."

"I think *Jansen* has faith in you." Millie tilts her head. "He trusts you to make wine from his grapes."

"Yes. He does. He's never questioned me." My heart contracts painfully. I do love him.

"Don't do it again," Ana says, her voice soft as velvet. "Don't put distance between you and him to protect yourself. Don't let your stubbornness come between you two."

"What?" I frown at her.

"I know how it affected you when your mom left," Ana says quietly.

They were my best friends when that happened; they know exactly what I went through. They stuck with me through my self-pity and existential crisis. And that's why I love them. They're the only two people I've ever let close. I will love them and be grateful to them and loyal to them forever because of that.

"You never let people get that close to you," she continues. "Not even Mark. When we graduated, you just said good-bye to him like it was no big deal."

"Yes. Because it *was* no big deal. And I did the same with Tomás in Mendoza."

"We know losing your parents at such a young age was hard. I think it's colored everything in your life since then. You expect people to leave you. You don't let them close because of that. When things get tough, you shut down and create distance."

I stare at her, my chest tight. "Gee, thanks." Then I bow my head. "You're right. Leaving here was creating the ultimate distance."

"It also made you strong and independent," Ana says. "Hard working. And empathetic and kind."

"Thank you." My smile feels lopsided. "It also made me resentful and stubborn. I know that. Since I've been back, I'm realizing I don't want that to be who I am. I want to be positive. I don't want all those old hurts to come between me and people I love. I want to trust people. I thought I was being so brave to tell Jansen how I feel."

"You were," Ana says.

"You said you've tried to put that resentment behind you and move forward. But I think..." Millie hesitates. "Maybe you're still using that as a reason to leave?"

I stare at her, then at Ana. I lean my head back against the couch. "I want to cry."

"I'm sorry," Millie says quickly.

"No, no! I want to cry because..." My throat thickens and I swallow. "Because you might be right." I hold up my glass of wine. "In vino veritas."

They both laugh softly.

"'Wine brings to light the hidden secrets of the soul,'" Ana recites. "'Gives being to our hopes, bids the coward flight, drives dull care away, and teaches new means for the accomplishment of our wishes.'"

"Horace," I murmur. "I've always loved that." I hold up my glass to study the garnet liquid, replaying the lines.

Wow. Those words are...powerful.

And teaches new means for the accomplishment of our wishes.

Maybe I need to think about that.

"For what it's worth—we'd love it if you stay here, too," Millie says.

Ana nods. "It's been so great having you back here."

They want me to stay, too. At least I know they love me.

Chapter 27

Jansen

When I walk into the Golden Cougar, I'm immediately met by Eugene, who I now know is the owner.

"Don't start any brawls," he says.

"What the fuck? I didn't start anything! You were here, you know that."

He grins. "Yeah. I'm just yanking your chain."

I shake my head, then spot Miles and Nolan over at a table against the wall. I head that way. "Hi, guys."

"Hey," Miles says. "How's it hanging?"

"Low and to the left." I take a seat.

He laughs and lifts his beer.

Nolan eyes me. "You look lower than a snake's belly in a wheel rut."

"Funny."

"Seriously." He pauses. "So you and Bianca have been riding the wild baloney pony."

I give him a long look. I guess I don't need to ask how he knows that. Does Bianca tell her friends everything? Jesus, they probably know my cholesterol levels from the check up I had last week. I sigh. "Yeah."

"But it's more than that," Miles says.

"You guys wanna explain it all to me?" I ask dryly.

"Sorry, man. But you talk about her all the time. I can tell you're crazy about her."

The waitress arrives and I order a shot of Jose Cuervo.

"So." Nolan taps his fingers on the table. "Do you confirm or deny that you're crazy about her?"

I throw my hands in the air. "Okay, sure, I care about her."

Miles hoists an eyebrow accusingly. "Does Bianca know that?"

"Yeah." One corner of my mouth pulls down. "Fuck me. She said she's going back to Argentina and I asked her to stay. Got my balls busted."

They exchange a look.

My tequila arrives. I knock it back and order another.

"Bring the bottle," Miles says to the girl.

"You want her to stay," Nolan states.

"Yeah. That's what I said."

"Huh. Good for you for telling her."

"Yeah, it felt really good when she walked out."

"Mr. Sarcasm tonight," Miles observes. "I respect it."

"I don't know why I bothered." I exhale enough air to sail a tall ship, then smile glumly at the server bringing me another shot of tequila. And the bottle. She also brought two more glasses and I pick up the bottle and pour shots for my new friends. "I really am better off alone.'

They exchange another look and Miles refills my glass. "That sounds like you've given up."

"I'm tired. I'm even a disappointment to my parents. They don't think I should have bought a winery. They're just waiting for me to fail and lose not only my shirt but my whole fucking wardrobe."

"Jesus." Miles frowns and tosses back his tequila. "You know, I don't think this is all due to Bianca. The thing is, if Bianca does leave, I get it, that'll be shitty. But you'll still be you. You'll still be a successful hockey player, running a successful winery. This isn't happening because you're a flawed human being. Fuck, we're all flawed."

"True." Nolan points at Miles. "You are always late. It drives me crazy."

"Well, you talk too much."

"I do not!"

"Yeah, you do. Also you interrupt a lot."

"What? Well, you're arrogant! You always think you're right."

"I am always right."

"Guys." I hold up a hand. "We're getting off track."

They give each other narrow-eyed glances, then turn back to me.

"What more can I do?" I ask wearily. "Get down on my knees and beg her to stay?"

"Yes," Nolan says.

"That usually works," Miles agrees.

I give him a look.

"I'm not joking."

I'm not going to admit it to them, but I have thought about doing that. The idea of Bianca leaving, when she loves me, is fucking *killing* me.

"Why does it have to be like this?" I ask dejectedly. "She said she loves me and she's leaving anyway."

"What happened when you told her you love her?" Miles asks curiously. "Wasn't she happy? Didn't she want to stay?"

I give him a blank look.

They wait.

"I...uh, didn't say that."

They recoil like I just said I enjoy kicking kittens.

"You didn't say that," Miles repeats deliberately. "You didn't tell her you love her?"

I move my head from side to side. "I...I'm not...I told her I don't want her to leave."

"Jesus Christ!" Miles's shout attracts attention from other patrons in the bar.

"YOU DIDN'T TELL HER YOU LOVE HER?" Nolan yells. "What the fuck, man?"

I edge back on my stool, eyeing them warily. I toss back more tequila.

Nolan closes his eyes. "I don't know if we can help you."

"I don't need help."

"Bruh. You definitely do." Miles shakes his head. "Okay. Telling someone you love them is a major relationship milestone."

"Sure."

"The fear of the other person not saying it back is real," Nolan adds.

"If one person says it and the other doesn't, it's a moment of truth in the relationship," Miles adds. "It shows your level of commitment to the relationship."

I stare at him, my mind spinning. "I asked her to stay! That's commitment! I thought she would know that."

"Oh man." Nolan claps a hand on my shoulder. "And you were married."

"*Were.* What does that tell you?" Then I jerk back as a painful memory slams into me. "Holy shit."

They give me expectant looks, waiting for more.

"I remember Stephanie—my ex-wife—said something to

me." I rub my forehead. "When we split up. She said...shit, I don't remember exactly, but it was something like it was hard being married to me because I wouldn't open up."

"You told *her* you loved her, didn't you?" Nolan narrows his eyes at me.

"Yeah, yeah. It was after I retired. I kind of spun out. Basically, I got depressed." I chomp on my bottom lip. "She said she felt like I didn't care enough to make an effort."

"Fuuuuuck," Nolan breathes. "And you just did it again. With Bianca."

I did. I fucking did.

I shove a hand into my hair. "Look, it's not easy talking about some things. My parents always told me to suck it up. Get back out there. Don't be a weenie."

"Is that hockey culture?" Miles asks.

"Who are you guys?" I stare at them. My hockey buddies are good friends, but not amateur therapists like these two.

"We know stuff." Nolan waves a hand. "Okay, tough guy, here's the thing. Talking about your feelings doesn't make you weak."

Is that what I believe?

"Huh. That's good, man," Miles says.

"Ana told me that." Nolan makes a face. "But it's true. Right?"

"Right." Miles looks at me.

Things are getting a little blurry. The tequila is hitting my bloodstream. "That makes sense. Although to be honest, nothing makes much sense at the moment."

"If you really love Bianca, you have to tell her. In those exact words. Not, *I love fucking you.* Not, *you make great wine.* Not, *I don't want you to leave.* Those. Exact. Words."

"I fucked up."

"You can make it right. There's still time."

"How?"

"Jesus. We can't tell you everything."

"Well, shit."

We finish off the bottle of tequila while switching topics to wedding talk and the argument Nolan and Ana had this morning about how to squeeze the toothpaste tube. But my mind is swirling with fuzzy thoughts of Bianca.

Miles ends up calling Millie to come pick us up and drive us home since we've all partaken of the Jose Cuervo beyond safe driving levels. They drop me off first, and I spend five minutes greeting Moose. I let him out to pee, and then trudge into my bedroom. Sleep sounds like a good idea right now.

Naked beneath the comforter, my fuzzy mind goes over what the guys and I talked about earlier.

I don't want Bianca to leave. I can't imagine my life here without her in it. I told her I want her to stay. I thought I was being brave to tell her that. Apparently I was just being a dumbass.

Talking about your feelings doesn't make you weak.

My therapist after the divorce told me much the same thing. It didn't mean as much then.

Did Stephanie really feel like I didn't care about her? I was a mess back then. Fuck. Sure, talking about my feelings might have been good, but I could barely get out of bed some days.

I had so many feelings—so many painful, exhausting feelings. I didn't even know I could feel like that. I would huddle in bed, overwhelmed, paralyzed.

I'd like to use that as an excuse for not talking about it, but... I'm not that stupid. It probably would have helped to talk about it to someone. But there was no way I was going to admit I was lost. Hopeless. I didn't know who I was anymore.

When I started going for therapy, I had a hard time talking about it even then.

Regret fills my chest with heaviness. Stephanie cheated on me. But our relationship was more complicated than that. I may have had a role in things falling apart. Maybe?

And then...yeah, just like Nolan said, I did it again. With Bianca.

I'm having a hard time getting air into my lungs. I don't want that to be the reason things end between me and Bianca. If it is. It's possible she wouldn't stay anyway. She does have a life to go back to in Argentina. That's always been her plan.

But...if it is the reason...if the reason I lose her is because of my own stupid fear of letting myself be vulnerable...I can't let that happen.

I need her. I crave her, with an aching, desperate need. I love everything about her—her beautiful body, that mouth I love to kiss, her quick mind and creativity, her humor and loyalty. Even her grape juice-stained hands and the weird questions she asks.

She's fresh air in my stale life. She's laughter and smiles and fun, with a dedicated, hard-working core. When she looks at me, it's like standing in a ray of sunshine, feeling the warmth of her admiration, her respect, her confidence in me that makes me feel like I can do anything.

She should have known. Have I not shown her how I feel?

Nah. I can't shift that onto her. I didn't know Stephanie felt like I didn't love her. But I know Bianca does.

Of course she does. She expects people to leave. She expects people to hurt her. And I realize how fucking lucky I am that she let me in. That she told me about her parents, her mother leaving, how her family overlooked her. How she has all that talent and wants to use it.

I need to do better with her. And I need to get over myself.

A crazy thought enters my murky head. I let it circle around and try to examine it. It's nuts. But maybe it's not.

"Moose."

He lifts his head.

"C'mere, buddy." I sit up and hold out my hand to him.

He pushes up to his feet and pads up the bed to me. I pick him up and set him on my lap. "Tell me what you think of this. Stephanie said I didn't open up enough. Do you think that's true?"

He cocks his head, one ear twitching, and I swear he's thinking, *Duh*.

"Maybe she was right."

Moose tilts his head the other way. He's a good listener.

"Okay," I tell him. "I have to open up more. Let's practice."

He makes a little whine.

I smile. "I love you, buddy."

He gazes back at me.

That was pretty easy.

Of course, he is a dog.

"I never had a dog, so I didn't know what it was like." I stroke a hand over the top of his head, then rub his ears. "I didn't know how much I would care about you. When I thought they were going to take you away from me, I—" My throat closes up. "I was wrecked."

His brown eyes are unwavering as he listens intently.

"You're a pain in my ass sometimes, but I love you."

He cocks his head.

"I love how you make me laugh. I love how you growl at me when you're tugging on a toy, but it's just playing. I love how you're so determined to catch those goddamn squirrels." I pet his back. "And I think you love me, too. You can't say it, but you show it. You're so excited every time I come home. Nobody's ever been that happy to see me."

I swear he smiles.

"But that's not enough for humans. Jumping all over them when you see them and licking their face isn't enough."

You're losing your shit, Dad.

I know that's what he's thinking. I give him a weak grin. "You could be right. I have an idea. Tell me what you think of this."

Chapter 28

Bianca

"I've booked my flight back to Argentina. I'm leaving Saturday."

Rosa's head snaps up. She frowns at me. "What? Really?"

I abuse my bottom lip with my teeth. "Yes. It's time."

Rosa sinks onto a kitchen chair. We just finished dinner and doing the dishes. Jake's at the sink rinsing it out. She glances at him, then back at me. "But we need you here."

I smile. "No, you don't. Jake's got things under control."

"He's not a winemaker, Bee. What are we going to do without you?"

Well, I haven't thought that through.

Which is actually kind of shitty of me. I own part of this winery. I'm going to leave Rosa here all on her own. Again. Who knows what's happening with Allegra. I feel my shoulders drawing up, tightening, and a twisting feeling in my stomach.

The panic that's been brewing inside me climbs, a tight, breathless squeeze.

"I don't know what to say," Rosa says quietly.

Jake comes and stands behind her with his hands on her shoulders. The tender, reassuring gesture makes me want to cry.

She looks up at him over her shoulder. He gives her a small nod. She looks back at me. "You're doing it again."

"Doing what?"

"Leaving."

I swallow. "Yeah."

"Why? Why are you leaving? We want you here. We *need* you here. We love you and we miss you when you're not here."

I give a soft snort. "I'm pretty sure no one missed me." Well. Ana and Millie said they missed me.

"Of course we missed you!" Her mouth drops open wide enough to fit a wine barrel.

With a quiet murmur about leaving us to talk, Jake disappears.

"Okay. Why are you leaving?" Rosa asks in a softer tone.

I sigh and sit down at the table. "I want to be somewhere I'm respected. Where I'm good enough. Where I'm not just pushed aside and treated like I don't matter."

Rosa moves her head slowly side to side, staring at me. "That's ridiculous. You're respected here."

That ache in my throat intensifies. I don't want to break down in tears while I'm trying to be an adult. I take a moment to swallow and get my voice under control. "I know you love me. We're sisters. I love you, too. But you've disagreed with me about things I want to do here. I feel like you don't trust me to make good wines."

Rosa presses her fingers to her mouth, eyes wide. "That's not true. Of course I trust you! That's why I want you to stay!"

"So we can argue over what wines to make and how much it'll cost and how long it'll take and—"

"Yes!"

Her nearly-shouted agreement startles me into silence.

"Yes! Of course we'll disagree on those things. And likely lots of other things. There are all kinds of decisions we have to make if we're going to run this place. We won't always agree. I know I'm focused on the bottom line. The business. You're focused on making beautiful wines. We just have to talk about things, work through them. Sometimes we'll have to compromise. But I'll always, *always* respect your knowledge and your talent."

Compromise.

My mind darts back to that conversation with Vitto here in the kitchen.

Good winemakers are really bad at compromising.

My heart squeezes. The stinging in my nose keeps me from speaking again. And I'm not sure what to say anyway.

"Why would you leave?" she asks again, more gently this time. "What is it you really want?"

"I just told you!"

"I know, I'm just trying to get underneath that."

"I want to be part of this family!"

Silence plunges over us, thick and heavy. I drop my head forward.

"Bee." Rose reaches over and grabs my hand. "You *are* part of the family."

"I know, but...sometimes...I don't feel like it."

"It's you who always pulls away. Puts up walls. You're the one who left."

Ana and Millie said the same thing.

I want to deny it and argue with Rosa, but hearing it from her and from my friends stirs up so many emotions. I feel defeated. But also a recognition of truth. And a bitter taste in my mouth that's remorse.

"I left..." I choke up and fight back the tears. "I left because...I was afraid."

Rosa squeezes my hand. "Of what?"

"After losing Papa and then Mama...always feeling like the middle kid who didn't matter because you were smart and perfect and Allegra was...challenging, but so much fun...I was so afraid I'd never truly be recognized. Or loved. So I left."

"I'm sorry." Rosa's voice thickens. "I didn't know you felt that way. You're a brilliant winemaker, Bee. So talented. We all know it. You're also a good person. You work so hard. Maybe I haven't said it, but I appreciate so, so much everything you've done for Caparelli. Coming home to help, and you've busted your butt working here. And helping Jansen on top of that. I know you weren't thrilled to be here at first, but lately you seemed really happy. And I thought maybe you've found your place. Where you really belong. With us. And I thought maybe you'd stay."

Jansen wants me to stay. Rosa wants me to stay. Ana and Millie want me to stay. Why am I leaving? So I can prove something to these people? To myself? Or...because I'm still afraid? "Oh God."

"The other night when we had the cousins over for dinner —you had to see that they consider you family."

I nod slowly.

"We share blood. A history. A legacy. They respect you. It was clear. And...you were the one who instigated that dinner. Bringing us all together. There's something about you that makes everyone feel good. Feel valued. You need to value *yourself.*"

My throat thickens and two plump tears threaten my mascara. I nod.

"And what about Jansen?" she asks quietly. "You've been spending a lot of time with him. When I see you together, you *both* look happy. The way he looks at you... I'm surprised he doesn't want you to stay, too."

"He does," I whisper.

"Ohhhh. And you're still going to leave?"

"I'm scared, Rosa."

After a short pause, she says, "Are you in love with him?"

Without looking up at her, I nod miserably. "But he doesn't love me."

Her eyebrows twitch toward each other. "He said that?"

"I asked him why he wanted me to stay. He didn't have an answer."

"Oh. Damn."

"Yeah."

She sighs. "Love is scary. Giving someone that much power to hurt you...it's terrifying. It takes a lot of trust."

Is she talking about me? Or...about Jansen? Is he afraid to trust me? Or is it because of what happened with his marriage...

"Even when you're *not* convinced everyone you care about will leave you," Rosa continues. "It wasn't easy for me to trust Jake again. I was scared, too."

"I told Jansen I love him and he couldn't say the same. I can't stay here now."

"You told him how you feel. You have to be brave to do that," she says. "And you are one of the bravest people I know."

I smile through the tears blurring my vision. "Thank you."

"The things you've accomplished...I don't know how you could feel that we didn't respect you for that. I mean, I believe you, I'm not trying to dismiss your feelings. We all have such different perspectives on things. I do regret that we didn't talk more, back when we were teenagers. About how you were feeling after Mama left."

"I regret it too. But we were kids."

"True. I'm sorry you didn't feel you could come to me, with anything."

Now we're gripping both of each other's hands. I nod. "I'm really happy for you and Jake, When I first got home, I wanted to be mad at him for how he hurt you, but he's a good guy and it didn't take long to see that he makes you happy."

"He does. And I don't know Jansen well, but I like him."

My smile trembles. "I like him, too."

"Don't do it again."

I blink. "Do what?"

"Don't leave because you're afraid. If Argentina is where you want to be, and you have people there you care about, who care about you, and you're accomplishing the things you want to do—then that's where you should be. I would never hold you back. But..." She meets my eyes. "Don't leave again because you're afraid."

I give a jerky nod. "I need to...I need to think. I'm still trying to sort out everything in my head."

She nods, "That's fair. I'm here for you. If you want to talk more, about the family, or Jansen, or wine...I'm here."

"Thank you. I love you."

"Love you, too."

I go upstairs to my room and lie down on my bed.

I don't feel so hopeless anymore. I play Rosa's words over and over in my mind. I think about my family. About how happy they were for me being nominated for that award. Vitto's admission of envy. Their respect.

Maybe not Uncle Geno. But if I feel the love and respect from everyone else, maybe that doesn't matter.

I'm drained. And yet I feel a growing lightness. Hopefulness. It was hard, but I'm glad Rosa and I talked and that she was honest with me. Hearing that I'm the one who shut down... I'm the one who left...it's true. I don't regret it—the experiences

I've had and the people I've met have made me who I am. But it has made me realize that my resentment toward my family probably wasn't completely well-founded. I may have created some of my own problems by not letting go of the past. In not letting go of the belief that my mother abandoned me because I was lacking. In not letting go of the belief that I need to prove my worth to be part of this family.

Nervous energy fills me and I jump off the bed and cross over to the window. It's dark but faintly, through the trees, I can see the lights of Bar Down. I lean against the sill.

Who I am...my worth...isn't determined by others. It's determined by me.

I'm a winemaker. I'm successful. I love doing it. I'm not musical, but I can create a symphony. I'm not an athlete, but I can create a team. I can bring people joy. Bring them together. That's something.

I love the history of wine. For thousands of years, wine has brought people together. It's friends and family and even strangers. Every bottle is a chance to create new memories. I love that I'm part of that.

Don't do it again.

I turn away from the window and run back downstairs. Rosa and Jake are sitting in the parlor watching TV.

"I'm sorry."

They both look up at me blankly.

Rosa blinks, her brown eyes soft and warm. "What for, Bee?"

I cross the room and sit on the chair next to them, leaning forward. "I'm sorry I've been so...so blocked. That I couldn't see things clearly. I couldn't see myself clearly." I swallow but hold her gaze. "We won't do the orange wine."

Her mouth falls open. "What? Why not?"

"It's not practical this year. You're right. We need to be more strategic to get started."

She blinks.

Jake smiles.

"I need to learn to compromise," I say. "Vitto made me see that. And you. If we're all going to run this place together, there are going to have to be compromises. I hate compromising, especially when it comes to the wine."

"I don't want you to compromise on wine."

"I know. And I won't. I'll make the best damn wines we're capable of. I can make orange wine next season. And it'll be amazing. But I'll listen to you, and to Allegra when she gets here, and we'll figure things out together."

She grins.

"Thank you for believing in me, when I didn't believe in myself."

She nods, her eyes suddenly shiny.

"And you're right about something else. I am running away. Again."

Chapter 29

Jansen

I pause on the sidewalk outside Atelier in Manhattan Beach. Here I am. This might be crazy, but I want to do it.

I got on a flight in San Francisco a few hours ago, rented a car at LAX, and now here I am. I have to do this fast because Bianca's leaving on Saturday.

I push inside and am greeted by a luxurious, feminine scent that pairs perfectly with the décor of the shop—brick walls lit with track lights, antique wood tables piled with neatly folded clothing, more clothing hanging on brass racks. I've been here before, many times, but not since Stephanie and I separated.

I see her behind the counter, tucking tissue paper around a customer's purchase. She smiles at the woman and slides her purchases into a glossy bag.

I amble closer, hands in my jeans pockets, and she sees me. Something flickers on her face, but at least it's not horror or hatred. She knew I was coming; I texted her yesterday. If she said no, I'd have to figure out something else, but she was agreeable to meeting up with me for coffee.

The customer moves away from the counter and Stephanie looks at me. "Hi, Jansen."

She's as pretty as ever—pale blonde hair, high cheekbones, dark blue eyes, wearing a black dress that's wrapped around her thin frame like a bandage, covering her from neck to mid-calf.

"Hi." I incline my head. "How are you?"

"I'm good! How about you?"

"Yeah. Good. Great."

"We can go into my office." She leads the way through a door, down a short hall, and into an office. It's decorated in a similar style to the front of the store, with an antique desk on the wood floor, a thick pink rug under a couple of armless chairs upholstered in turquoise, pink, and green.

She holds out a hand to one of the chairs and I sit.

"Coffee?" she asks, nodding at the Keurig on the credenza.

"Sure."

"Just milk, right?"

She remembers. "Yeah. Thanks."

When we each have a mug in our hands, she sits too and gives me a curious but wary look. "This is a surprise."

"I'm sure." I grimace. "You're probably wondering what's going on."

"Oh yeah." She grins and nods.

I pull in a long breath. "I'm not sure where to start. I have questions for you."

Her eyebrows shoot up.

"But mostly I want to say some things, also."

"Okay." She lifts her mug to her lips, regarding me with interest.

"Did you know I moved to Napa?"

She nods slowly. "I did. Austin told me you bought a winery."

"That's right."

"That was a surprise."

"Yeah. I know it sounds nuts." I lift one shoulder. "But I really like it. It's hard work and I have a lot to learn but it's going okay."

"Well, that's good."

She's being very patient.

I rub my mouth and look away briefly. "I met someone."

"Oh." She nods. "That's...good."

"Yeah. Except I kind of screwed up." I want to vomit. I fight back the nausea.

She doesn't react. Just waits.

"I remember when we split up you said some things about how you felt. You said you felt like I didn't love you anymore."

She purses her lips, nodding slowly. "Yes."

"Because I wouldn't talk to you about how I was feeling after I retired."

"Right." She blinks a few times. "You were obviously having a hard time. I tried to talk to you about it, to get you to see someone, but you kept saying you were fine, you just needed to figure things out."

"Yeah. But I wasn't figuring things out."

"No. You weren't."

"Is that why you cheated on me?" Fuck, it's hard to ask that.

She closes her eyes, then sighs. "No. Maybe. Partly? I don't know. I felt like you were shutting me out. Like you didn't care enough to talk to me. Or share things with me. We were supposed to be partners."

A burning sensation traces down my chest and into my gut. "Yeah."

"I'm not blaming you," she adds quietly. "I screwed up. I guess neither of us was that great at talking. I should have told you how I was feeling. Instead, I...well, I thought someone else would make me feel...wanted."

"I'm sorry." I lower my chin then lift it. "I am so, so sorry I made you feel like that."

Her face softens and she presses her fingers to her mouth.

"I'm seeing now that I did have some responsibility in why our marriage ended. You're right. We should have been partners." I pull in another big breath. "So I apologize for that. Not an excuse, but I was having a hard time. I was pretty depressed, although I didn't realize it. It was hard to make myself care about anything." I wince. "That sounds bad. I did care about you. But I just had no interest in anything. I had zero energy. And I had zero interest in talking about it. I kept telling myself nothing was wrong. I tried to pretend I was okay. My parents kept telling me to get over it."

She covers her face with one hand. "I don't think it works like that."

"No. It doesn't. I felt...like a failure." Yeah, talking to Moose was easier than this. But I forge on. "I gave up my career and I had nothing else. I didn't know what to do. I felt worthless."

Her face tightens like someone just punched her in the stomach.

"And hopeless," I add. "I had nothing to look forward to."

She ducks her chin. "Not even me."

"It's not a reflection of you, Steph. It was me."

"Okay."

"Like I said, that's not an excuse, I just wanted to explain to you. And apologize. And I wanted to understand how you felt because I don't want to—" My windpipe squeezes shut and I cough. "I don't want to make the same mistakes again. I remember my hockey coach in Ottawa always said 'you either win or you learn.' It's taken a while, but I want to learn from what happened."

"What happened with your new girlfriend?"

I've never really thought of Bianca as my girlfriend. But I

like it. I want her to be my girlfriend. "She's going back to Argentina."

"Whoa. She's from Argentina?"

"Well, no, but she was working there. She has a great job. She's a winemaker."

"Oh." Her eyes widen.

I tell her about what happened, like I told Miles and Nolan, and she too slaps her forehead. "Jansen."

"I know, I know. I'm going to tell her how I feel. I am. But I wanted to learn. And to apologize to you. Maybe it's closure?"

She drops her head back against the chair. "Well. It takes two people to make a marriage work. Maybe it takes two people to make a marriage fail?"

I don't want to take *all* the fucking blame. She cheated on me. Bottom line, I couldn't get past that. But I do recognize that she felt unloved and unwanted. "I wish things could have been different."

She nods.

"But they weren't. And here we are. You and Bones are okay?"

Her mouth lifts at the corners at my use of his nickname. His last name is Boness. "Yeah. We're good. But...thank you. Because I needed to learn some things, too."

I smile thinly. "Let's hope we both don't make the same mistakes." I set down my cup on a small round table in front of us. "Thanks for making time for me. I appreciate it."

"Of course. I'm actually glad we talked."

We both stand and she leads me out to the front of the store. At the door, she says, "Go get your girl."

Now I grin. "I'm gonna try."

I have two more things to do before I fly back to San Francisco.

Chapter 30

Jansen

I'm in the cave at Caparelli, the place Bianca loves. I hear voices on the stone stairs and I snap to attention

Bianca appears and stops as she sees the candlelight. "What is going on?" Then she glances around and sees me. Her eyes widen, her lips part, and her chest rises on a big breath in. She's wearing ripped jeans and a black T-shirt that says BITCHES BE SIPPIN' and she looks messy and brilliant and so damn adorable.

"Hi," I say quietly.

"Go on," Rosa says from behind Bianca.

Bianca turns and looks at her over her shoulder. "What is this?"

"You two need to talk." Rosa smiles at her sister, then at me.

That smile reassures me that I'm doing the right thing.

Yeah, I recruited Rosa to help me. Luckily, she was a willing accomplice. And with that smile, she disappears back up the stairs.

Bianca slowly steps down the remaining stairs. She eyes me

warily, a small groove between her eyebrows, a troubled bow to her mouth. "I thought you were in Los Angeles."

"How did you hear that?" I only told one person where I was going.

"Millie said she heard it from Oren at the market."

I throw up my hands. "How the hell did he know?"

"Millie said his sister works at the airport in San Franciso and she must have seen you."

"Jesus Christ." I rub my forehead.

Bianca shrugs. "That's how it goes here." Her top teeth sink into her bottom lip briefly. "Why did you go to Los Angeles?"

I can read the apprehension and worry in her expression. "I had to talk to Stephanie."

Her bottom lip quivers but she catches it her teeth again. "That's what I thought. You're still in love with her, aren't you?"

"Fuck, no." But I sigh because I don't blame her for jumping to that ludicrous conclusion. Serves me right.

I'm standing next to an oak barrel that I'm using as a table. I reach for the bottle of wine there and pour some into two glasses. "Here. We do need to talk."

"Well." She walks closer. "You know I can't turn down wine." Her gaze lowers to the bottle and she lifts eyes that are now as big and round as hockey pucks. "That's my wine."

"I had to taste it." I hand her a glass.

She lets out a short puff of air and a ghost of a smile passes over her lips. "Jansen."

I shrug.

"Where did you get it? I don't think you can find it here."

"Los Angeles. I had to hunt all over the fucking city for it, but I found it."

Her lips twitch. "So taste it," she prods me gently. "Tell me what you think."

I swirl the glass, inhale the aromas. "Complex," I say. "Although I'm probably the least qualified person to be judging this."

Her lips curve upwards a little more.

I taste the wine and savor it, concentrating. "Intense. I taste minerals."

She nods.

"Am I crazy to say I taste peppers? Like, roasted red pepper."

Her smile broadens. "Not crazy at all."

"Mmm...black cherry. Chocolate. And..." I sip again. "Spices. I'm not sure what they are. Cinnamon, maybe? And a hint of vanilla, which I think is from aging in oak."

"Yes."

"It's amazing, Bianca. Mouth watering. I can see why it's nominated for an award."

"Thank you." Her eyes glow with pleasure.

"Would you please sit?" I gesture at the chairs I brought down here.

"Um. Okay." She lowers her cute butt to one of the chairs., taking in the flickering candles and bouquet of purple flowers.

I sit, too. "I had to talk to you before you leave."

"Oh. Okay."

"I want to apologize. And I want tell you everything. Things I'm not proud of. Things that are humiliating."

Her forehead pinches together between her eyebrows.

"I know you're leaving." I clear the sudden thickness in my throat. "I know I screwed up when I asked you to stay. I'm not good at this."

She watches me with a faint droop of her eyelids.

"I'm not going to ask you again," I assure her. "If you want to go back to Argentina that's what you should do. You know what's best for you. And your career. I want that for you."

She gives a tiny nod, emotions flickering in her eyes. I sense her guardedness.

I don't blame her.

It's fucking terrifying, opening yourself up to someone who might kick you in the nuts, knife you in the gut, break your heart. I know pain—I'm a hockey player. But this is different. This is Bianca. This is more than just a broken bone or bruised ribs. This is everything.

I set my wine glass on the table and slide off my chair and onto my knees in front of her. Her eyes fly open wide and she blinks rapidly. "What are you doing?"

"This is me being vulnerable." My eyes are burning and I squeeze them briefly shut.

She sucks in a shaky breath, her eyes glossy.

"I'm so sorry, Bianca. I'm sorry I've been an asshole."

She watches me, her wine forgotten.

"I have a hard time talking about my feelings. Hell, some-times I have a hard time even knowing I *have* feelings."

She huffs out a small laugh. "Yes."

"So even if it's too late for us, I wanted to get my shit together and man up and tell you the truth. I screwed up with my marriage. I don't want to screw up again. That's why I went to talk to Stephanie. She had some harsh truths for me. She told me them years ago, but I kind of tuned them out. I felt like she was blaming me for her cheating. And that pissed me off. I didn't want to hear that."

Her eyes grow larger. "She blamed *you?*"

I shake my head. "No, not really. She was trying to tell me why she cheated. How she felt. She felt like I didn't love her anymore. She felt alone." I suck in a breath, inflating my tight lungs. "And that was my fault. I haven't told you how bad things were after I retired."

I tell her more details about my depression and how my

friends helped me get out of it. That part's embarrassing, too, but she doesn't seem horrified or disgusted. No judgment from her, either.

"I came here for a fresh start. Something to give my life meaning, something I could start over with. But I wasn't letting go of the past. I wasn't being honest with myself. And I wasn't being honest with you. Again, I'm sorry. I know that building real connections with people takes honesty. And vulnerability." I cough. "The way I was raised was to be tough. You definitely don't cry when you get hit on the ice. You don't talk about feelings, except maybe tough masculine feelings—" She opens her mouth but I keep going. "Which is bullshit, because feelings aren't masculine or feminine. We all have them."

She smiles.

"I want to let go of the past. I think talking to Stephanie will help with that. I apologized to her, too." I exhale sharply. "I'm sorry I didn't tell you she cheated on me. It was embarrassing."

Her forehead puckers. "What? Why?"

I shake my head, rubbing my forehead. "The other thing I didn't tell you is that Stephanie cheated on me with one of my teammates."

She gulps in air, her eyes flying open wide. "Oh no."

"Yeah." My mouth twists wryly. "That made it even harder. It was humiliating enough, but everybody knew about it. All my former teammates, all the gossip blogs." I shake my head. "I might have been able to stay in touch with the team better if that hadn't happened, but the last thing I wanted to do was see Austin. Or most of the guys, really. Everybody feeling sorry for me. At least my buddies Frenchy and Copper made an effort to see me."

"I'm sorry," she says quietly. "I already hated Stephanie, but now I do even more."

I let one side of my mouth hook up at that. "My self-image had already taken a big hit after retiring. I didn't know who I was anymore. I felt like nobody. Then...when you get cheated on, it feels like there's something wrong with you. And it was with someone I knew, who I thought was a friend, and they're still together." I shake my head. "I didn't want to talk about it at all."

Her eyes slowly close, then open again. "I...yeah. I felt hurt that you didn't tell me, though. I felt like you didn't trust me, or care enough about me to talk about things like that, when I'd shared so much with you."

"Fuck." I groan miserably. "I am so, so sorry. Hurting you is the last thing I ever want to do. I was being a selfish dickhead. I thought making myself vulnerable would get me hurt. And yeah, that happens. But..." I drag a hand down over my face. "The other thing I did in LA was see the therapist I worked with. She told me...when you don't let yourself be vulnerable, you're basically telling yourself you're not worthy of acceptance and love. Like, it's the opposite of what you think. You think you're protecting yourself. But when you open up, you make the conscious decision that what you're showing other people is worthy." I blow out a breath, my heart rampaging in my chest. "For a long time I didn't feel worthy. But then I spent time here, making friends, with Miles and Nolan and Ana and Millie, with the people who work for me. And you. You made me feel like maybe I am worth it."

She makes a small, distressed sound, eyebrows pulled down.

"I don't want to feel like a loser. I don't want to make the same mistakes I did in my marriage. You reminded me—you either win or you learn."

Her eyes flicker and a hint of a smile brushes her lips.

"So if it takes being brave enough to tell you the truth about me, and tell you how I feel about you, then that's what I'm gonna do." I meet her eyes. "I love you, Bianca."

She gazes at me wordlessly, eyes big and shiny.

"I love your crazy questions. I love your passion for wine. I love your intelligence and your sense of fun and how hard you work."

Her bottom lip quivers.

"I love that you love my dog. And I also love your spectacular tits and ass and—"

"Jansen!" She drops her head back. But she's smiling.

"Sorry. I mean, not sorry, I do love your body and your beautiful face and your stained fingers." I grin. "And I know you're leaving. Like I said, I won't ask you to stay. It's your decision and if you go back to Argentina, I'll support you. It'll break my fuckin' heart, but I want you to live your dreams."

There's a moment of silence. She looks like she's fighting emotion. Then she says, "I'm sorry, too."

"Sorry for what?"

"I'm sorry I was a mess. I guess I still am, but I've been told some hard truths, too, and I've reflected on them and I've figured out some things—I think." She takes a breath. "And you're right. Letting go of the past is something we have to do if we want to move forward. I let the past control my feelings about being back here. About my family and how they see me."

"I know you want their respect. But your value doesn't decrease because they can't see your worth. And if they don't, they're just boneheads. *You* have to see your worth."

Her eyes go glossy and her bottom lip trembles. "Yes. That's exactly right." She composes herself. "Rosa told me not to do it again—to leave because I'm afraid. And the truth is...I *am* afraid."

Jesus. It's even hard to ask about *other* people's feelings. But I want to know. And...it's Bianca. I *need* to know what she's afraid of so I can slay those dragons for her. So I can defend her and protect her and cherish her. So I can be her warrior, her guardian...so I can give my life for her.

I may be getting a little dramatic.

"What are you afraid of?" I ask gently. She seems so confident and sure of her abilities, so self-possessed and fearless. But we all have things we're afraid of.

A chirping noise has us both straightening.

"That's a fucking cricket," she mutters, eyes sweeping around the cellar.

"It is." I grin. "Sorry. I was just thinking that we all have things we're afraid of and then the damn cricket pipes up."

Her lips twitch. "Well, that's one thing, yeah. But...I'm afraid of so many things. I'm afraid my mother left me because there's something wrong with me. I'm afraid that *anyone* I care about will leave me. I'm afraid I'll never live up to the family name."

"Bianca."

"I know." She holds up a hand. "I know. My career in Argentina was going great. I'm nominated for a big award. But coming home, I still felt I had to prove my worth to my family. To this community. But you're right. I don't need to prove myself to anyone. Just to me."

I smile.

"And Rosa was right. I've always been afraid to let people in because it hurts being left. So *I* left. When I came home, I didn't want to get involved with people. All I wanted was help my sisters get things started with Caparelli and then high tail it back to Castillo Lorenzo. But things...changed."

My heart thuds faster. Harder.

Chirrrup. Chirrup. Chirrup.

Bianca's eyes flicker.

I huff out a frustrated laugh as I push up to standing and

follow the noise. The little creature is behind a barrel. I peer down there, but it's dark, so I pull out my phone and turn on the flashlight. Aha. I grab the broom I used earlier to sweep down dust and cobwebs and brush the insect out. It immediately leaps, trying to get away. I bring the broom down on it, not too hard; he doesn't deserve to die. Then I manage to scoop him into my hand. "Be right back."

After depositing him outside—"Be free, little one"—I return to the cellar.

Bianca's sitting there wide-eyed, gripping her wine glass. "You saved him."

"Yeah."

She smiles, a slow, soft smile. "My hero."

Fuck, yeah. I want to be her hero. Even though I know she doesn't need rescuing, I want to be her refuge. Her champion. I return to my position on the floor, on my knees, which are now feeling the hardness of the stone. I repress the wince. I take her wine glass and set it next to mine, then curl my fingers around hers. "Okay." My voice is scratchy. "Where were we? You said things changed."

"Right. Um. Actually, maybe things didn't change. Maybe *I* changed."

I lift my chin.

"I came home reluctantly. I left because I wanted to get away from the family baggage, make a name for myself. This place is insular. Everyone knows you. They know your history, good and bad. Rumors spread fast. But also...the people are good. My friends are good. My family is...well, Uncle Geno is pretty stubborn, but my cousins are good people, too. So maybe it's me. *I'm* seeing things differently. I'm seeing myself differently. And..." She swallows. "There's you."

My heart goes into high gear, blood pumping wildly in my veins.

"I already told you I fell in love with you. That wasn't supposed to happen. We were supposed to just have fun. But I started feeling more. That night I found out about your wife cheating on you. I had just realized that I was in love with you. And things felt...not like a business dinner and I thought maybe you felt the same. But then you told my cousins something important about you, that you'd never told me. And it hurt. Because bam bam in the ham is hot, but—"

I choke. And sputter. "*What?*"

She grins. "Sorry. Ana said that. What I'm saying is, sex is great but it made me sad that that's all you wanted from me."

"Jesus." I close my eyes on the stabbing sensation in my chest.

"It was how I felt! I was good enough to bang but not good enough to talk to. To tell me all the things that make you *you*. You didn't trust me with your story. Your vulnerabilities. It wasn't enough for me anymore, and I got scared. I wasn't supposed to fall in love with you."

A wave of hot shame washes through me. "I'm sorry." I tilt my head back, then open my eyes to meet hers. "I was doing the same thing. Trying to protect myself." I let out a low laugh. "I really thought I was being brave and open when I asked you to stay. I thought you would know what that meant."

She lowers her chin, pouting a little. "I thought it meant you wanted to keep boinking."

My heart burns behind my sternum. "That wasn't it. But how would you have known? I'm an idiot, as Miles and Nolan helpfully pointed out. I'm sorry. I am so sorry."

Her lips tremble.

I reach for a small shopping bag sitting on the barrel. "I have a gift for you. I bought it a long time ago. Because I think I fell for you the first night we met."

She takes it, eyeing me curiously. With her head cocked,

she opens the bag and pulls out purple tissue paper, then unwraps a puddle of purple silk. Her eyes widen. "Oh my God." She holds up the slip. "Oh my God."

I swipe a hand down my face. "I don't know why I bought it. I couldn't get you out of my mind, and I kept thinking about you wearing that. I felt like a bonehead, but..." I shrug.

She looks up at me, eyes glowing. "So you really did think I'd look sexy in this."

A smile tugs my lips. "Oh, hell yeah. Of course you look sexy in cut-offs, rubber boots, and a stained T-shirt."

Her smile is luminous.

"Even if I'll never have a chance to see you in it, I thought you should have it. So you know that you are sexy and beautiful and fascinating."

The candlelight glimmers on the wetness at her eyes. "I want you to see me in it."

My heart stutters. And literally stops. I try to talk, but my throat is sandpaper. "I won't hold you back from your dreams. What I want most of all is for you to be happy."

She gazes back at me, her beautiful face wearing an expression of steady calmness. "I'm not leaving."

Chapter 31

Bianca

Jansen goes very still. His eyes meet mine. His eyes have a tired look about them, but he's still so rugged and handsome. His striped button-down shirt is open at the throat, giving me a glimpse of that place I love to kiss. I admire his big hands and his strong forearms where he's rolled the sleeves up.

And he's on his knees in front of me, apologizing. Am I a fool to believe him? He seems sincere. He seems wrecked that he messed things up. I don't love that he went to see his ex-wife, but it seems like he needed to hear what she had to say.

And he says he loves me.

Hope is a fluttery feeling in my belly. A floating sensation.

"I'm staying," I say again.

"Yeah?"

I nod, smiling. "Yeah."

He lowers his head, resting it on my knees, his big body vibrating with emotion. I slide one hand free of his and thread them through his hair, my heart thrashing wildly. His chest and back expand on his deep inhalations. Then he lifts his head, his eyes blazing, and reaches for me. He stands, taking me with him, and I move into his arms without hesitation because I need to touch him, to feel him, to have his solid strength against me. His heart thuds against me and his hand slides down my spine.

"Are you sure?" he asks. "I don't want you to give up something that's important to you."

"You're important to me. I love you," I say quietly. "And I want to be with you. And make wine with you. And go on dirty picnics with you."

His lips quirk.

"But I'm not staying just for you. I'm staying for me, really. I'd already decided to stay before I came here." I tell him about my conversations with Millie, Ana, and Rosa, and the things I've learned about myself. "And even though I thought you didn't love me, I had to be brave enough to leave my past in the past and truly commit to my family."

He nods, and the admiration on his face calms my fears and doubts, "I'm glad. Because I love you, too."

Emotion swells in my throat, strangling me. I quickly nod. "Good. Because you are my favorite person and I like you a lot, on top of wanting to ride you like a Harley on a bad stretch of road."

He chokes on a laugh, shaking his head. "Jesus."

I grin. "Seriously. I've told you before how much I admire you. I love how you love Moose. I love how you look out for the people who work for you. I love how you try to answer my crazy questions. I love how you've made friends with Nolan and Miles, and I love how everyone who works for you respects you even though you're totally new at this. I love how you admit what you don't know. You're my favorite person."

For a moment we sit and gaze at each other, my chest feeling light and fizzy, my mouth pulling into a smile that I can't stop. Jansen smiles too, and I was right the first time he almost smiled—when he smiles a genuine, happy smile it makes me feel like I could float away.

"Let's go home," he says, voice husky.

My throat pinches. Home. With him. "Yes."

AT HIS PLACE, JANSEN GETS WINE GLASSES AND POURS US each another glass, but then he leads me into the bedroom.

"I thought we learned our lesson. No wine in bed."

"Okay, which is it? Wine or bed?"

I press my finger to my lip and look skyward. "Hmmm." Then I set my wine glass on the dresser and run at him. He catches me, grabbing my ass and I wrap my arms and legs around him and kiss him.

Our mouths join in long, hungry kisses, lush licks, tiny nibbles. I want him so much my bones are melting.

"Yeah," he whispers against my mouth. "This. You."

"Mmm."

He makes a rough sound in his throat and changes the angle, coming at my mouth with even deeper greed. Then he carries me over to his bed. I expect both of us to end up on top of it, but he lowers my feet to the floor.

"Can I put on the slip?"

"Please." It comes out like a groan.

"I didn't plan for this, obviously," I say as I remove my ripped jeans and old T-shirt.

"You're beautiful, Bianca." His heated gaze slides over me like melting chocolate as he opens my bra and tugs it off, and it makes me feel so beautiful and cherished.

The silk slides over my skin in a sensuous glide, the straps settling on my shoulders. The embroidered bra cups barely cover my breasts.

"Look at you. Perfect." He traces my cleavage with a fingertip. "Gorgeous. Sexy."

He cups my cheek in that way of his that tells me I'm everything to him and kisses me again, his firm lips moving on mine, with gentle sucks and smooth licks.

My fingers start working open the buttons of his shirt and he backs away to shrug it off, both of us staring at each other longingly. I'll never get over the sight of Jansen naked. He *is* beautiful. So much strength and grace. My gaze roves over his muscle-packed torso, rounded biceps, and firm stomach as he undoes his jeans and steps out of them, along with his briefs. His thick thighs flex as he stands on one leg, then the other, and my attention drops to his heavy cock. Hot sparks sizzle over my skin, the ache inside me deepening.

He kisses me again, nudging me toward the bed and then we're on it, me on my back, him coming down on top of me. His substantial weight on me is erotic, also gratifying. I need it. His kisses are so tender, so thorough, I feel them in the ache in my pussy. I push my heels into the mattress and arch against him, holding on to his shoulders, kissing him back. I want to open wider, drink him in, lick inside him, devour him. "I love you."

"I love you. I need to taste you." He shifts me under him, then kneels between my legs.

I'm shaking with need, my fingers in his hair, pulling him closer, and he complies, pressing his mouth to my center. I make a strangled noise at the contact and tighten, nerve endings lit up, inner muscles twisting. He groans, a broken, needy sound, his mouth searching and hot, devoted to eating me like he's starving, his fingers digging into my thighs. I come apart, a trembling, brilliant burst of sensation that ripples through me, over and over, and Jansen coaxes me through it with soft sucks and licks,

I'm wrecked. Gasping. Quaking.

He stays there, nuzzling my swollen, sensitive clit, his breath alone enough to make me shiver, gliding his hands up and down my legs. Then he lifts his head and his eyes blaze directly into mine. "Okay, baby?"

"Unhhhh."

He has a condom and rolls it on, moves closer and finds my entrance. He's burning hot, solid, pushing inside me, filling me with that luxurious length and breadth, sliding over tender nerve endings still pulsing. He tugs down one embroidered cups of the slip. "Look at this beauty. Just begging to be sucked." Bending, he kisses one, then the other, then sucks my flesh into his mouth in a greedy pull, making more noises of hunger and longing.

I moan too at the exquisite sensation that streaks through me. "I'm coming again already."

"Fuuuuck." His jaw clenches, and he stares down at me with an intensity that has my heart exploding into a frantic rhythm. "Yeah. Come on my cock. I fucking love that."

He slides out, back in. I squeeze him, and another orgasm tears through me, blinding me, burning me, spiking tears in the corners of my eyes. I cry out and hold onto him and then he comes, too, shuddering, gasping, coming down over me and clinging to me so tightly more tears gather.

"I'll try to do better," Jansen mumbles later. "To

communicate better. No, I *will* do better. Kick my ass if I don't."

I smile against his chest, wrapped up in his strong arms. "Okay."

"I practiced with Moose."

I go still, then tip my head back to look at him. His lips tug up into a half-smile. "You practiced what with Moose?"

"Communicating."

"What did he say?"

He grins. "He didn't say much. He's mostly a good listener."

"Ah. Yes."

"I told him I love him."

I smile. "I knew you did."

"I thought he should know."

"I think he did know. But it's good that you told him."

"And I talked to him about you and how I felt about you and what a dumb fuck I was. It felt good."

I relax back down against him. "That's good." I trace my fingers over the tendons of his neck. "I thought I could do this. I thought I could have a fling with a hot hockey player and then leave. I failed."

"What is failure?" he asks. "What is success?"

I lift my head and stare at him, then burst into giggles. "Excellent questions. And why is success sometimes scarier than failure? Also, I think this *is* actually success, not failure."

"Sometimes failure is better for you than success."

Happiness bubbles up in me. "Yes." I pause. "When I was at Ana's place the other night, she reminded me of this quote from Horace."

"Who?"

"Horace. A Roman poet from...well, way back."

He snorts softly.

I recite it for him. "And that line 'and teaches new means for the accomplishment of our wishes' really made me think."

"Oh. Yeah. Totally. I'd say we're both doing that. Finding new ways to get what we want."

"And figuring out what it *is* we really want."

"I want you."

"Same. I want you. And I want family. And friends. And a community, even if rumors here spread faster than a lizard on hot asphalt."

He laughs.

"The people here are good people. There's just Uncle Geno to deal with."

"I've got your back with him."

"Thank you. I've got your back with everyone."

I adore him. He's comfort and strength and pleasure. He's everything I didn't know I wanted, everything I need—the hidden secret of my soul.

Chapter 32

Bianca

I need to talk to Uncle Geno again. When I came here, I was going to get him to give us the wine. To get him to stop sabotaging us, if not help us. And to get him to admit I know what I'm doing when it comes to wine.

But...things have changed.

I've changed.

It doesn't matter what Geno thinks. I'd like him to acknowledge my accomplishments, but in the end, they're my accomplishments and what matters is that I'm proud of myself and I know what I'm capable of. I think what I really wanted was to feel like part of the family. And I have felt that.

I always thought my cousins were the same as Uncle Geno—oblivious to me and my dreams of creating beautiful wines. But after our family dinner that night, I see they're not. I felt such a sense of family that night—shared memories and laughter, common experiences. Rosa and I have gotten closer, understanding each other better now. I even consider Jake part of the family and I love him for loving my sister. We all have a history together and I feel part of it. Part of the family. Part of the Lamberti saga, but also my own person.

But I need to talk to Uncle Geno.

I know Jansen would come with me and support me, but I want to do this myself. So I don't tell him I'm going over to Belmonte.

I find Uncle Geno in his office.

"Bianca. What brings you here?"

"I need to talk to you. Do you have a few minutes?" I'm being polite, because I'm going to talk to him no matter what. I close the office door behind me.

He crosses his arms and his ancient chair creaks as he leans back in it "Are you here to beg for the wine again?"

I smile. "No. After thinking about it, I realize that's not fair to you. You grew the grapes. You harvested them and cared for them while they fermented."

He narrows his eyes. "Indeed."

"It will make things harder for us, but that's okay. We have a plan and we're working hard. I've decided not to go back to Argentina."

His eyes widen then narrow again. He sits up straight. "Really."

"Yes. That wasn't my plan when I came home, but it's what I want to do now. I want to honor Nonna. I want to work with my sisters. I want to make beautiful wines. I *will* make beautiful, award-winning wines. Here."

"I see."

I can't read his reaction. He's not horrified, but he's not happy either. I don't know. It doesn't matter.

"For a long time, it bothered me that my own family wouldn't give me a chance. It made me so resentful." Emotion creeps up into my chest and throat, squeezing. I fight to control my voice and keep it steady. "But that resentment is keeping me from being happy with what I've achieved. I don't want to be ruled by the past. I keep thinking I need to do more. Maybe *something* I do will show everyone what I'm capable of. I thought I had to prove myself to you. But the truth is, I don't need to prove myself to anyone."

"You're being dramatic." He rolls his eyes.

I shake my head. "You've been actively trying to stop us from being a success. I don't know why. It's one thing to just overlook us, but to try to stop us—that's not how you're supposed to treat family."

"You're one to talk about how to treat family!"

I don't even flinch back from his raised voice. Like Jansen told me, being vulnerable makes me safe because I know on the inside that I'm good enough. If Uncle Geno yells at me, that's not a reflection on me.

"Family doesn't split apart our legacy!" he adds sharply. "I've done so goddamn much for Belmonte. And this is how you repay me."

Now I'm taken aback. "First of all, *we* didn't do that. Nonna did that. It was her decision, remember?"

"You didn't have to go along with it. With this crazy idea of running your own winery. You'll destroy the family legacy."

"Is that what you're worried about?" I ask slowly, remembering Vitto saying how rooted in tradition his dad is.

"Of course it is. Our family is generations of quality wine making."

I nod. "I know. And I'm sorry you think that we can't continue that. We believe we can. And...I also think you should let Vittorio have more independence. He has talent, too, but I don't think you allow him to shine."

His face turns thunderous. "Now you're lecturing me how to run Belmonte? Che cazzo!"

I blink at his curse—*what the fuck!*—but then laugh. "I'm

not lecturing you." Hmm. I wonder where I get my oversensitivity. "Just my opinion. Something to think about." I wave a hand. "It was Nonna's wish that we would stay a family and support each other. We haven't been doing that. And I take some responsibility, too. That's why I'm agreeing that you should keep the wine." I smile, a genuine, happy smile. "I'm compromising."

His brows lower over his eyes.

"Winemakers aren't good at compromising," I tell him, repeating Vitto's words. "But I'm learning." I tilt my head. "It would be great if you did, too. If you would stop interfering with us. We don't expect you to come and stomp our grapes with us, but we won't tolerate any more bullshit trying to obstruct us." I meet his eyes directly, letting him see my resolve. My conviction.

I don't get a response from him. I mentally shrug.

"Thank you for listening. Rosa and I are planning another family dinner. We'll let you and Aunt Janet know when it is. Have a great day."

I walk out. Inside, I have to admit, I'm quivering. But I keep my shoulders back, my chin up, and I stride out the front door.

I pull my sunglasses down onto my nose in the bright sunshine. The air I pull into my lungs holds a crisp autumn chill. I tip my head back to gaze up at the clear blue sky stretching above me, then look around at the vineyards blazing with fall color, scarlet and bronze, pumpkin and gold. The ginkgo trees around the parking lot positively glow yellow against the sky, some of their leaves already carpeting the ground, crackling beneath my feet as I walk to my car.

Moments later, I turn into Caparelli. Nonna's house—I mean, our house—still needs work. The yard needs grooming. But the pumpkins sitting on the veranda are charming and the vines...they're magnificent. It's home.

As I near the house I see Jake and Jansen standing near the house talking. They're both relaxed and smiling. My heart swells with love and affection and gratitude.

Rosa appears at the front door, throwing it open and flying out. Uh oh. What's got her undies in a tangle? I park and slide out of the car.

"Bee!" she calls to me.

"What?"

"We have to go! To the sheriff's office!"

"Oh my God. What now?" I just left Uncle Geno. Surely he isn't up to more nonsense already!

"It's Allegra!"

My feet stop dead and I gape at Rosa. "What?"

"She's here! She's home. She's at the sheriff's office!"

I throw my hands in the air. "You have got to be kidding me. What has she done now?"

"I don't know," Rosa frets. "But we have to go pick her up."

I take a breath and look at the beauty around me once more. This is my legacy. This land, these vines...these women. My sisters. We may not always agree but we'll always be sisters. And we'll always be there for each other. Even if it's bailing one of us out of jail.

"Let's go."

What's going on with Allegra? Find out in Que Será Syrah by P.G. Forte!

https://books2read.com/Que-Sera-Syrah

And have you read No Way, Rosé? Be sure to read Rosa and Jake's story!

https://books2read.com/u/3JA8oP

And do you want more of Bianca and Jansen?
Click here and add your name to my mailing list to get the free epilogue!

Acknowledgments

First, I have to thank my co-writers in this project, Kate Davies and PG Forte. It took so long to make this happen and I'm so glad it finally did! You are both amazing writers and friends, and I've loved creating this world with you. Especially the wine.

Also thanks to Kristi Yanta who worked on developmental edits for this book when it was a complete pile of dog doo doo. Thank you so much for your invaluable feedback on how to make the book better!

And most of all, thank you, readers. I love to share my stories with you. Thanks for taking a chance on a non-hockey romance!

About the Author

Kelly Jamieson is a best-selling author of over sixty romance novels and novellas. Her writing has been described as "emotionally complex," "sweet and satisfying," and "blisteringly sexy." She likes coffee (black), wine (mostly white), shoes (especially high heels) and hockey!

Kelly appreciates your help in spreading the word about her books, including sharing with friends! Please leave a review on your favorite book site! You can also join her Facebook group, Kelly Jamieson's Sweet Heat Reader Lounge, to hang out with her, and for exclusive giveaways and sneak peeks of future books.

Visit her website at www.kellyjamieson.com or contact her at info@kellyjamieson.com

Other Books By Kelly Jamieson

HELLER BROTHERS HOCKEY

BREAKAWAY

FACEOFF

ONE MAN ADVANTAGE

HAT TRICK

OFFSIDE

POWER SERIES

POWER STRUGGLE

POWER PLAY

POWER SHIFT

RULE OF THREE SERIES

RULE OF THREE

RHYTHM OF THREE

REWARD OF THREE

SAN AMARO SINGLES

WITH STRINGS ATTACHED

HOW TO LOVE

SLAMMED

WINDY CITY KINK

SWEET OBSESSION

ALL MESSED UP

PLAYING DIRTY

BREW CREW

LIMITED TIME OFFER

NO OBLIGATION REQUIRED

ACES HOCKEY

MAJOR MISCONDUCT

OFF LIMITS

ICING

TOP SHELF

BACK CHECK

SLAP SHOT

PLAYING HURT

BIG STICK

GAME ON

LAST SHOT

BODY SHOT

HOT SHOT

LONG SHOT

BAYARD HOCKEY

SHUT OUT

CROSS CHECK

WYNN HOCKEY

PLAY TO WIN

IN IT TO WIN IT

WIN BIG

FOR THE WIN

GAME CHANGER

BEARS HOCKEY

MUST LOVE DOGS…AND HOCKEY

YOU HAD ME AT HOCKEY

TALK HOCKEY TO ME

THE O ZONE

GOOD HANDS

SCORING BIG

MERRY PUCKING CHRISTMAS

LIGHT 'EM UP

STORM HOCKEY

CROSSING THE LINE

STANDALONES

THREE OF HEARTS

LOVING MADDIE FROM A TO Z

DANCING IN THE RAIN

LOVE ME

LOVE ME MORE

2 HOT 2 HANDLE

FRIENDS WITH BENEFITS

LOST AND FOUND

ONE WICKED NIGHT

SWEET DEAL

HOW SWEET IT IS

HOT RIDE

CRAZY EVER AFTER

ALL I WANT FOR CHRISTMAS

SEXPRESSO NIGHT

IRISH SEX FAIRY

CONFERENCE CALL

RIGGER

YOU REALLY GOT ME

SCREWED

FIRECRACKER

BIG WITCH ENERGY

HATE ME UNDER THE MISTLETOE